DREADNOUGHT

WAR MAGE: BOOK TWO

CHARLES R CASE

Illustrated by
MANUEL CASTANON

Edited by
JEN MCDONNELL

CASE BY CASE PUBLISHING

CONTENTS

Chapter 1	1
Chapter 2	7
Chapter 3	13
Chapter 4	21
Chapter 5	31
Chapter 6	37
Chapter 7	45
Chapter 8	51
Chapter 9	59
Chapter 10	67
Chapter 11	73
Chapter 12	81
Chapter 13	87
Chapter 14	93
Chapter 15	99
Chapter 16	107
Chapter 17	115
Chapter 18	121
Chapter 19	131
Chapter 20	139
Chapter 21	151
Chapter 22	157
Chapter 23	163
Chapter 24	171
Chapter 25	177
Chapter 26	183
Chapter 27	189
Chapter 28	195
Chapter 29	203
Chapter 30	211

Chapter 31   215

Chapter 32   221

Chapter 33   229

Chapter 34   231

Chapter 35   241

Chapter 36   249

Chapter 37   255

Chapter 38   259

Chapter 39   265

Chapter 40   269

Chapter 41   275

Chapter 42   281

Chapter 43   287

Chapter 44   295

Chapter 45   303

Chapter 46   309

Chapter 47   317

Chapter 48   323

Chapter 49   329

Author's Note   333

CHAPTER 1

SARA LAY on her back in the shade of a stubby tree. She had her arms crossed behind her head, her carnelian red hair splayed out like a fan all around her to let the cool breeze tickle the back of her neck. The long grass of the central park in the ancient human city was matted down to form a nest that gave her a little privacy in the bustling grounds.

She could still smell the smoke of the previous day's battle, but laying on her back, she could at least block it from her vision. The sky was a deep blue, with fluffy white clouds scuttling across it, unaware of the carnage that had taken place beneath it the day before.

Alister lifted his head from Sara's chest, coming awake from his cat nap at the sound of grass swishing against legs. He was laying down, spanning the length of her sternum, his black tail swishing across her belly, and his paws between her breasts. Sara didn't move, knowing full well who was approaching.

"It's a beautiful day, Captain," Sargent Major Baxter said, stopping just inside her peripheral vision and taking a deep breath through his nose, looking to the sky along with her.

He had left his Aetheric armor back in the command tent, and was wearing the same skin-tight black battlesuit she was.

Alister settled his head back down on his paws, and with a few smacks of his lips, closed his yellow eyes and feigned sleep once more. Through their new empathic link, Sara knew he was miles from sleep, just as she was. Her actions at the end of the battle weighed heavily on both their minds. She had tried to kill her own men in a berserker rage; if not for Alister, she would be laying here all alone on this planet, covered in the blood of her own people. She shuddered at the thought, and felt a sympathetic feeling of regret from her familiar.

Pushing the dark mood to the side for now, she turned to Baxter. He was tall and strong, and cared deeply for his men and their well-being. She admired him greatly for that, and for other things.

Hours ago, you tried to kill this wonderful man in a rage you could not control. She felt a guilty pang try and slip in, but she quashed it. *'Control' is just one more item I need to add to my 'Things Sara Doesn't Know How to do Yet' list.*

"Hello, Baxter. It sure is. Any word from the *Raven*?" Sara asked, shading her eyes from the sun behind Baxter's head.

He looked down at her, giving a halfhearted smile. "The repairs are done, and the reactors are back online. The ship seems to be in fully working order, but…" He trailed off and ran a hand over his short-cropped, white hair that was such a contrast to his dark brown skin. His deep brown eyes wandered away from her gaze.

"Cora's still not awake?" she guessed.

He gave a nod, putting his hands to his hips and taking a deep breath through his nose. He indicated a spot next to her. "Do you mind?"

She smiled and patted the ground on her other side,

"Over here; that way the sun won't be in my eyes. This tree is shit for shade."

Baxter, ever the practical thinker, took a large step over her prone form, causing Alister to twitch in surprise. Sara put a hand on his back to calm him, and, after judging the situation, he closed his eyes once again.

Stomping down a section of grass, Baxter sank to a cross-legged position, his back straight and strong so he sat high enough to block the sunlight hitting Sara's face. He plucked a long piece of grass and began to chew on the end while contemplating his next words. With a grimace, he spat out the grass. Then after a moment spat again, to clear the bad taste.

"It may look like grass, but that stuff tastes like rotten fruit," he said in explanation before spitting again. "Sorry," he said, wiping his mouth with the back of his hand.

Sara shrugged, sliding her hands back behind her head. "That's okay. I did the same thing half an hour ago."

"And you let me do it?" he asked, raising an eyebrow.

"I like the solidarity of bad experiences. Years from now, we can say something like, 'It's not good, but it's not as bad as the grass on Colony 788', and we will laugh while everyone around us scratches their head."

Baxter's eyebrows came together. "You're an odd one, if you don't mind me saying, Captain." He leaned back on an outstretched arm. "So, you think we will be working together for years?"

Sara kept her eyes closed, but smiled. "I'm counting on it, Baxter. We will go out among the stars, and have countless adventures. Didn't you know the Navy is all about seeing far-off and exotic places?"

Baxter grunted. "That hook didn't work back on Earth. Their line should be, 'See exotic places, where everyone will try and kill you'."

Sara gave him a chuckle.

A silence built up between them as they enjoyed the short break from organizing the evacuation of the Elif researchers and their security force. The sound of people moving equipment and tearing down temporary structures sounded far away from her grass cocoon, and Baxter seemed to be enjoying the distance, as well.

They had received word from the United Human Fleet Command (UHFC) after the battle: the Elif had packed up and left the Sol System, saying that they were needed to defend Effrit, the Elif homeworld. No one had heard from Admiral Setti or the High Council in the days since. Fearing another attack on Colony 788 by the Teifen, the UHFC decide to evacuate the Elif themselves and take them to Earth until communications could be re-established. A scout ship had been sent to the Elif home system to determine what had happened, but the ship was not due back for a few more days.

A destroyer, two cruisers, and a transport ship would be arriving any minute to begin the evacuation. Then Sara would be able to leave this place—and all her guilt—behind. More importantly, she would be back on the *Raven,* able to figure out what that core had done to her sister.

Sara's comm buzzed, and Ensign Mezner's cool voice broke her contemplation. "Captain, we picked up four ships jumping insystem. They have been verified as UHF through their transponders. They should be arriving in orbit in two minutes."

Sara tapped her earpiece. "Thank you, Mezner. How's the ship doing?" she asked, unable to help herself. She knew exactly how the ship was doing; it was Cora she wanted to know about.

Mezner knew what she wanted, too, and her voice took on a slightly somber tone. "No change, ma'am."

Sara sat up, making Alister jump to the ground and give her a slightly dirty look. She mouthed 'sorry' to him, and he flicked an ear in response before cleaning an already immaculate paw.

"Thank you, Mezner. We should be up shortly," she said, tapping the comm to end the call. "You ready? The transport should be here in a few minutes," she said, looking at Baxter.

They pushed themselves to their feet and began the short walk to the command tent, which was being taken down a section at a time. She could see that both hers and Baxter's Aetheric armor had been moved outside, along with a small mountain of crates holding the command center's hardware.

A STREAMER of fire and white smoke dove through the atmosphere like a meteorite. Unlike a meteorite, the object slowed until the fire abated, and then it swung low over the open plain that surrounded the ancient city. Its belly glowed orange for a brief time, then cooled to a white finish streaked with soot. The rumble of the gravitic drives became a tickling in her chest, as the transport ship crossed the ruined city wall.

Sara could see the broken and still-smoking heaps of the Teifen transports she had smashed in her final assault, and gave a shudder at the feelings that stirred in her. She had killed thousands, and felt nothing but the joy of battle. No remorse, no fear, just pure elation at what her powers had done. Now that elation was replaced with fear and shame. Fear that she would not be able to stop herself next time, and shame that she'd had to be stopped by Alister against her will.

Alister hopped up onto her shoulder and nudged the side of her head as if to say *'It's okay. I'm here for you.'* She smiled and gave him a scratch under the chin.

The transport came straight in, its stubby landing pads extending from the sleek body like legs of a malformed beetle. A rush of air washed over her and Baxter as the huge transport settled on the grassy field in front of them.

The ship was five stories tall, with a bank of windows overhanging the top lip, where the bridge was positioned. A hissing sound preceded the entire front of the ship splitting open to reveal three floors of cargo space. A ramp extended slowly to the ground as the gravitic engines cut off, leaving a deafening silence in their wake.

Baxter opened his battalion-wide comm channel. "All right, people. Let's get this boat loaded," he said, whipping his hand over his head in a circular motion. He marched off toward a group of Elif and continued to bark orders.

Sara muted the channel, not needing to hear what should be loaded first and who was going where. Instead, she looked up to the sky and spotted the three silvery flashes: the destroyer and two cruisers, flying in formation. She then looked to the small moon just coming over the horizon. The *Raven* was on the surface of that moon, and she couldn't wait to get there.

Don't worry, Cora. I'll be there soon. I can fix this, she thought, hoping she could.

CHAPTER 2

THE LOADING of the transport took far too long for Sara's liking. She knew the troops were moving as fast as they could, and she didn't want to push them too hard, after the last few days of intense battle. They had lost friends and comrades in the fighting, and some were still recovering, even if their wounds had been healed by the mages. They had lost over a hundred Marines and twice as many Elif. Sara felt some shame at her impatience when the long line of coffins was being carried aboard the transport.

She didn't think to ask, but guessed that there were enough foldable coffins stored on the *Raven* to bury them all. That thought shut down any irritability her mind was trying to push. She was responsible for those deaths; they were her troops, and she had ordered them to the surface to defend a place they had never seen, and would never see again. One hundred and twenty-seven Marines were going home in a box because she had been too scared to complete the Familiar spell.

Alister gave her head a light smack from where he perched on her shoulder. She glanced his way, and he gave her a disapproving glare. She could feel his reproach at her train of thought, even if he didn't know the specifics.

This empathic link is going to take some getting used to, she thought, giving him a little nod and trying not to be too hard on herself.

After a few hours, the transport and the three dropships were loaded and ready to go. Sara and Baxter watched as the transport lifted off, folding its landing struts into its belly. The rumbling of the huge gravitic drives made her chest rattle till the transport was high in the atmosphere and gaining speed for orbit.

They were the last two to board the final dropship. Sara looked out the window at the smoking and abandoned city falling away, until it was obscured by clouds and distance, as the ship rumbled and swayed its way off-planet. Colony 788 would be remembered, if never visited again. It was where the second core had been discovered, full of plans from a long-dead, human civilization that had called the stars home. It was the place the first Teifen / Human battle had taken place. It was where the first War Mage in thirty thousand years had been born. It was the place where she had lost the first of her men.

She knew it would not be the last.

"WE TRIED to have Ensign Boon do it, seeing as she was the one who installed the core in the first place, but the damn thing keeps throwing up an error message," Chief Engineer Sabine said, frustration etched into his olive-skinned features.

Sara was standing in front of Cora's tank on the engineering deck of the *Raven.* She looked over her shoulder at her cabin girl, Alicia Boon, who was trying not to be in anyone's way and failing miserably.

"Oh, excuse me," Boon said, stepping out of Caroline Green's path, only to have Teichek ask her to move so he could plug a cord into the back of the console Boon had scooted behind. The small, blonde woman scowled at her predicament and took a step back.

Sara felt bad for her, but was also a little fascinated that she was able to handle and initiate the core that was now spinning happily in the box attached to Cora's tank. She would need to talk with Boon more, once this was all over.

"Show me the error," Sara said, stepping up to Sabine's console and leaning over his chair to better see the display.

He pulled up a screenshot of the screen he was currently on, but in the center was a box containing a warning that read, 'Unauthorized user attempt. Core unable to complete boot process. Final User required'.

Sara frowned at the message. "Is it talking about Cora? She would be the 'final user', right?"

Sabine's shoulders slumped. "We don't think so. It's pretty obvious that the controller needs to be in the tank as part of the boot sequence."

"We're picking up some brain activity," Caroline interjected. "Cora's interacting with the core. The readings were all over the place for the first twenty or so hours, then kind of dropped off to a pattern indicative of sleep, but with a repeating spike. Like it's periodically looking for signal or something."

Sabine nodded along with the technician's report. "We think it's talking about you," he told Sara.

"Me? I didn't have anything to do with its installation. Why would it need me…" She trailed off as she thought about it. "Oh. The twin thing. Right. Genetically, we're the same person."

Sabine touched his nose conspiratorially. "Exactly."

"That makes the Elif's behavior about twins sort of make sense," she mused.

"Uh, what behavior?" Sabine asked.

"The Elif refer to a set of twins as the same person. They understand that we think of ourselves as separate, but in their culture, twins are viewed as singular. They even have the same names," Sara said, walking up to the tank and pressing a hand to the glass.

"That's… odd," he said.

Sara could almost feel her sister's presence through the glass, but she decided the feeling was in her head. Alister wove his way between her legs, rubbing his cheeks on her ankles in solidarity.

"Okay, what have you tried so far?" Sara asked, still looking at Cora's floating form. Her sister's silver bodysuit caught the light as she gently drifted back and forth.

Boon stepped up at the question, snapping to attention. "The scanner, ma'am. I just pressed my thumb to it, and we got the error message," she said, back rigid and arms straight by her sides.

Sara gave the young woman a warm smile. "At ease, Ensign. You're not on trial."

Boon relaxed, but only slightly. "Thank you, ma'am. I did my best. If I did something that put Captain Cora in danger…" She trailed off, not knowing exactly what the punishment for activating ancient tech would be.

Sara gave her a half-smile. "You did nothing wrong, Boon. In fact, I'm very happy to know that there is someone else I can trust to handle the cores. I'm sure your services will be needed again. I can't be everywhere at once."

"Thank you, ma'am," she said simply.

Sara turned back to the tank and examined the box containing the core. It was nearly identical to the one she had taken from the vault on Colony 788, but the lights around the edge were green instead of blue. She saw the scanner pad at once. "Here goes nothing," she murmured as she pressed her thumb to the pad.

A green line rolled down the screen, scanning her. What it was scanning, she was not sure; she didn't know what a thumbprint could tell the machine if it didn't have a database of people to connect the print to, but it did its magic, and the lights running around the edges of the box turned from green to blue.

Sabine gave a shout of triumph. "Now we're cooking!" he yelled. His eyes were scanning left to right as he tried to read everything on the screen as it scrolled by. "It worked. Everything beyond basic systems is coming back online. Aether Amplifiers, thrusters, weapons, Aether cannons…" He read out each system as it booted up.

Sara was only half paying attention to him, watching Cora for any sign of life. She wasn't sure what she would see, considering Cora's body had been asleep since they first took command and initialized the tank, but she watched closely anyway.

"Her brain waves are returning to normal," Teichek said, eyeing the readings. "She should be waking up any second."

Sara held her breath, the moment drawing itself out like the pregnant pause of a bad actor.

Just as Sara opened her mouth to ask Teichek what was happening, Cora's body spasmed. Her arms and legs jerked out as the muscles became rigid and tight. Her eyes snapped open, and she took a deep lungful of the fluid she was suspended in.

Sara leaned against the glass, her hands pressed flat to the cool surface, not knowing if Cora was in trouble, or if this was part of the process. Cora's eyes rolled in her head until they caught Sara's. The twins stared at each other until Cora's lids became heavy, and her arms and legs relaxed. Then she drifted back to her normal fetal position, and her eyes closed once again.

"Is she okay? What happened?" Sara asked, panic in her voice.

"I'm fine. Why? Did something happen? Wait, Sara? How did you get here?" Cora said over the speaker.

Sara nearly sobbed in relief. "Oh, man. Do I have a story for you."

Cora was quiet for a breath. "Holy crap. It worked."

"What worked?" Sara asked, confused.

"The core. I know what happened."

"You mean the battle?"

"No," Cora said. "I mean I know what happened to the ancient humans. I know how we got to Earth." She paused. "The core downloaded all kinds of information into my brain. It's like I have memories that aren't mine. This is going to take some getting used to."

Sara was relieved that Cora was awake again, but she didn't know if she liked the idea of the core implanting memories in her sister of its own accord. "Are you okay? It didn't hurt you, did it?"

Cora thought about it for a second. "No. It didn't hurt me. I'm just going to need a little while to get my head straight."

The tension in Sara's chest finally let go. "Good. I'm going to contact the destroyer in orbit and have them tow us back to Sol. I don't want you doing anything 'til we are in safe space. Do you hear me? Nothing."

Cora's light laugh gave Sara a boost she didn't even know she needed. "I hear you, Captain. I won't do anything but organize this mess in my head."

"Good. We'll talk later. For now, I need to get that destroyer on the horn."

CHAPTER 3

THE *RAVEN* BUMPED up to the hard point on the destroyer *Regis,* and the ship shuddered slightly as the docking clamps engaged.

"We have good connection, ma'am," Ensign Connors said, releasing the thruster controls, and scratching at his short, auburn hair.

"The *Regis* is giving the green light as well, ma'am. They say they will be making for warp in seven minutes," reported the ensign on comms.

"Thank you, Mezner. Let them know we are good to go on our end." Sara sat down in her command chair and turned to Grimms, who was in the seat next to hers. He was going over something on his tablet, as usual. "I'm not used to the slower speed the rest of the fleet travels at. This ought to take a while."

Grimms gave a grunt as he switched off the tablet and joined the conversation. "They're estimating three days. The fleet has some upgrading to do when we get back."

Sara smiled. "Thankfully we're one step closer to getting the tank systems online. I have a feeling with the cores we have, making more is just around the corner. Though, I think Cora's going to be too busy learning what her new capabilities are to be teaching anyone anything, so they will be on their own in that respect."

"True enough. I've already begun setting up a series of tests for her, to be completed when we get back to the Sol System. It's going to be an interesting few weeks," Grimms said, patting the tablet.

Sara gave him a smile. *He does like his procedures.*

They sat in silence for a few minutes, as the timer that Mezner had put up in the corner of the viewscreen counted down to warp.

Alister jumped up onto Sara's lap and bunted her chest with his head, wanting some attention. She began roughing him up with both hands, ending with him curled in her lap while she spanked him rather vigorously. Sara could feel through the empathic connection that he loved the treatment, though his loud purring was also a good indicator.

Grimms raised an eyebrow at her handling of the small, black cat, but said nothing.

"What? He likes it. He's a weirdo like that," she said, giving her familiar's belly a scratch.

"If you say so, ma'am," the commander said with a smile.

Sara was having a difficult time coming to grips with Alister being a pixie. She knew he was a man, but he was also a cat, and liked to do cat things. She would never even consider doing this to him when they met in the Aether, but here and now, he was having the time of his life. The next time they spoke, she would have to bring it up. At least he seemed to have dropped the morose mood he had picked up after the battle. He was probably just happy they got out alive.

The counter was down to three minutes to warp when she turned to Grimms again. "So, about Boon."

"Hmm, yes. Boon. She's an interesting case," he said, readjusting in his seat to better look Sara's way.

"I had no idea she was a mage," Sara said, resting a hand on Alister, as he purred with his eyes closed.

Grimms took a breath. "She's not. She has some abilities, but never went to the academy, or had formal training of any kind. She came out of one of those religious compounds in western North America. They were not so keen on the idea of magic, and forbade anyone from using it. In her record, she stated that as soon as she turned eighteen, she left and joined the Navy. She told me that she was thinking about becoming a mage, but wanted to wait 'til her tour was over."

"So how did she have enough power to handle a core?" Sara asked, half to herself.

"It must have to do with her being a twin," Grimms mused.

"She's a twin?" Sara asked, eyes wide in shock.

Grimms frowned. "Yes, but her sister died when they were children."

Sara leaned back in her chair, trying to work it out. *If being a twin is the only stipulation to handling a core, then my having Alister had nothing to do with it. It was enough that I was a twin, because ships utilizing a core would recognize that authority. But Boon couldn't initialize the core for Cora because it needed to be done by **her** twin, so it could recognize the bond between us. That's why I needed to be the one to initialize the final boot up.*

Sara sat up, "Wait. We've been thinking about this all wrong. Cores are artifacts for *twins*; it makes a lot more sense than requiring a War Mage on every ship. Or maybe Boon has the potential to be a War Mage, and the core somehow recognizes that."

Grimms' eyebrow rose once again, "If the core can recognize the potential, that would mean that being a War Mage is somehow genetic, not a matter of practice."

Sara leaned her chin down on a palm, lost in thought. She got an idea.

"Do you think I should teach Boon the Familiar spell? We're going to need War Mages to win this war, and so far, we don't know how to find them. I'm going to present the spellform to the UHFC in my debriefing, but you know how long they can take to make decisions."

Grimms considered this before replying. "I agree that we will need War Mages. I just don't know that I like the idea of making them without approval." He weighed his next words. "However, if she were able to do the spell and become a War Mage, we as a ship would be able to operate at a much higher potential. And you haven't been forbidden from teaching anyone."

"That's because they don't know it's an option yet. I just came into my powers yesterday," Sara said, giving him a sly glance.

"Like I said; they haven't ordered you not to."

Sara nodded. "You have the bridge, Commander."

Grimms gave a salute and a smile. "Aye, ma'am. I have the bridge."

Sara got up, dumping Alister to the floor, where he stretched before following her off the bridge.

"You wanted to see me, ma'am?" Boon said from outside the open door of Sara's cabin, standing at attention.

Sara looked up from her tablet, where she had been doing some reading on Alicia Boon and her particular circumstances. Sara stood up from the couch and indicated the small table and four chairs, where she normally had her meals. "Would you like to take a seat, Alicia?" she asked, using her first name to let her know this was not a formal meeting.

Boon, however, didn't seem to understand the gesture, and stayed at attention. "I'm fine, ma'am. I wouldn't want to be an imposition."

"Boon, get in here and close the door. This is not a formal meeting. I want to talk to you, and I need you to be honest with me," Sara said with a sigh. She walked over to the small liquor cabinet and pulled out two glasses and a bottle of something clear. After a moment's consideration, she put the clear liquid back, and took out a brown one with a grin.

Boon stepped inside, and with the press of a button, the door *swoosh*ed closed. She drew a breath and took a seat at the table, not knowing what to expect.

"Why are you so nervous? We see each other every day. You're my cabin girl, for crying out loud," Sara teased, taking the seat opposite Boon and pouring a few fingers into each glass. She slid one across and indicated to the girl that she should drink it.

Boon, not knowing what else to do, sipped at the whiskey. She made a face that told Sara Boon was not a drinker. Then Sara remembered that the girl was only twenty, and—being the by-the-book kind of person she was—she'd probably never had liquor.

Sara smiled. *This is going to be easy.* "Drink it all. That's an order. Do it in one gulp, it helps with the taste."

Boon took a few breaths, and stared at the brown liquid like it was going to bite her, but she did eventually down the stuff. She even managed not to cough up most of it.

Sara grabbed a napkin from the small shelf of utensils above the liquor cabinet and threw it to Boon.

"Thank you," she said, wiping the whiskey from her chin,

and dabbing at the spot on the leg of her battlesuit.

Sara felt a little bad and gave her water to wash down the taste. "So, Grimms tells me you are thinking about becoming a mage?"

Caught off-guard by the question and the effects of the whiskey, Boon stammered, "Oh, uh. I guess so." She wiped at her pants a second longer before her face turned red and she blurted out, "Uh, ma'am."

"What are your plans to make that happen?" Sara asked, taking a sip of the whiskey herself. She licked her lips in appreciation. It was no craft beer, but still pretty good.

"Oh. Well, I was planning on testing into the academy when my tour finished."

Sara could see that the flush on Boon's cheeks had not abated, and figured the alcohol was loosening her up. "Your plan is to wait two years and then try to get in? Then what, serve another eight years in academy training?"

"I guess so. It's not like I have anything else going in my life. I assume you read my file, and know that I don't exactly have a home to go back to," she said, sipping at her water.

"Hmm," Sara mused, squinting at the small, blonde woman. "What would you do with your power? The Marines is the most likely place for you, but there are positions on the larger ships, like the destroyer that's towing us home. Would you be interested in either of those?"

Boon took another sip of water, thinking it over. "I would do whatever they needed me to do, but I would hope it was something that made a difference. You know, really help people. Like a medic."

"Could you fight, if you needed to?" Sara asked, getting to the meat of her query.

Boon didn't hesitate this time. "Absolutely. The Teifen have shown us that they are incapable of mercy. We need to fight to keep ourselves safe."

Sara nodded. She liked Boon—had ever since the girl had served her first meal on the ship. "Did you see what I did on Colony 788?"

Boon's eyes widened. "Yes, ma'am. Some of the Marines had video from their Aether suits. You were incredible."

Sara bit her lip. She didn't want to scare the girl by telling her how close she had come to killing her own troops. It was a balancing act; on one hand, she was scared of what a War Mage could do on a rampage, but on the other, she knew humankind would never survive the war without more of them.

Maybe Boon's temperance will serve her well as a War Mage. If she becomes one. Sara wanted to know more. "What would you do with the kind of power I have?" she asked the slightly swaying woman.

Boon gave a laugh. "I would take the fight to the Teifen. Make them understand that humans are not just going to stand by and be annihilated."

Sara leaned back in her chair, sizing Boon up. Alister jumped into her lap and regarded Boon as well, his yellow eyes just coming over the table's top.

Sara looked down at him. "What do you think? Should we let her give it a try?"

Alister looked up at her so his face appeared upside down. "Merp," he said with conviction.

"Yeah. I think so too," she agreed, giving him a pat. She looked up at her cabin girl. "I have a proposition for you, Boon. How would you like to skip the whole training part, and become something better?"

Boon squinted one eye. "Skip it? Like, become an engineer or something?"

Sara laughed. "I was thinking more along the lines of a War Mage."

Boon's eyes went wide, and she hiccupped.

CHAPTER 4

SARA RUBBED at her sleep-deprived eyes, fighting off the urge that Alister had succumbed to hours ago. The little shit hadn't even tried to keep her and Boon company.

Sara had to smile at the little black cat, though. He was curled up in a ball, breathing slow, deep breaths. He was too cute by far.

One of Alister's ears twitched, and Sara rolled her eyes. "You little faker."

"What? I'm not faking it. This spellform is unbelievably complicated," Boon half-whined, thinking Sara was talking about her. She was sitting cross-legged on the carpeted floor, showing no signs of fatigue.

Sara chuckled. "I was talking to Alister. He's faking sleep."

Boon's mouth opened in an 'O' as she breathed out with understanding. "Sorry. I'm a little on edge. I don't know how you did this without help; I can barely cast a normal fire spell. I just wasn't trained for this," she said, leaning over her tablet and looking at the 3-D models of the spellforms for the hundredth time.

"It was hard, but I've been practicing spellforms my entire life. This isn't supposed to be easy; in fact, it's supposed to be nearly impossible. From what I can tell, War Mages were rare."

Boon let out a breath, blowing a strand of blonde hair that had come loose sometime in the last few hours away from her face .

Sara had started by explaining what a War Mage was. She'd given Boon the small amount of history she knew, which was not much, but Sara's own abilities were all it had taken to convince Alicia that she wanted to be a War Mage. Sara explained that she might not be able to cast the spell at all, but the girl had said she would try until it became obvious she was unable to do it.

People make all sorts of promises to themselves, 'til the real work comes and smacks them in the face.

Oddly enough, when Sara mentioned that a Familiar was the basis of a War Mage's power, she was unable to tell Alicia that they were also actually pixies. It was as if there was a block in her mind, a gag.

I'll have to ask Alister about that next time we meet in the Aether.

"What makes you think I have the ability to become a War Mage in the first place?" Boon asked, raising her arms above her head in a stretch.

Sara considered this. Rationally, she knew it was because Boon had been able to handle the core, but that could have just been because she was a twin. The reality was that Sara just had a feeling. She couldn't explain it, but it was there.

"I don't know. There's just something about you. Chances are you're not a War Mage, but I figure it's worth a try."

Cora's voice cut into the conversation from the speaker in

the ceiling. "Actually, the chances may be higher than you think."

Sara sat up excitedly. "Cora! How are you feeling? Back to normal? Shit, it's good to hear your voice."

Cora laughed lightly at Sara's exuberance. "I feel great. Sorry I've been keeping to myself, but I had to get all this new information sorted in my head. The core downloaded a lot of history into my brain, and I've been struggling to make sense of it. We have a lot to talk about."

"Hang on, I need to get Grimms in here. He should hear this," Sara said, tapping her comms and connecting with Grimms.

"Hmm? Hello?" Grimms' normally deep baritone was well past gravelly.

"Grimms? Are you okay?" Sara asked, concerned at his unusual tone.

His voice perked up, now sounding only slightly woozy. "I'm fine, Captain, I was just asleep when you called."

"Asleep? What time is it?"

"Three twenty eight," Boon said, reading the time on her tablet and raising her eyebrows at the late hour.

"Oh, sorry to wake you, Grimms," Sara apologized, embarrassed.

Grimms cleared the last of the sleep from his voice. "It's no problem, ma'am. What can I do for you?"

"Can you come to my quarters? Cora and I need to chat with you about what she's learned from the core."

She heard him grunt his way out of bed as he said, "I'll be there in a minute, ma'am."

"There's no need to get into uniform for this. Just put some pants on," Sara said, smiling at the red-faced Boon.

There was a pause on the line, then a "Yes, ma'am," and he disconnected.

Sara rubbed the lateness off her face with both hands. "I'll bet you five bucks he comes in uniform."

"You're on. I'm getting to know our commander pretty well; I bet he comes in sweats and a robe," Cora challenged.

"There is no way he comes in a robe. You're on," Sara countered gleefully, getting up and starting a pot of coffee.

By the time Sara put three cups of steaming coffee on the table, Grimms had arrived. To Sara's amazement, he was wearing sweatpants, a tee shirt, and a fuzzy, black robe.

"Well, shit," she grumbled, taking in the slightly disheveled Grimms.

He looked older than when he was on duty. He had the beginnings of a white five o'clock shadow, and the robe put a few years on him, if for no other reason than Sara had never seen anyone but her father in a robe.

"Did you lose a bet?" Grimms teased, a half-smile melting a few years from his face.

Sara squinted at him, then, handing him a coffee, said, "Cora told you to wear that robe, didn't she?"

He didn't answer, instead hiding his smile behind the mug before taking a sip. Sara rolled her eyes and waved for Boon to join them at the table.

"Shouldn't I leave, ma'am? I don't want to intrude," the girl said, inching closer to the door.

Before Sara could say anything, Cora spoke. "You should stay. This is going to be common knowledge soon enough, and if your training goes like Sara and I think it might, you'll need it. You should probably just get used to being near Sara from now on, Alicia."

"Oh, um, okay," she mumbled, and slipped into an empty chair at the table, taking a sip of the hot, black brew.

Grimms took another empty chair and, adjusting his robe, asked, "What's this all about?"

Cora took the lead. "My time sleeping in the tank was

not wasted. The core downloaded quite a bit of information directly into my brain, which was a bit like an update patch for an old operating system."

Grimms' eyebrows rose slightly. "That's helpful."

"Quite. As you know, Sara is teaching Boon how to cast the Familiar spell, testing her ability to become a War Mage. Sara had mentioned that War Mages were pretty rare, and that the chances were low that Boon would be able to cast the spell at all. I told her it was more likely than she thought."

Grimms took another sip. "Why is that?"

"Because being a War Mage—or any mage, for that matter—is about genetics," Cora explained.

"Like eye color?" Sara asked, making sure they were talking about the same thing.

"Exactly. We knew the Elif genetically manipulated humans to be receptive to the Aether. What we didn't know was that the gene was already a part of our DNA, but had been turned off thousands of years ago to keep humanity from being found by the Teifen and Elif," Cora said excitedly. When no one reacted, she said, "I should start at the beginning."

Sara gave a laugh. "Please do. I'm already a little lost."

"The Ancient humans suspected they would eventually be betrayed. So, in secret, they prepared four planets to hide away a number of humans, ensuring their survival . But the betrayal came much faster than anticipated, catching humanity off-guard. The plan had been to send four dreadnoughts, flown by War Mage twin sets, full of refugees and supplies, to set up a society on each of the planets. But in the end, only two of the dreadnoughts were able to escape, and with only their naval crews on board. The Navy had an unusually high number of Mages in it, so the crews started with an unusually high concentration of the Aether gene,"

Cora said, her voice taking on the motherly, slightly condescending tone Sara knew all too well.

"Okay, but what does that have to do with there being more War Mages? It sounds like there were only two War Mages per planet," Sara asked, draining her coffee and getting up to refill it.

"Well, for a quick and dirty explanation, I'll keep it simple, but understand that the actual mechanisms are a little more complex," Cora warned.

"Simple is good. I'm too tired for a thorough genetics lesson," Grimms grunted, holding his empty cup up for Sara to refill.

"The Aether gene has two expressions: dominant and recessive. Everyone has the gene, so everyone can channel Aether. If a person has two dominant genes, then they can only channel. If they have one recessive and one dominant, then they are able to split their mind in two and become a mage. And if they have two recessive genes, they can combine two spellforms while maintaining the integrity of them both, and become a War Mage. There is a whole lot more to it, but in the simplest terms, this is how it works. I'm telling you all this because there is evidence that all identical twins have at least one recessive gene, which means they can all at least become mages."

Sara nodded along with Cora's explanation, "So, if you start with a higher number of recessive genes in the pool, you end up with more people having them. Like if you have an unusually high number of blue-eyed people, the number will increase over time."

"Exactly," Cora said.

Boon spoke up, to everyone's surprise. "So, couldn't I just take a genetic test and see if the Familiar spell would work for me?"

"Theoretically, yes. But I don't know how to do that. The

core doesn't have a human genome map on it. I assume we could eventually find the specific gene, but that would be a job for geneticists back on Earth, and I would guess it would take them a few years to get it down. For now, trial and error are our best options," Cora answered.

"You heard the woman, Boon. Practice is the best medicine," Sara said with a smile as she slid Grimms' refilled mug across the table to him, and sat down.

Boon hung her head a little. "Yes, ma'am."

"It's not all bad, Boon; you're at least learning how to create complicated spellforms, which will help you in your studies if the Familiar spell doesn't work for you," Sara assured her.

"So, are you saying that only twins can become War Mages?" Grimms asked, getting the conversation back on track.

"No, but twins are much more likely to have the ability. According to the core, it was very rare in the past for the recessive trait to be passed down, even if both parents were War Mages. This is where the gene expression gets fuzzy; it's a lot more complicated than a simple binary gene expression, and there are other genes that determine the final pairing. Long story short, anyone has the potential to have the pairing to become a War Mage… it's just more likely if they are a twin." Cora paused for a beat before continuing. "Though I wouldn't be surprised if we find out that a lot more individuals can become War Mages, with the concentration of Mages that came to Earth in that final escape."

"Are you saying that all humans on Earth are descended from those who landed there on the dreadnought? Didn't that happen, like, thirty thousand years ago? Fossils of human remains exist that are older than that. Where did *they* come from?" Sara asked, cocking her head, trying to make the numbers work.

"Funny story, that. Before the core on Earth—the one from the dreadnought—went offline, it reported to the rest of the cores that there were humans already on Earth when they arrived, but then it was switched off before it could explain where they had come from," Cora said thoughtfully.

"The cores can communicate with each other?" Grimms asked, latching onto the strategic information like the good commander he was.

Cora gave a good-hearted laugh. "Right, I knew you would pick up on that, Grimms; ever the thinker, you are," she noted, genuine admiration in her voice. "It amazes me you're not higher ranked than a colonel."

Somewhere along the way, these two became a team. I haven't heard Cora talk that way to anyone in a long time. I would be jealous if it weren't so good for the ship. Okay, maybe I'm a little jealous, Sara thought, sizing up the half-smile Grimms was sporting.

Grimms, his face flushed at the compliment, waved it away. "I wouldn't want anything higher. Too much desk work."

Cora laughed and then answered his original question. "The cores can communicate with each other, which is the reason we need to have this conversation. They do so instantaneously, and over any distance. They are all connected through the Aether, almost as if they are the same core, just in different locations," Cora said, unable to hide her excitement.

Everyone was quiet while the implications sank in—except for Boon, who was a little lost. "Why is that such a big deal? Mages can already send messages through the Aether."

Grimms gave a grunt. "But it still takes time. Even at a hundred times the speed of the best warp, the amount of time it takes for a message to reach the recipient is a disadvantage, and slows down response times. Reactions are the key to winning any battle," he explained to her, then turned his attention back to Cora. "We need to get this system installed on all the ships in the fleet. How do we make more cores?"

"That's the rub. The plans are not on the core itself. It mentions that the War Mages kept the process secret, even from their own people. The advantage a core gave was far too great to fall into enemy hands."

Sara smacked the table in frustration. "Great. So the only ones who know how to make a core are all dead. What are we going to do now?"

"I think you should go find the Dreadnought hidden on Earth. Maybe we can find some answers there," Cora proposed.

"Do we know where it is?" Sara asked, liking the idea.

"Not a clue."

CHAPTER 5

"You ready?" Baxter asked, leaning into Sara's quarters with a big smile on his face.

Sara was in the middle of a yoga routine, not quite having worked up a sweat, but getting close. Her shift on the bridge had put a crick in her neck, as she'd sat for six hours with nothing to do while the *Regis* towed them home. She figured a quick set would work out her muscles without much trouble. She was currently in Downward Dog, and peeked under her arm to see the large man leaning against the doorframe, arms crossed.

"Ready for what?" she asked, frowning slightly as she lifted her right leg and swung it forward, her torso coming up into Warrior One.

"For that beer I owe you," he said, his white teeth brightening his face with childlike glee.

Sara had to laugh at his enthusiasm. A beer did sound good right then; even if what they had on the ship was all non-alcoholic. She was determined to finish out the routine, however.

"Can you give me ten minutes to finish up and change,

or is this a limited time offer?" she asked, flowing into Warrior Two.

He came in and sat at the small table. "Take your time. I'm not on duty for a few shifts." He leaned back with his hands behind his head, as if the hard plastic chair was a recliner.

Sara shook her head in exasperation, but didn't tell him to leave. She felt comfortable around Baxter; He was like a rock in the tumultuous waves of her first command, something she could grab onto if she felt overwhelmed.

That was a weird way of putting that, she thought as she floated down to Plank, and proceeded through the Chaturanga. *I mean, Baxter is a solid guy, and I trust him, but I don't want to **grab** onto him.* Her face reddened, and not from exertion.

She suddenly decided having an audience was a little too much for her, and cut the yoga short. She stood and smoothed her red hair back, redoing her ponytail, making sure she didn't have any wild hairs. She grabbed the towel beside her mat and wiped at her face, but, not having really broken out in a sweat, managed only to smudge her mascara.

"Shit," she said, looking at the black smudge.

Why do I even bother with this stuff? She looked over her shoulder at Baxter, who was messing with an app on his arm tablet, oblivious to her makeup tragedy. She noted that he was not wearing his uniform, but instead had put on a pair of old jeans and a black tee shirt. If it weren't for the cuff on his forearm holding his military issued tablet, he would have looked like he was just heading out to the bar with friends. She smiled. *Looking nice isn't a crime. Besides, the mascara brings out my eyes.*

She rolled up the yoga mat and stuffed it in her closet. She picked out a thin knit sweater, deciding her black yoga pants were fine for a beer with a friend. *Plus, he seems to rather like them. Not that that matters,* she amended quickly. She slipped the sweater over her head, and after a small internal battle, reapplied her mascara in the small mirror on the closet door.

She could see in the reflection that Alister had jumped up onto Baxter's lap, and was being vigorously petted.

Slipping on some ankle socks and black running shoes, Sara declared herself ready for beers.

They walked down to the dining area, a slightly awkward silence accompanying them. It wasn't unusual for the crew to dress in their civilian clothes if they were off-duty, but most people just wore their battlesuits. The suits were extremely comfortable, but sometimes not wearing a skin-tight suit was nice. Seeing Baxter in jeans and a tee shirt made Sara think of him as someone more than just the Sergeant Major.

Finding an empty table in the corner, Sara sat down while Baxter went to the drink dispenser and grabbed them two beers. He returned and twisted the tops off the plastic bottles, handing her one.

He took a long pull before saying, "I don't know that I've ever seen you in anything but your uniform or battlesuit."

So we're going straight for the elephant in the room. Sara flushed, taking a gulp of 'beer' to cover it up. "Same to you. I didn't even know you owned anything that wasn't government-issued."

He laughed. "To be honest, this is about it." He leaned in conspiratorially, his voice low and without a trace of humor. "Don't tell anyone, but this tee shirt came from boot camp."

He said it so seriously that it took Sara a second to realize it was a joke. She barked out a laugh that surprised them both, and quickly took another drink to mask the burning flush that was creeping up her neck. She noticed a few heads turn their way and then quickly look away when they saw who it was.

God, I wish this beer was real. What is wrong with you, Sara? It's Baxter; no need to be nervous. You're just two friends, having a beer.

Baxter gave an easy smile, chuckling at his own joke. "So, where are you from? Originally?" he asked, leaning back and giving her some room to breathe.

Having something to pour her unexpected nervous energy into, she was happy to tell him all about her life in the American Midwest. "Columbus, Ohio. My parents own a farm just outside the city that they inherited from my dad's parents. They still work it, though it's not all that big... mostly fruits and vegetables that taste better than the printed versions. They have kids come from the local schools to learn about farming techniques and practices, and they still sell the produce locally. My dad said that, before the Elif came and the molecular printers started to provide everything, they were struggling to stay afloat. Now the farm is there for educational purposes and because he didn't really know what else to do. He was a farmer all his life, then overnight, it became a boutique business. They make a little money for luxuries, but it's not like money is all that important anymore." She was rambling, but Baxter was following every word.

He nodded when she finally took a breath. "That must have been fun; growing up on a working farm. Not many people can say they've done that."

"Cora and I were off to school at seventeen, so we didn't really ever get into it."

Baxter took another swig of beer. "Yeah, I was in the Marines at eighteen, and never left, obviously," he said, indicating the ship in general with a wave of his hand. "But my dad was a cop in L.A., so I kind of followed in the family business. Though I'm sure he never thought his son would be seeing action on another planet."

After the ice was broken, the conversation took an easier turn. They ended up talking about everything from school to what the holidays were like back with family, and how long it had been since they had gone home.

Sara found it easy to talk to the dark-skinned man, with his generous smile and white hair that somehow didn't add years to his face. Halfway through the conversation, dinner was being served, so they grabbed trays and fell in line with the rest of the crew, continuing to talk the whole way through the queue.

Once they had eaten, Alister crawled into Baxter's lap, purring and rubbing his face on Baxter's fingers. Sara felt a stab of jealousy; he only acted that way with her.

Alister stopped purring and turned to look at Sara, a perplexed look on his face. His yellow eyes narrowed slightly, and she could feel his confusion through their empathic link.

Then she got it. He liked Baxter so much because her own feelings were bleeding into him. Alister was just acting on what she was feeling.

Oh, my god. I like him. Shit… shit. I can't. He's my subordinate. This isn't good. What would people think? What would Cora think?

"I'm sorry, but I have to go," she said, standing up and interrupting Baxter right in the middle of a story about his time in boot.

The look of shock on his face quickly turned to something more somber. "Ah, right. Wouldn't want to keep you. Have a good night, Captain," he said with a nod, putting Alister on the floor.

"Sorry, it's not you. I have a… few reports that I need to get done before my shift tomorrow," she said lamely.

He gave her a smile, but she could see the disappointment it hid. "I understand. Please, don't let me keep you. I had a nice time." Sara was well aware of the lack of the usual

'We should do it again sometime' that accompanied the end of most nights like this one.

Fuck, Sara. You're an idiot.

She didn't know what to do, though. So she gave him a nod and made a beeline for the door.

She looked back right before exiting and saw that Baxter had his head down slightly, and his brows furrowed in confusion, more than likely wondering what he had done to drive her off.

Alister trotted up next to her as she walked down the corridor toward her room. He gave her a sideways look. "Merp?"

Sara frowned. "I know. I'm a big ol' chicken. You don't need to rub it in."

He flicked an ear, but didn't say anything more.

CHAPTER 6

THE NEXT DAY and a half passed with Sara trying to avoid Baxter and the feelings she was burying. Her shift on the bridge became a relief instead of the monotonous chore it had been in the previous days of transit. She wouldn't have to deal with any feelings while staring at the slowly expanding view. Grimms had picked up on her odd mood, but said nothing, gleaning that it was a personal matter he was best left out of.

Sara took the time she wasn't on duty to talk with the Elif on board. Dr. Hess and Dr. Romis had caught a ride with the *Raven,* and had been spending time with Ambassador Foss in his quarters. The Ambassador had training on how to handle being alone, but he was relieved to have some company.

The Elif were a very social species, and spent the majority of their time in small groups, even sharing quarters on starships. The doctors had taken the time to reacquaint themselves with each other, and Sara was glad to see that Ambassador Foss was a welcome addition to their reunion. Sara did feel a little uncomfortable at the thought of all three of them sleeping in the same room together, but to each their own. She wasn't about to judge them for finding happiness, after the battle they had survived.

The doctors were currently keeping busy talking with Cora. They pulled up old descriptions of human ships and the fascinating things they could do both in battle and in peacetime. Cora was finding the detailed records immensely helpful, seeing them as a glimpse of what was to come from the tests she and Grimms had set up. All three of the Elif made it clear that they would like to be onboard when the testing commenced, in order to see firsthand what they had been studying for the majority of their lives. Cora welcomed them with an enthusiasm that mirrored their own.

Sara, however, was still having a little trouble trusting the Elif as a whole after watching the video of the War Mage dying at their treachery. But that was her problem, not the doctors' or Ambassador Foss's; they had been nothing but kind and helpful since before Colony 788. She needed to remind herself that what she had seen had happened a long time ago, carried out by long-dead rulers of a desperate race of people. The circumstances were far different now. She didn't think she could ever sacrifice an entire race of people to save her own, but then again, she had never been confronted with that choice.

On the third day, the *Regis* dropped out of warp, and, with a sweep of the sensors, the Sol System showed itself on the bridge's holo projector, looking the same as it had when they had flown out on their maiden voyage just under two weeks ago.

They were towed insystem, all the way to the orbital ship-yard, where Connors detached the *Raven* from the destroyer's hard points and flew them into the dock under thrusters. Sara still didn't want Cora doing any heavy lifting, even the relatively short warp across the system, despite her twin's reassurances that she was fine.

Sara was packing up her Navy-issued duffel bag for the short stay back on Earth during her debriefing. The Admiralty wanted her to come in person, and with the sensitivity of the information she had gathered on their short mission, she thought an in-person meeting was a good idea.

"Well, we have our testing parameters. Grimms' suggestions were all accepted, as I figured they would be," Cora said from the room's speakers.

Sara smiled. "He is rather thorough. Are you sure you don't want me onboard for the tests?"

"No, Grimms and I can handle it. We're not going to be looking for a fight, and the jumps we have planned are into deep interstellar space and back. There shouldn't be anyone even remotely close to us; if there is, I can get us out of there quickly," Cora said, amused at the idea that Sara would want to hang around for a boring battery of tests. "You're going to have your hands full, anyway. With the debriefings and searching for the dreadnought, you'll be busy. Do you know where you're going to start looking, by the way?"

Sara had been thinking about this ever since Cora had brought it up the first time. "I have an idea, but I need to talk to Alister about it." The cat perked up at the mention of his name.

"How are you going to do that? He's a cat," Cora said, reminding Sara that she had not told Cora about their meeting in the Aether. Or the fact that he was a pixie—though now she wondered if that was even possible. Sara told herself she'd kept it quiet so that Cora would not be distracted while adjusting to the core, but she wondered why she really felt the need to keep things like this from her sister.

Some habits die hard, I guess. It's your sister, dummy; who else do you trust even half as much? Now is as good a time to tell her as any, she supposed.

She opened her mouth to explain how she could talk to

her cat, but found she couldn't mention anything about it. Her mouth opened and began to move, but she couldn't get the words out. It was like when she had tried to tell Boon about the pixies. Something was keeping her quiet about anything even remotely concerning the creatures.

I really should have met with Alister to talk about this, she admonished herself. "We have our ways," she finally told her sister, knowing it sounded lame.

Sara could hear Cora's disbelieving expression. "Uh, okay, weirdo."

She changed the subject before she was talked into a corner. "How long will the testing take?"

"A few days, a week at the most. I'm sure the UHFC has plenty of plans for us, so they don't want the tests taking too long, but of course they want a thorough examination, at the same time. Don't worry, we'll be safe." She paused. "How is Boon doing? Any closer to getting the spellform?"

Sara had just come from Boon's bunk before packing her own bag. "Don't you watch everything that happens on the ship?" she asked, realizing she had no clue how Cora operated from her tank.

Cora laughed. "I can, but I don't. People deserve their privacy. Besides, I can't look everywhere at once. I'm still human."

"You spy on me all the time!" Sara argued, standing up from her half-packed duffel bag and planting her hands on her hips.

"Well, you don't count. You're my sister. And besides, someone has to keep an eye on you," Cora said smugly.

"Great, my own personal voyeur," Sara said, rolling her eyes, and she snatched a folded shirt from the bed and stuffed it into the open duffel. "Boon is doing well, for your information. She can make both forms, but is having trouble combining them; I can say from experience that's the hard part. I'm really impressed by her ability, though, considering she hasn't had any formal training. With a little more work, I think she'll have it."

"Good, then I don't feel so bad that I ordered her to accompany you."

"What? I'm going to be in with the Admiralty most of the time. Doesn't she have duties here on the *Raven*?" Sara asked, immediately regretting the question, because it let Cora know that she wasn't paying attention to her crew's duties.

"God, I can't believe you're in charge of a warship," she said with a sigh. "Yes, but nothing that can't be covered by someone else. Besides, most of Boon's duties are related to you. She is *your* cabin girl, after all."

"I knew that," Sara lied. "It's probably best if she's with me, anyway. I'm hoping to learn more about being a War Mage, and she may as well learn it with me." Sara kept her fears about being unable to control her powers to herself; no need to worry Cora.

There you go again, she scolded herself, before shaking her head slightly to dislodge the worry.

"How long will it take her, do you think?" Cora asked, bringing Sara back to the conversation.

"To be able to cast? I have no clue. She works on it constantly, but it's a really hard spellform. Besides, if this whole thing is determined by genetics, she may not be able to do it at all," Sara said, dropping her makeup bag on top of her clothes and zipping the duffel closed.

"It is a hard spell, but I think the fact that she can hold the two separate forms is proof she's a War Mage. I never met anyone able to hold two forms at once, but after what I learned from the core, I gave it a try. After some practice, I was able to do it, though I still can't combine them," Cora said mischievously.

Sara cocked her head. "You're trying the Familiar spell?"

Cora gave a light laugh. "Of course I am. We're twins, remember? If you're a War Mage, then so am I."

Sara blinked a few times, trying to let that sink in. "I didn't even think about that. Holy shit, Cora. We would be unstoppable if you had a familiar, too. "

"The problem is I'm stuck in this tank, and the last I checked, there are no small animals onboard for me to bond with," her sister reasoned, sounding slightly disappointed.

Knowing that the familiars were not animals at all, Sara had an idea. "Let me worry about that. Don't cast the spell if you figure out how, not until I can arrange for a potential familiar to be close by. I don't know what will happen if they can't get to you."

"I figured you would say something like that. Don't bring me a rat or anything creepy; make it something cool," she laughed.

Sara looked over at Alister, who was paying close attention to the entire exchange. He gave her a very slight nod, though she didn't know if it was to indicate he agreed that Cora could be a War Mage, or if he was saying they could bring her a pixie. Either way, they had a plan of sorts.

Sara checked her arm tablet. "Shit, I have to go. Is Boon ready?"

"I'm ready," a high voice chimed in from the doorway. Boon was in her dress uniform, and her bag, gripped in both hands, hung in front of her.

Sara threw the strap of her own bag over her shoulder and headed for the door. "Let's go. We have some admirals to impress," she said, closing the door behind them once Alister was out in the hall. He jumped up on her shoulder as they made for the airlock.

"Does he always do that?" Boon asked, looking at Alister

perched on her shoulder, doing his best impression of an Egyptian god.

He caught her gaze with his yellow eyes, and raised an eyebrow at her. Alicia started, and turned to face forward.

Sara gave a chuckle. "He does. I think it's because he's a lazy bastard that hates to walk anywhere."

His head snapped around to her, and he let out a high-pitched "Meep?"

Sara regarded him with squinted eyes, then said to Boon, "Don't worry, you'll have your own little bundle of joy riding you like a horse in no time."

The girl let out a long breath through her nose, dispelling the pent-up frustration that the spellwork had brought on. "I hope so."

CHAPTER 7

Sᴀʀᴀ ᴛᴏᴏᴋ ᴀ sɪᴘ ᴏғ ᴡᴀᴛᴇʀ, sitting straighter in her chair. She was at a table facing a semicircle of admirals, all of whom were old enough to remember a world without magic. Boon sat next to her, holding a tablet and scrolling through the reports Sara had written during the mission, presenting the pertinent information to her captain when the time came.

Sara cleared her throat and continued. "That's right, Admiral Franklin, a familiar." Alister sat at attention on the table beside her as exhibit A.

Admiral Franklin, a man in his mid-sixties with a neatly trimmed white beard, regarded the cat. "And you say that this familiar," he looked down at his own tablet, "Alister, is no normal cat, but a conduit for the power you've harnessed in becoming a War Mage?"

"That's right, sir. The spell is extremely difficult, and new evidence from one of the cores we recovered suggests that the ability to cast this spell is somehow genetic in nature; though the details of those genes are, unfortunately, not on the core. The important thing is that my abilities as a mage have escalated. According to the records of the Ancient Humans, a

War Mage was like an army unto their self, and that was all possible because of…" She hesitated as the word 'pixie' was stricken from her mind. "Creatures like him," she finished, resting her elbows on the table and giving Alister a smile. He rolled his eyes at 'creature', but he knew the restraint she was under.

It must be part of the contract Alister mentioned when we met in the Aether. I really need to talk to him. Tonight, she thought, playfully pulling on the tip of his tail. He gave her a dirty look before sitting up straight, ignoring her pestering.

"I just want to be clear. You're telling us that, because of this spell you found in a schoolbook, you are now able to take on an entire army? I find that hard to believe, Captain," a female admiral with her hair in a severe bun said with a smirk.

Alister looked at the woman and flipped an ear in irritation.

Sara suppressed a smile. "With all due respect, Admiral, you have the reports. You have the video from a dozen Aether suits. I can pull this building down around us, if you would like a personal demonstration," she offered snidely, regretting the flippant comment immediately.

Admiral Franklin frowned. "Despite Captain Sonders' ill-advised offer of a demonstration, the footage does not lie, Admiral Smith. It is not unreasonable to think there is a type of mage we have not heard of, or a set of spells the Elif don't know about." Admiral Smith gave a conceding nod, and Admiral Franklin turned back to Sara and Boon. "Ensign…" he checked his tablet once more, "Boon. What is your impression of this union between Captain Sonders and Alister?"

Boon looked up from the tablet, blinking a few times, as the color drained from her face. Her long, blonde hair was pulled back in a bun, better for showing the rising flush of her skin at her sudden involvement in the proceedings.

I'm just supposed to be Sara's secretary for this meeting!

After a strangled swallow, she cleared her throat. "Sir, to be honest, I had no knowledge of the union until after the battle of Colony 788. But I have to say, the things the captain was capable of were nothing less than amazing. You have the reports, but seeing the wreckage left behind after her attack on the Teifen carrier and their ground troops…" She trailed off in thought. Coming back to herself after a moment's reflection, she continued. "Sirs, to ignore the possibility of a working union with the familiars is folly. We are facing an un-winnable war, and we are going to need all the help we can get. Right now the only defense we have against the Teifen and Galvox is that they don't know where Earth is; if they ever found out, we would be extinguished in less than a day. Humans are short-lived and slow breeders, on the galactic scene, but we dominated the galaxy for thousands of years. It seems pretty obvious that the War Mages made that possible. It took the combined forces of three empires to take us down. That tells me we have an ace up our sleeve, and, to be honest, if we don't play it, we may as well give up now and save the ammunition. Sir."

Sara's mouth nearly dropped to the floor. Boon, normally so reserved and quiet, had broken the problem down perfectly. They needed the United Human Confederation to adopt the idea of creating War Mages; even if they could only find a few dozen on Earth, they would have a huge advantage.

The admirals sat back, each officer quietly contemplating Boon's words. Then they leaned in and talked amongst themselves for quite a while. They seemed to be torn about what to do with this unexpected development. Normally Sara would be concerned that they would try to study Alister, and any like him they could summon, but she knew there was nothing the Navy could do to the pixies.

Pixies only show themselves to their summoner, and after that, the two become inseparable. The Navy can't just catch one and study it with no consequences, Sara thought, relieved that the pixies would be safe. *And no War Mage would ever give up their Familiar. This is an all-or-nothing move, and the admirals know it. They're just worried about not being in control, about putting their hopes in a nuclear option with a will of its own.* She understood where they were coming from, but she still hoped they'd make the right call.

Admiral Franklin cleared his throat. "Captain Sonders, you have sent all the information you have on the familiars—and the process for obtaining them—to Naval Intelligence, correct?"

"Yes, sir. I have given them the spellforms and all the notes I have taken on the subject. My sister, who helped with the creation of the spellform, has sent her reports as well. They have everything they need."

"Good. We're going ahead with the project. Ensign Boon is right: we need every edge in the coming conflict. The Elif leaving to defend their home system has left us with a gaping hole in our own defenses, but the core you have brought us will go a long way in filling it. We are already shifting production to the new designs, and upping the schedule for the second and third fleets, and a few surprises will be coming out of the printers in a few days; I just hope it's fast enough." The old man referred to his tablet once again. "Captain Sonders, I understand you have requested to take some leave while the *Raven* undergoes its testing, is that right?"

"Yes, sir. I need a little time to come to terms with my new power and the responsibilities that come with it. I wish to serve at my best, sir, and I don't think I've given myself enough time to adjust," Sara admitted, arranging her face to convey seriousness and loyalty.

The admiral nodded. "I can understand your desire to become better, Captain. Be sure to stay close to your comms; I'm sure there will be many questions for you in the coming days."

Sara stood, making a quick hand motion for Boon to do the same, and they both saluted. "Yes, sir. I'll be at your disposal, sir. Thank you."

She turned and started down the aisle of empty seats, toward the back of the room and the double doors that led to freedom. Alister was on her shoulder before she'd gone two steps, Boon right behind them.

Before she could open the door and step out, Admiral Smith called out for her. "Captain?"

Sara cringed slightly, but turned and smiled at the elderly lady. "Yes, ma'am?"

Smith narrowed her eyes slightly in consideration before asking, "Could you really pull this entire building down?"

Her question caught Sara, and the other admirals, off-guard. The surprise on their faces was replaced with questioning stares, and Sara realized they wanted to know the answer as well.

"Easily," she said without hesitation.

CHAPTER 8

Two DAYS of endless talks and debriefings awaited Sara and Boon when they landed at the capitol building in Hawaii. For two days, they watched footage and explained decisions, and—while never actually having to—justified Sara's new powers. At the end of the two days, the only thing the captain was sure of was that the UHFC was very nervous.

Having someone who could literally take out an army under the command of someone who could not was a dynamic they had no experience with. While Sara tried to convince them that she would follow orders, she knew there would eventually be someone who would not.

Sara had talked with Cora right before getting on the tram. After a day and a half of scientists who had no clue what was happening trying to tell them what was happening, Cora said the tests were finally getting started. The *Raven* was making its first test warp with the core in a few hours. Sara wished her luck.

Boon shaded her eyes from the bright afternoon sun, as she and Sara stepped out of the tram that had brought them down the mountain from the capitol complex on the side of Mauna Kea.

Sara handed her a spare pair of sunglasses. "Here, I figured you'd forget to bring some," she said, putting on her own pair of silver-rimmed aviators. Boon quickly followed suit, and Sara had to smile at the too big glasses on her small face.

"Come on, let's find you some that fit properly. I have a feeling we're going to need them over the next few days." Sara tightened the straps of her backpack and headed for a line of shops on the edge of the square outside the tram station.

They were both dressed as civilians: tee shirts, blue jeans, and, in Sara's case, a white knit hat that she could stuff her fire-engine-red hair into to make herself a little less conspicu-ous. Boon had opted for a ballcap, with the adjustable snaps in what Sara thought of as the 'child-sized' position. She had pulled her ponytail through the hole so that it bounced around her shoulders as she walked. Each of them carried a backpack containing a few changes of clothes, their arm tablets, and some metal water bottles strapped to the side. A few weeks ago, Sara would have wanted to bring a gun, just to be safe; now she brought a cat instead, and felt much more comfortable about it.

They stepped up to a kiosk where a young woman sat inside, playing on her tablet. The entire cart was covered in sunglasses. Boon took off the too large pair and began trying on various styles—none of which, Sara noted, were aviators.

Sara loved her aviators, but she knew they weren't for everybody. She crossed her arms as Boon tried on pair after pair and checked herself in the mirror. Alister poked his head out of Sara's backpack and rested his paws on her shoulder, watching Boon with interest.

"So, how do we know where to look?" Boon asked,

trying on her fourth pair of glasses, then going back to the previous ones and checking them again.

"Right now, we don't. I'll find out tonight, after I go to bed," Sara said, reaching up to scratch Alister's chin. They had finally made plans to meet in the Aether for the second time. "First I want to get us a hotel, then we can go to the beach. This will probably be the last opportunity either of us has to relax for a long while."

"Okay." Finally choosing the pair she liked best, Boon reached over the counter and pressed her thumb to the payment pad. It scanned her identity, and the price was deducted from her account.

The economy of Earth had changed quite a bit, if Sara was to believe her dad. In the old days, people had to work for basic survival; now they only worked for luxuries. Everyone's housing and food and medical care was provided for free, and Earth was no longer in the resource game. With the molecular printers, an asteroid could be towed in and broken down to its elements, then reassembled into anything—food, clothing, buildings, starships. Now people only worked if they wanted something more. The population used to be divided into 'haves' and 'have nots'... now there were just 'haves,' and nobody suffered for it; there was plenty to go around.

"What do you think?" Boon asked, tilting her head to the side slightly as she looked up at Sara, showing off her choice. She had picked out a pair of black plastic frames with oversized black lenses. She looked like a fabulous bug.

Sara smiled. "Marvelous, darling. Simply marvelous," she complimented, rasping her voice a little to sound like she was from the golden age of cinema.

Boon flashed a smile then turned to look down the street that headed toward the beach. "Where did you want to get a room?"

"Come on, Baxter told me about a little place he stayed the last time he was on leave," Sara said, starting down the wide avenue that was full of tourists on day trips.

"Baxter, huh?" Boon asked playfully, but Sara acted like she didn't hear.

Am I that obvious?

They passed many glass-windowed storefronts, lining the main road. Boon had to scoot out of the way of several people when something caught her eye and she stopped watching where she was going. Eventually, Sara noticed that Boon had disappeared completely, and stopped in the middle of the sidewalk, looking around for her. She spotted the small woman standing in front of a boutique shop, her thumbs tucked into the straps of her backpack and her mouth hanging open as she stared into the window.

Sara backtracked, fighting the current of people, until she was beside the girl. "See something you like?" she asked sarcastically, then looked in the window.

It was a dress shop. 'Handmade, classic dresses! Made to order' the graphic on the window read. Sara leaned back and saw the name of the shop. 'Mr. Green Jeans'—despite a total lack of jeans on display in the front window.

"It's beautiful," Boon murmured, leaning in so close to the window that her nose nearly touched the glass.

Sara looked past the graphic to see what had grabbed Boon's attention, and wondered how sheltered the poor girl had to have been, raised on that compound with her family. She was looking at a dress. A simple, sleeveless, skater dress.

"The color is amazing," Alicia said, nearly drooling.

Sara had to look around to be sure she wasn't the butt of some elaborate prank. "It's blue," she noted, cocking an eyebrow.

"I know, isn't it pretty?"

"You know your uniform is blue, right?" Sara asked, still not sure this wasn't a setup.

"I know, but it's not the same," she almost whined.

"Don't you own a dress? I mean, you have to own a dress; every girl has at least one dress," Sara pressed, cocking her head to the side. Alister bumped his forehead against her ear and purred at her closeness. She reached up and scratched his chin in acknowledgment.

"No. Where I grew up, everyone wore white pants and shirts. Divinity's Light preached that no one should stand out, so they took away everyone's individuality," she explained, not looking away from the dress in the window. "When I left, I immediately joined the Navy, and they provided all my clothes. These jeans and a few pairs of shoes are the only clothing I've ever bought. Even this tee shirt is Navy-issued."

Sara rolled her eyes, grabbed the shoulder of Boon's tee shirt, and dragged her through the store's open door. Boon was stumbling along behind her until she got her feet under herself and was able to pull out of Sara's grasp.

"What are you doing?" Boon hissed, half-hiding behind Sara.

"Making you try on the dress," she said, waving to the young woman working a handheld stitching machine behind the counter.

The boutique was filled with bolts of cloth of all different patterns, and had that smell that lingers when there's just a little too much dust in the air. Three mirrors stood around a low platform where, Sara guessed, a customer would have her measurements taken.

"I can't afford that," she argued, glancing at the dress on display.

The woman waved back to Sara and set down her work

in progress, then came around the counter and headed their way.

"What do you mean you can't afford it? You're a fucking officer in the Navy. I mean, a low-ranking one, but still. How do you not have money? Everything is provided for you, we don't sell anything on the ship, and you just told me the only things you've ever bought were some shoes and a pair of jeans," Sara recounted, looking down at Boon's red face.

"I bought a hover bike," she said out of the corner of her mouth as she smiled blankly at the approaching woman.

"A hover bike? Seriously?" Sara marveled at this whole new side of the normally-reserved woman.

"Yeah. I've always wanted one, and I found a shop that does them up custom. I'm too small for one off the salesroom floor."

"A hover bike?" Sara asked again. She couldn't picture Boon racing around on one of the death traps. Now she was sure this was an elaborate prank. "Why?"

Boon gave her a puzzled look. "Because they're awesome."

"Hi, what can I do for you?" the saleswoman asked in the overly polite, customer service manner.

Sara smiled and pointed at the blue dress in the window. "Is that for sale?"

"Oh, yes," the young woman said, brushing back some mousy brown hair that had escaped her ponytail. "I normally make dresses to order, but I do have a few in stock."

She led them around a stand full of rolls of cloth to a rack on the wall filled with dresses of various designs. It looked like she just made whatever struck her fancy, because no two garments were alike—or from the same decade, it seemed. She slid a section to the side, revealing a copy of the blue dress from the window.

"It's one of my most popular designs, so I always have a

few on-hand in different colors," she explained, showing both a red and a yellow version. "Would you like to try it on? It may be a little short on you, but you look like you have the legs to pull it off."

Sara reddened slightly at the compliment. "Actually, it would be for my friend, here," she said, pushing Boon out in front.

The woman's eyebrows rose, and she said, "Oh, well then, I may have to take the hem in just a bit. Come with me, dear," she said, guiding the stunned Boon to a curtain and pulling it back to reveal a changing room. "Slip it on and come out so I can see about adjustments."

Boon stumbled into the changing room, and the woman slid the curtain closed.

This woman knows how to get a sale. Sara smiled. "So, are you Mr. Green Jeans?"

The sales associate laughed. "Oh, that. Well, I started out making designer jeans, but got bored with it and switched to dresses. I kept the name because it was such a hassle getting the sign up on the building in the first place. Oh, I think she's ready. Are you decent?" she asked the curtain.

"Um, I can't reach the zipper."

The woman whipped back the curtain and revealed a barebacked Boon, who yelped and clutched the front of the dress to her chest. "Let me help you out with that, darling," she offered, deftly zipping the dress before Boon could even move. "Come out and take a look at yourself in the mirror."

Sara had to smile. Boon looked great; the dress was the perfect cut for her small frame, and the blue color made her blonde hair seem richer, and complemented her blue eyes perfectly.

The look on the girl's face when she saw herself in the mirror was worth making her put the thing on. Her jaw dropped as she took in the halter style top that ended in a

high waist, and the layered skirt that flared out around her
just slightly.

Sara stepped up, making a 'not bad' face as she nodded
her approval. "Damn, Boon. You look great in that," she said
admiringly.

"Thanks, but you know I can't—"

"My treat," Sara cut her off. "Think of it as a training
gift, if there is such a thing. Fuck it, we'll call it a thing. It's
your training gift."

The woman began to fuss with the cut and fit of the dress
with practiced hands, making marks with a small piece of
chalk. The last thing she did was pin the hem of the dress
four centimeters shorter, revealing more of Boon's legs. The
effect was that she now looked six centimeters taller.

"Do you like it?" the woman asked, smiling at Boon's
overwhelmed expression.

"I love it," she breathed, smoothing down the skirts with
both hands.

"Good! Take it off, and I can make the adjustments while
you wait. It shouldn't take more than ten minutes," she said,
shooing Boon back into the changing room and closing the
curtain.

Sara saw a rack of bathing suits to her left, and, realizing
they didn't have any swimwear, picked out two string bikinis
with a nice crocheted design along the edges. She figured if
they only had to tie them, they wouldn't have to try them
on. She grabbed a white one that matched her knit cap and a
red one for Boon, just to mix it up a little, then wandered
back over toward the changing room.

She and Mr. Green Jeans stood in silence for a minute,
until Sara said, "You're really good, you know that?"

"At what, making dresses?" the woman asked, a half-grin
on her face.

"That too," Sara grinned back.

CHAPTER 9

THEY CHECKED into the little hotel that Baxter had mentioned, after wandering down two wrong side streets looking for the place. "The Quiet Hideaway" only had ten rooms, but it seemed all ten had been built with meticulous care. Their room's floor plan was open, with the two king-sized beds in small, private rooms on either side of a shared living space that opened out onto a furnished balcony. While the entrance to the hotel had been down a tight alley, the rooms were on the top floor, so that the view was uninterrupted all the way to the water.

Baxter has some good taste, Sara noted as she threw her bag on her bed.

"We're really just going to go hang out at the beach for the rest of the day?" Boon asked, yelling from the other bedroom to be heard.

"It's not like we have a lead just yet. I'm going to see if there's anything on Cora's core that can help, but I can do that anywhere, so why not take advantage of the beach while we're here?" Sara answered, pulling the two bikinis from the shopping bag.

"I don't have a suit," Boon said, turning just in time to have both the top and bottom of the red bikini hit her in the face. She quickly snatched them from the air, taking a second to recognize what they were. "Oh, wow. I've never worn so little in public before."

Sara laughed from the doorway, "That's a pretty conservative suit compared to what I'm sure we'll be seeing. Get changed. We're burning daylight, Blondie."

SARA LEANED BACK on the wooden beach chair. She was still wearing the white knit hat, but it matched the crocheted bikini perfectly, and she rather liked not having people stare at her unusual hair color. The bikini fit just right and complemented her pale skin. She knew she would be a little burned that night, but her burns usually tanned by the next day, and she could really use the vitamin D.

She closed her eyes and let the sun warm her skin, making up for the last few weeks she had spent under artificial light. The drone of people speaking and kids playing and the ever-present sound of the crashing waves became a white noise she could clear her mind to.

Until she heard Boon cursing under her breath and rummaging in their bag. The hotel had provided a woven bag, along with some beach towels and flip flops, and Alicia was in the process of dumping the contents of the bag out on the sand.

Alister had been curled up under Sara's chair, out of the sun, but when the towels hit the ground, he climbed out from under the seat and burrowed his way into the heap, his tail sticking out and slowly flicking back and forth.

"What the hell, Boon? Don't get sand all over everything," Sara scolded, reaching into the pile of towels and personal items to grab her arm tablet. "I don't want to be picking sand out of the ports on this thing." She banged the side of the tablet on her palm to dislodge a few granules.

"Sorry, I can't find my sunglasses. I think I left them in the room," she said, looking inland toward the hotel, as if she could escape.

"They're right there." Sara pointed at the neck of the tee shirt Boon had insisted on wearing over her suit.

Boon looked down and saw the black glasses hanging from her collar. "Oh. Right."

She sheepishly pulled them out and slipped them on her face. She then looked around to see if anyone was looking her way. When she was satisfied that there was not a crowd forming to stare at her, she pulled off her tee shirt and laid back, feigning comfort.

Sara just watched her for a while, paying special attention to the tendon that stood out more and more prominently from her neck the longer she 'relaxed'.

Wow, how can she be this shy?

"Boon," Sara said, still staring at her sideways from her beach chair.

Boon didn't move, but Sara could see she was staring up into the sky like an animal frozen with fear.

"Boon," Sara said, louder this time.

Jumping at her name, Boon stiffly swung her head to face Sara. "What? Do I have something on my face?"

"No, but you look like you're going to pop a blood vessel. Relax. What's got you so tight?"

With a sigh, she said in a loud whisper, "I've never been this naked in front of strangers. It's freaking me out."

Sara sighed. *I should have guessed. They had one-piece suits, why didn't I just grab one of those?*

Clearing her throat and giving Boon a bright smile, she said, "Listen, if you're that uncomfortable, just put your shirt back on. But just so you know, you don't have anything to be embarrassed about. You're in the military, and we tend to be in pretty good shape. You look good. But if it makes you feel more comfortable, cover up. Just understand that no one is judging you."

Boon gave her a smile, "Thanks, Captain."

"None of that 'captain' shit. We're on leave, remember? It's just 'Sara'," she said, leaning back again. She noticed Boon slip the tee back on over the blood red bikini before she closed her eyes.

SARA FELT the presence of a hulking figure behind her, felt the power emanating from it. Even through the protective plating of her Aetheric armor, she could feel its heat, like standing too close to a campfire. A bead of sweat rolled down her neck inside the suit, making her itch.

She turned around, bringing her hands up in a defensive posture, ready to face her enemy. She was a War Mage, and this creature stood no chance against her might.

She froze when she saw what she faced. Or rather, *who* she faced.

Standing three meters away was Cora, surrounded by swirling flames. Her eyes glowed a molten red as power surged through her. She opened her mouth, and flames poured out, rippling up her face to dance atop her head like a crown of flames. There was joy in her expression, as if she were reveling in the uncontrollable, evil power that rolled off her in waves.

Sara knew she needed to stop her sister before she could hurt anyone. She mustered her will to snuff out the thing Cora had become, but no spellform came to her. She looked around her feet for Alister's ever-present form, but he was nowhere to be seen. She tried to make the spellform in her own mind, but like always, it wouldn't form properly. She was powerless.

She took a step back, trying to gauge the situation better, and noticed a small cat jump onto the flaming figure's shoulder. It was Alister; he, too, was wreathed in flame, his normally yellow eyes a deep crimson as they regarded her with hate.

Sara took another step back, realization hitting her like a blaster to the stomach.

That's not Cora. That's me.

The burning Alister leapt forward from the shoulder of the twisted version of herself, and landed on her chest, the heat of his flames scorching her face. She was frozen with fear as he stared into her soul.

He reached up a paw and smacked her face—not hard, but firmly. He did it again. And again. Then he bit her nose.

SARA SHOT up from her lounging position, her sudden movement throwing Alister to the sand from where he had been perched on her chest. Her heart was racing, and she couldn't seem to be able to catch her breath. She put a hand to her chest and squeezed her eyes closed, trying to will her beating heart to calm.

Alister hopped up onto the chair beside her, shaking the sand off and looking at her in concern, but he seemed distracted. He kept glancing over his shoulder.

They were still on the beach.

I must have fallen asleep. She looked down at Alister. "Sorry, I didn't mean to toss you like that. I was having a nightmare," she explained as way of apology.

Alister didn't seem to care, as he began smacking her leg and looking in Boon's direction.

Her heart slowing to a manageable level, Sara turned to see the girl kneeling in the sand, her eyes wide open, and tears streaming down her cheeks. She seemed to be frozen in place, as if she were being electrocuted.

"What's happening?" Sara asked, rolling off the chair to kneel in front of Boon. "Can you hear me? What did you do?" She reached out to shake Boon's shoulders and received a nasty shock of Aether for her trouble.

A flash of movement caught Sara's attention, and she saw Boon's tablet half-buried in the sand beside her, with the image of the spellforms for the Familiar spell rotating on the screen.

"Oh, my god. Alister, did she cast this?" she asked the near-panicking cat.

"Merp!" he said, scrambling to her side and looking up at her with concerned eyes.

"Shit," she swore, looking around the crowded beach. So far, no one had seemed to notice anything was happening, but Sara knew that would not last. She leaned in close to the girl and said, "Boon, can you hear me? Alicia? If you've begun casting the Familiar spell, I need to know you can hear me."

Boon's eyes flicked to hers, making brief contact before glazing over again.

Sara gave a half-smile. "Okay, good. Now, this is going to be the hard part. The spell is going to want to take every last bit of your Aether; I know they teach you not to use it all, but this time I need you to let it go. All of it. In fact, push it out. The spell won't work unless you make a full connection." She bit her lip, hoping Boon had understood.

Sara could remember when she had cast the spell, and how frightened she had been. She didn't know if her previous magical training had helped her or hindered her. If she were less practiced back then, she may not have been able to stop the last little bit of Aether from flowing out. However, now that she had completed the spell, she knew she had gone through an ordeal she hadn't needed to. The spell had to be completed with intention as much as action.

"You need to give up that last bit willingly, or it won't work. Trust that everything will be fine. It will, I promise," Sara said, her eyes welling with tears as she watched Boon suffer.

Then a change came over Boon's face. She went from tight-jawed and struggling to serene in the blink of an eye. Her features softened, and her shoulders sagged in relaxation. Boon closed her eyes and rolled sideways to the sand, her body sending up a small puff of dust.

Sara sat in stunned silence, not sure if she should touch her. She pushed the fear of being shocked to the back of her mind and felt for a pulse. She found none.

"Oh, fuck," she said in panic, rolling Boon onto her back to begin CPR.

Before she could begin compressions, Boon's skin began to glow slightly with Aether, the blue light difficult to see in the midday sun. Sara leaned back, not sure what to do. The light was getting brighter, and a static charge was building in the area. The hairs on Sara's arms stood up, and she could feel little zaps on her head as her hair built up a charge. A small radio a few meters away cut to static, making its owner pick it up and start fiddling with it in confusion.

The light of Alicia's skin quickly built in intensity, soon overpowering the glow of the sun on her skin, and gaining the attention of a few passersby. Sara had to shield her eyes from the light, and she scooted back a meter or so.

As the light became brighter and brighter, Boon's body slowly lifted into the air until it hovered half a meter off the ground. Then it began to pulse with light—slowly at first, but increasing in frequency with each blip until they were right on top of each other.

A crowd was now gathering to watch the odd light show. They were keeping their distance, but Sara could see several tablets held up as people thought to record the event.

The pulses were flashing so fast they became one, continuous, bright light, too harsh to look at directly. Then in one final pulse, the light exploded out from Boon's body and through the crowd, causing everyone to duck and a few to scream. Sara could see the wave of light dimming as it traveled out in a sphere, racing across water and land, passing through objects as if they were not there.

Boon landed on the sand with a *thump*, her power spent. Sara reached over and found a pulse, to her great relief.

The gathered crowd made her nervous; she needed to get Boon out of there. With a thought to Alister, he provided her a shield spell to power. It was a sphere that encircled her and Boon and a considerable chunk of sand, along with all of their belongings. Alister provided a second spell, and the sphere rocketed up off the beach and quickly shot into town.

Sara was sure to move fast and stay low, keeping them from being seen, only popping up to arc over the rail of their balcony. She dropped the shield, spilling sand all over the deck boards. She didn't care about the mess in the least, but she wondered what the cleaning staff would make of it.

She scooped Boon up and carried her to her bed, laying the unconscious girl down. Then she pulled up a chair and sat down, leaning close to watch over her.

Alister climbed onto the bed and, pressing himself up against Boon's leg, laid down.

"That could have gone better," Sara admitted, resting her chin in her hands.

"Merp," Alister agreed.

CHAPTER 10

THE REST OF THE DAY, Sara alternated between pacing and sitting in the chair beside Boon. She ordered some room service, but had no appetite when it arrived. Alister made quick work of a piece of succulent pork before returning to Boon's side. He gave Sara a nod of reassurance, and then closed his eyes to nap again.

By midnight, Sara was sitting in the chair, her head slowly sinking to her chest as sleep began creeping its way in. She was nearly gone, her head bouncing a few times as she tried in vain to fight off the warm embrace, when Alister sat up, startling her back to wakefulness.

"What? What happened?" Sara asked, leaning in to check on Boon. She was sleeping comfortably, but unchanged.

Alister however was not looking at Boon. He was staring over his shoulder, toward the front door. He swung his head around, his yellow eyes wide with excitement. "Merp!" he said, with a flick of his ear.

He jumped to the floor and raced out into the main room, disappearing around the corner, meowing and chirping the whole way.

Sara jumped up and chased after him. He was sitting at the door, looking up at the handle and then back to her. Sara reached out and opened the door, expecting to see an animal waiting, like when she had first summoned Alister, but there was nothing there.

"What the hell, Alister?" she asked, looking down, but he was gone. She stuck her head out the door and looked down the hall just in time to see him turn and head down the steps at the end of the passageway.

Fuck, he's fast, she thought. She stepped out into the hall, but went back for her room key. *It wouldn't do to get locked out when my roommate is passed out.*

She rushed out onto the balcony and sifted through the pile of sand, finally finding the card key. A few seconds later, she was running down the hall after Alister. She took the stairs two at a time and was in the lobby of the small hotel a minute later.

She looked around the empty, marble-floored lobby, but didn't see the little stinker anywhere. There was a young man at the front desk, reading a tablet and not paying attention to anything. She ran to the desk, her bare feet not making a sound, and slapped her hand to the marble counter right in front of the guy. He jumped and tossed the tablet in the air, fumbling it between his hands a few times before finally catching it.

"Have you seen my cat? He came down here a second ago," Sara said, her intensity making the poor guy cringe away from her.

"Uh, um, what? W-where did you come from? Were you at the beach? It's closed at night, you can't go down there," he blurted, confused and frightened at her sudden appearance.

"The beach? What the fuck are you talking about? I'm

looking for my cat," she repeated, trying to understand his rambling.

He waved a hand at her chest. "You have a bathing suit on, I just assumed…"

Sara looked down, noticing she was still wearing the white bikini. She'd been so intent on watching over Boon that she hadn't bothered to change. She shook her head in irritation, and turned away, scanning the lobby again.

"Alister? Alister, where are you?" she shouted to the empty area.

"Who's Alister?" the clerk asked.

"My cat!" she shouted in exasperation. "Have you seen him?"

"A cat?"

She growled in frustration and ran for the front door, bursting out into the lit alley. She looked left, then right, spotting Alister's tail whipping around the corner onto a side street. She took off, calling his name, her bare feet smarting when she stepped on the occasional pebble. She rounded the corner and hopped to a stop, almost trampling Alister, who was sitting on the empty sidewalk.

He looked up at her, his eyes bright and glowing in the streetlights. "Merow," he said excitedly.

Sara put her hands on her knees, inhaling deeply to catch her breath from the intense run and fighting off the panic she had felt at losing him.

"What the fuck, man? Where are you going?" she panted.

He looked down the street, causing her to look as well. At first she didn't see anything. Then there was a flash of white fur, darting between doorways. She squatted down behind Alister, her anger and fear dissipating in a breath.

"Is that him?"

"Mrow," he said, furrowing his brow.

Sara's eyes widened a little. "Sorry. Her. Is that her?"

He gave a short nod, rising from his haunches as the white animal darted to a closer shadow. Sara couldn't make out what it was, but it was too low to the ground to be a cat, and it moved more like a rat. She didn't think it was a rat, but she'd only gotten a quick look before it disappeared from her view. She could see two eyes regarding them from the shadows.

Sara stuck out her hand, looked to make sure the street was clear, then whisper shouted, "Were you summoned?"

The creature didn't move.

She tried again. "This is Alister, and I'm Sara. He's my familiar." She checked to be sure they were still alone and then added, "My pixie," she added, surprised she could say the word after all the times it hadn't come out.

The eyes rose, as if the creature were standing higher at that statement. Then, in a sudden movement, it darted out from cover and ran at full speed, right toward her and Alister. It was moving so fast she couldn't make it out. Then it tackled Alister, and they rolled past Sara's feet.

"Oh, shit! Are you all right?" she asked, dancing back from the rolling ball of white and black fur.

The two separated and faced each other, Alister's face bright and excited, putting Sara at ease.

It was just a greeting, like a hug or something, she realized with relief.

The creature had finally stopped moving enough for Sara to get a good look at it. It was a stark white ferret. Not an albino—it had a black nose and black eyes—but it was snow white. The ferret stood on its back legs and gave Sara a pretty good approximation of a bow while emitting a chirping grunt.

"Oh, my," Sara said, blushing at the gesture for some odd

reason before returning the bow. "It's a pleasure. Would you like to meet your mage, and get off the street?"

The ferret began her low chirping again and shot off down the alley, toward the hotel.

Sara and Alister looked at each other, and Alister shrugged before taking off after the little white streak. Sara gave a laugh and began jogging after them.

They were waiting for her at the door to the hotel, leaning against each other and chattering. Sara opened the door, and they both darted in, scooting across the lobby floor toward the steps at a dead run. The clerk behind the desk gave a yelp and pulled his legs up, as if they were going to run over and bite his toes.

"I found him," Sara called out, waving to the guy, who waved back slowly with wide eyes.

Sara followed them up the stairs and, after following the two excited animals as they pounced on one another the entire way down the hall, slid her key into the slot and opened the door. Alister and the ferret got stuck in the barely opened door as they both tried to be the first through. Sara opened the door further, and they spilled inside, Alister leading the ferret into Boon's bedroom.

I don't think I've ever seen Alister this excited.

She came around the corner to see both Alister and the ferret on the bed. Alister had taken his spot against Boon's leg, and the ferret was curled in the nook between Boon's head and shoulder. Somehow, in the time it had taken Sara to walk from the door to the bedroom, both familiars had calmed down and settled in for the night.

She just shook her head in amazement. "So we're staying in here tonight?" she asked Alister. He flicked an ear, keeping his eyes closed. Sara rolled her eyes.

She went and changed from her bathing suit into a tee shirt

and panties, and tossed the knit hat onto her bed, combing out her red hair with her fingers. Crossing the living room, she nearly stubbed her toe on a chair in the dark. She threw a curse at the offending furniture before crawling into the bed beside Boon. Curling up on her side, she watched the sleeping woman until her eyes became heavy again, and she finally let sleep take her.

CHAPTER 11

SARA OPENED her eyes to the soft, all-encompassing, white light of the Aether. She closed them again and took a breath.

"Are you here?" she asked.

Alister cleared his throat. "I am. How do you feel?"

"Naked," she said, sitting up to a cross-legged position.

Taking another deep breath, she opened her eyes again and saw Alister sitting in a high-backed, brown leather, Victorian style chair. He was wearing a pair of dress trousers, and a white shirt beneath a royal blue vest with gold buttons. He looked like a tiny lord from a steampunk novel. There was a small side table, with a brandy snifter a quarter of the way full of brown liquid. He was holding a small book with his thumb between two halves, marking his page.

"What the fuck?" she asked, looking down at her own naked body. "How do you have clothes on?"

Alister took a swig of the brown stuff and smacked his lips in satisfaction before answering. "This is the Aether," he said, as if that explained everything.

Sara gave him a sour look. "No shit, Sherlock. Is that supposed to mean something?"

He smiled. "Everything, in fact. When we are here in this dream state, we can command the Aether any way we like. It's just a representation of how we see ourselves. Long before I was a cat, I was this." He waved a hand over himself. "Just will it to be, and the Aether will show you the way you want to be seen."

She thought of the battlesuits she'd become so used to since joining up with the Navy. When she looked down, she was wearing the skin-tight, black suit. She smiled. "Well, that's handy."

"Really? A battlesuit? You can wear anything you like here, and you chose your work uniform?" Alister asked incredulously, shaking his head and taking another drink.

She considered that, then changed her outfit.

"Now we're talking," the pixie said, holding up his snifter in appreciation.

She was wearing a corn-yellow sundress, and her feet were bare. The area around her turned from the blank white of the Aetherscape to green grass and sunshine. She wiggled her toes in the grass and let out a contented sigh.

Alister smiled, taking in Sara as she basked in the light. "Sorry we haven't made contact since we completed the summoning spell. I figured you needed some time to recuperate."

"It's not like we had much chance. It's been crazy since the fleet evacuated the colony. Nothing but debriefings and reports." She snarled, rolling her eyes. "Today was a great day, though. Right up until Boon cast the Familiar spell in public. That's going to be all over the news feeds by morning."

"I know. I'm glad she could do it, though. We're going to need all the help we can get. Plus, Silva seems nice; I think she and Boon are going to be a good match," he commented, smiling and holding up his snifter in salute. Sara materialized a beer in her hand and clinked glasses.

"Silva? That's the ferret's name?"

He nodded. "Yeah. We can communicate in animal form —not in full conversations, just snippets. I told her to join us tonight, if Boon is conscious enough. Now that Silva's here, Boon should be coming out from under the spell's influence."

Sara nodded and then sat in silence for a minute before bringing up what she thought was going to be an important conversation. "So, about Colony 788…"

Alister slid his book onto the side table before leaning forward, putting his elbows on his knees. He rolled the brandy snifter between his hands while he spoke. "That was quite the show we put on. I thought I may have lost you at the end…" He trailed off.

She bit her lip and looked down. "Yeah, we need to talk about that. Why was I so…" She waved a hand when her words failed her.

"Crazy? Out of control? That's what happens when a human goes too far," he said, staring into the brown liquid.

Sara raised an eyebrow. "That can happen to any human mage?"

He shook his head, then leaned back and crossed his legs. "Only a mage with a familiar. Now that we are connected, you have access to far more Aether; if you channel too much, you become a little drunk on the power. That's the drawback with the arrangement that humans and pixies have. There is so much power available that we can get out of control easily if we're not careful. My teachers told me that many War Mages went down like this—throwing themselves into battle and fighting until they burned up. They used every last bit of Aether and snuffed themselves out. Not before ripping cities from the ground, mind you, but they were still dead when the dust cleared."

"Couldn't their familiars stop them?" she asked, leaning back on her arm and sipping at the beer.

"No. I assume you're asking because I was able to cut you off, but we were in a special circumstance. Because the spell had not been completed properly in the beginning, there was a build-up of potential Aether; that's why you had so much available right after we connected in the vault. But there hadn't been time for our empathic link to form, so I was not influenced by your emotions, like I would be now. Boon and Silva won't have the same spike in power you did since they completed the spell right away." He let that sink in before saying, "We got lucky, Sara. We'll have to be much more careful in the future."

Sara let the weight of his words really reach her. She had almost destroyed her own men in her Aether-fueled rampage. If it weren't for the pixie, she would be locked in a brig or worse right now. Not to mention crippled by her guilt.

"Good to know you have my back, Alister," Sara said, smiling and looking him in his yellow eyes.

"That's my job, Sara. I guess we will see how good I am at it. I heard you talking with the admirals… The Elif are no more?"

"We don't know yet, but there's been no word from them. Their fleet bugged out of the Sol System around the time we were getting bombarded from that Teifen carrier. The core we recovered from Colony 788 is at the defense ministry now, and they're digging through it to see what they can find. The plans on that thing are going to change the tide of this war. I just hope it's fast enough."

"Should be, if the old teachings are to be believed," a young female voice said from their right.

Sara started at the strange voice, spilling some of her beer into the grass. She turned to see a woman in a white, flowing gown, with white hair that came to her waist. She was walking toward them, and at first Sara thought she was far off in the distance—due to her size—but quickly realized she was just small, like Alister.

"Silva?" Sara asked.

The tiny woman approached and extended a small hand, which Sara took between her thumb and forefinger to shake. "Yes, Silva August; a pleasure to meet you, Sara." Silva gave a smile, and looked her up and down. "I have to say, you don't look like the War Mages in the stories. They were all serious and stern. You look, I don't know, light and airy?"

Sara had to laugh at that. "Light and airy? Like a dinner roll?"

Now it was Silva's turn to laugh. "It sounded better in my head." She turned to Alister, who had stood up and approached during the conversation.

Before Silva could say anything, Alister engulfed her in a bear hug. "Oh, it is so nice to see one of my own kind. We have so much to talk about," he gushed, a smile trying to split his face in half.

"Oh, my. Well, I suppose you have been cut off for a bit." She struggled to break free, but Alister kept hold. "Uh, it's very nice to meet you, Alister; the real you, that is," she said, awkwardly patting him on the back.

Sara looked around for Boon, but didn't see her anywhere. "Is Boon joining us?"

Silva finally broke free of Alister and his excitement, and smoothed her gown. "No, it's better for the two in contract to meet alone the first time. It makes things easier. I'll join with her after we are done talking. She could use a little more rest."

"I can understand that. Be sure to warn her not to get out of control; there are only two of us, and we're still trying to figure all this out. I don't want either of you getting hurt," Sara said.

"Don't worry. This is something pixies are taught from childhood. There hasn't been a War Mage pairing for a long, long time, but we still learn the history of them. As I'm sure Alister told you on your first visit here," she said, turning to Alister. He looked away, his face turning a little red. "You did warn her, didn't you?"

"Uh, well, you see…" He started to trail off, but then blurted, "I kinda skipped that part of my schooling."

Silva stood with her mouth open, regarding Alister like he had grown a second head. "Skipped it? Why on Earth would you skip it? It's important to learn about your role as a War Mage."

"Well, I mean, it had been thirty thousand years since the last War Mage…" He put his hands in his pockets and bashfully kicked a stone he'd materialized for effect. "I thought it was a waste of time."

Silva smacked her forehead with the palm of her hand. "I can't believe this." She turned to Sara. "So has he shown you the modified forms?"

"Uh, I don't know. What are those?" Sara asked, wide-eyed at the realization that her familiar was as lazy as she was when it came to schooling.

"Oh, god. You guys are so lucky I'm here. Where to begin? Okay, there is an ebb and flow to Aether management; did he talk about that?"

Oh, man. Mrs. Dontis was right; it all comes back to Aether management. I really should have paid more attention in her class.

Sara swallowed. "No, I don't think we got to that part."

Silva plopped down to a cross-legged position and put her face in her hands. "Okay, here's the quick of it. There are two kinds of spells: damage and healing. Being a successful War Mage is all about balancing the two. A really creative War Mage pair can use them in conjunction to fight far longer without being overwhelmed and going berserk."

Alister sheepishly sat at the third point of a triangle between Silva and Sara. His face was red, but he wanted to know this, he *needed* to know this. Sara felt a surge of emotion at how similar she and Alister were—something she had not noticed until this very moment. She reached over and gave him a supportive pat on the knee. In response, he reached down and squeezed one of her fingers with his hand and gave her an apologetic smile.

"So, are you saying I need to heal people while fighting?" Sara asked to clarify.

"You could, but that's just one option. Remember, healing isn't always about living things. You can 'heal' a torn piece of cloth by mending it. Or you can make a plant grow rapidly. It's a general term, but basically, if you are adding or fixing something, it is considered healing; if you are taking away or destroying something, that is damage. There are neutral spells as well, like shields, that don't push you one way or the other." Silva demonstrated by flipping her hand one way and then the other.

"That one, we've got down," Sara laughed.

"What happens if she uses too much healing magic? Does she go berserk then, as well?" Alister didn't want to sound stupid, but he needed to know the answer.

Silva repressed a frown at his lack of knowledge and answered, "Not 'berserk'. The opposite. She would fall into a coma that she would never wake from."

"So, in theory, we could fight forever, as long as the powers balance," Sara mused, thinking she found the loophole.

Silva shook her head. "No. The more Aether you channel, the narrower your margin for error becomes. If you balance your spells perfectly and push till the that margin is razor thin, even a small fire spell would send you into a berserker's rage, or mending a slight rip would put you into a coma. There is only so much you can do, and the closer you get to your edge, the finer the line you have to walk."

Sara nodded. *That makes a kind of sense.* "Okay, something for us to work on. We need to think outside the box a little," she said, nodding to Alister to show she felt confident they could make it work. She held up her hand. "Okay, we do need to work on this, but it's more important that we find the dreadnought the humans landed here at the end of the war. We need cores, and the one Cora is using said that ship contains a way to build them. Do you know where it is?" she asked both Alister and Silva.

They looked at each other and shrugged. Alister said, "No, but I think I know who might."

Silva nodded. "The Elders."

"Pixie elders?" Sara asked.

Silva nodded, but it was Alister who answered. "At the capital. They keep records all the way back to the beginning of our time on Earth. If anyone knows where that ship is, it will be them."

"Great! Let's go. Where is it?" Sara asked excitedly. *I wonder what a pixie city looks like. How has no one found it in all this time? It's probably magic. I'm going with magic,* she decided.

"It's in Atlantis," Silva said, smiling at Sara's slack-jawed expression.

CHAPTER 12

GRIMMS SAT in the captain's ready room just off the bridge, sipping at a cup of hot, black coffee. They were still an hour or so away from Cora's first test, and he was taking a break from all the UHF scientists that were crawling all over his bridge. They were in everyone's way, setting up monitors and taking readings and doing whatever else scientists did. All he knew was that his patience was running thin; he just wanted to get the test underway.

"How are you holding up, Commander?" Cora asked through the room's speakers.

Grimms gave a grumpy smile. "Oh, just peachy, Captain. Nothing like what you must be going through, though, having them all poking and prodding at you like you're a lab rat."

Cora laughed. "It's not like they're climbing into my tank. I can ignore them most of the time. To tell you the truth, I've been catching up on my TV shows."

Grimms cocked his head. "You can watch TV in there?" he asked, surprised the activity would be an option for her.

"Oh, yes. I can access pretty much anything that has to

do with electronics. I have to do something to pass the time, while these scientists set up their equipment and argue over how best to gauge the tests. I only sleep for a few minutes every couple of hours, so I have a lot of down time," she mused. "I've been going over the core's data, but there is so much… I need to take breaks. The history of humanity is, well, long," she said with a smile.

Grimms grunted his assent. "Any more info on the core design? We're going to be dead in the water if we can't provide cores for the ships the Navy has started building from the new plans."

"Sara and Boon are working on it. They're done with the debriefings, and have had a little time to collect their thoughts. She said she would update me when she found something. In her classic, cryptic fashion, she said they had 'a lead', as if she were some detective from an old movie," she said, the eyeroll obvious in her voice.

Grimms could feel she wanted to say more, so he stayed quiet.

Eventually, Cora continued. "I don't know what to do with her sometimes. She's brilliant, but she's always hiding things she thinks I'll disapprove of, so I don't have any clue if she's heading into danger or not."

Grimms considered her assessment. He respected Sara as a captain, and her willingness to fight for her people made him swell with admiration, but Cora was right in some respects. Sara did play her cards a little too close to the vest for his liking. She was a captain of a warship—it was his opinion that she needed to keep her people more informed of her plans.

"I feel the same way," he finally agreed. "Which is why I have Baxter looking out for her." He took a sip from his mug.

"You sent Baxter to follow her? She's not going to like

that," Cora said, a little shocked at the bold move. "Actually," she chuckled, "she might like it just fine, if their last interaction was a clue."

Mezner stuck her head in the ready room's door. "Sir, they're ready for you."

"Thank you, Ensign. I'm on my way." Grimms downed the rest of his coffee, almost choking on the hot liquid, before placing the mug in the coffee bar's dish recycler. "You ready, Captain?"

"I've been ready since I woke up on that moon over Colony 788. Let's get this started," Cora said enthusiastically.

Grimms stepped out onto the bridge and made his way to the projection table between the front view screen and Sara's command ring. A holo projection of the surrounding star systems rotated slowly, with a golden icon hanging over the Sol System, indicating the *Raven*'s position.

Dr. Hess stepped up beside him and gave him a nod. The Elif doctor had been given a position on the assessment team due to his knowledge of ancient human ship designs and culture. He was working with Dr. Romis, his colleague—and his lover, if the rumors were to be believed—along with several human scientists that had come aboard for the tests.

"Dr. Hess, I hear you're ready to begin?"

The tall, middle-aged Elif gave a nod, tugging at one of his ear tips. "Ready as we can be. I want to start with this new jumping ability Cora has been talking about."

Grimms nodded. He wanted to try it out, as well. From what Cora had described, it was a little like warp, but without all the pesky traveling between locations. She would be able to jump instantaneously from one location to another—not for long distances, compared to the vastness of space, but it would still grant them a huge advantage in battle.

"Will we need to provide coordinates?" Grimms asked,

and it took Dr. Hess a moment to realize he was talking to Cora.

"No, I don't need to be accurate. In battle, I'll need Sara to guide me to exact positions and headings, but for this test, I'm just going to point toward empty space," Cora said.

"All right. Doctor, are you recording or whatever it is you are doing?" Grimms asked, turning to Dr. Hess.

"We are ready, Commander."

"Cora. You have the conn. Take us out at your leisure," Grimms said, zooming in the projection to show only the Sol System and their golden icon in high Earth orbit.

They had come out past the moon's orbit, and were positioned far from any other ship, just in case. There were a few probes monitoring outside the ship to determine what impact the jump would have on the space around them.

"Three, two, one," Cora counted down softly, her voice flat with concentration.

Grimms waited a beat, but felt nothing. He looked around the room and saw a few other baffled faces.

"Oh, by the Seven," Dr. Hess breathed.

Grimms noticed that he was closely observing the holo display. When Grimms took a closer look himself, he saw that they were halfway across the Sol System, out around the orbit of Jupiter.

"Well, that was intense," Cora gushed, sounding a little giddy. "I pushed it pretty hard on that one. My Aether well took a big hit, so I wouldn't recommend a jump that far if we're going into battle. I don't think I could charge an Aether cannon for a few minutes afterward."

Connors spoke up from the helm. "I have us at just over a billion kilometers from our starting position, sir."

"Well, that's impressive," Grimms said, leaning over the holo display and getting a good look at the planets' new positions. "What is our elapsed time of flight? And why didn't we feel anything?"

Cora answered before Connors could speak. "The time was less than a picosecond, so not instantaneous, but close enough to call it such. And we didn't feel anything because, technically, *we* didn't move. Space moved around us. Sort of."

"You're going to have to explain that better, Captain. We have obviously traveled a billion kilometers," Grimms said, raising an eyebrow.

"Basically, I dematerialized the ship then rematerialized it, and in that instant, we no longer existed—we were completely in the Aether. The power I used pushed us through the Aether, to rematerialize here. So we skipped space entirely, and, from a relative perspective, space moved around us.

"I still can't tell if we were moving in the Aether or not, but I'll know more when we do the next jump. I plan on only doing a short one, to compare times, but I would bet it's the determining factor to distance traveled. When we are in the Aether, my well flows out at an incredible rate; only when we rematerialized did it stop. The timing is what the core controls, otherwise I wouldn't be able to think fast enough to get us back out," Cora said, obviously making a few discoveries of her own.

Grimms thought about this for a minute then said, "So, we died and were reborn a picosecond later?"

Cora considered this. "I suppose you could think of it that way."

"Amazing," Dr. Hess said, his eyes wide in wonder.

CHAPTER 13

GRIMMS LOOKED over the report of the morning's tests, leaning back in the swivel chair in the ready room. In front of him was another cup of coffee, along with a light lunch that someone had left for him while he was in the last test. With one hand, he undid the clasp at the collar of his uniform, trying to relax as best he could before the warp test in an hour.

In all, Cora had made twenty-two jumps throughout the Sol System. After her initial long jump, she started over at the bottom of the distance scale, making a short jump of only a few hundred meters. She concluded that she could make an even shorter one if Sara were there to give her a precise location. From there, she slowly expanded the jump distance, gauging her Aether well after each jump to determine just how nimble she could be in a fight.

After the single jumps allowed her to get a baseline for the amount of Aether it took to make them, they did a multiple jump test. At first, it was only two jumps, one after the other in quick succession, but they ended with a ten-jump string that had taken them nearly two billion kilometers when the sequence was finished. Cora reported that she would still be able to power the Aether cannon at least twice after the ten jumps.

"It looks like the Aether requirement uses the inverse-square law," Grimms said after swallowing a bite of his sandwich.

"Good eye, Commander. That's what my calculations show, as well; twice the distance equals four times the power. I'm working on an optimal set of jumps for distance, and one for power conservation. Honestly, I think those numbers are going to change, though," Cora said, slightly distracted.

Grimms put down his sandwich, wiping crumbs from his beard. "Why do you say that?"

Cora huffed a breath. "Well, I can't say for certain just yet, but I feel like me and the core are… I guess you would call it 'getting to know one another'. The more I use my Aether, the better the core seems to be able to distribute that power. If you take a look at the jump distances on that ten-jump run, you'll see what I mean."

Grimms pulled the numbers up and scanned them. "The distance increased a little with each jump. You didn't do that on purpose?"

"No. I was trying to keep my Aether output the same for all ten jumps. I may have gotten it slightly wrong, but not that wrong. There's a nearly twenty percent difference in the distance, for the same energy output, between the last jump and the first one. There is a bit of a precision problem, without me having an exact position to jump to, but I don't think it would account for twenty percent," Cora said.

"So you're becoming more powerful?"

"No, not more powerful. The core is just using my 'brand' of Aether—for lack of a better term—more efficiently. It's as if the core is talking with my Aether flow and coaxing more out of it. I honestly don't see what it's doing differently, mechanically, so it has to be a question of efficiency," Cora reasoned, and Grimms thought she would have shrugged if she still had control of her body.

"It could be a question of potency," Grimms mused, leaning back again and picking up his coffee.

"Hmm, I hadn't thought of that. How would it make the Aether more potent, though?"

Grimms gave a shrug. "I don't know, I'm not a mage. I can barely channel enough Aether to activate a lighter, much less the level of Aether you're channeling on a daily basis. I'm just the idea guy," he said with a smile while stroking his short, white beard.

"Well, it's an idea… it may even be the answer, but I have no way of testing it 'til Sara finds out how the cores are made. Right now, we don't even know what element it's made from; nobody wants to damage it by studying it too aggressively, and a surface scan just throws up errors, as if it can't get a sample, or even recognize the structure on a molecular scale." Cora sounded defeated.

"Don't worry. Sara will find something; even if she has to blow up a city to find it," he said, with a chuckle. "You two are more alike than you are different, you know. You'll push yourselves beyond any reasonable level to get the results you need to do what's best for your people. Honestly, I've never felt safer than I do when I'm here on the *Raven*."

"Even though we're being pushed to the front line of an ancient conflict?" Cora asked quietly.

Grimms gave her a smile he wasn't entirely sure she could see. "Especially when we're being pushed. You work harder under pressure; that's a trait I love to see in my captain."

Cora laughed lightly. "Commander Grimms, that sounded like a compliment. Don't go all soft on my account."

"Wouldn't think of it, ma'am," he said, taking the last bite of his sandwich.

"God, I miss sandwiches. And beer," Cora whined. "When I come out of this tank, you're taking me to go get sandwiches and beer. That's an order."

Grimms gave a laugh at that. "It would be my pleasure, ma'am." He checked his watch before continuing. "It's time for the next test. You ready?" he asked, getting up and circling around the desk, making his way for the door.

"Oh yeah. It'll be good to get out and stretch my legs."

Grimms entered the bridge just as Mezner was approaching. She stopped and gave him a quick salute before taking a seat at her station. Grimms stepped down to the holo projector, occupying the space next to Dr. Hess, and placed his coffee mug on the flat surface of the table-like projector, causing a small distortion in the image of the local star systems.

"Do we have a heading?" Grimms asked the doctor.

Dr. Hess nodded. "Intelligence gave us the coordinates. According to the information they gathered from our communications network, it should be far from any traffic."

"Good. The last thing we need is to run into an enemy ship without Captain Sonders onboard. How far is the warp?" he asked, noting the two icons in the projection—one golden and one flashing blue—a good distance from any systems.

Dr. Hess referenced his notes, then said, "We are making a fairly long first warp, about halfway to my home system. Just over twenty-five hundred light years."

"How long does it take an Elif ship to travel that far?" Grimms wanted to know.

Dr. Hess looked to the ceiling, doing some quick math. "At a hard burn, it would take roughly six of your days."

"One hundred forty-four hours," Grimms calculated.

"Let's see if we can't cut that down a bit, Captain Cora." He smiled with anticipation. Before the core was installed, their first journey to the derelict shipwreck had been estimated to be around two thousand light years, and Cora had managed that one in three days. He was eager to see what she was capable of now.

"You got it, Commander. Engaging warp in three, two, one."

The view screen smashed its image down to a pinpoint, as the destination and their current location connected through a thread of Aether. After a slight shudder under Grimms' feet, the image began to slowly expand again.

"Mezner, what is our ETA?" he asked the blonde woman.

She was already checking her calculations, and quickly said, "Twelve hours and sixteen minutes, sir."

Dr. Hess began excitedly tugging on his ear tip at the news, his eyes wide as he mumbled, "Amazing. Simply amazing."

Grimms smiled. "Ten times the speed of the Elif ships. Impressive, Captain."

"Thank you, Grimms. I could probably have eked out a little more power, but I didn't want to go all out, just in case." Cora sounded to be in high spirits.

Grimms picked up his coffee mug and took a sip. "We really need those cores. I hope Captain Sonders is making headway."

"I'm sure she is," Cora said, her voice not quite as confident as Grimms would have liked.

CHAPTER 14

"ATLANTIS?" Boon asked, double-checking that her new Aetheric armor was strapped into the shuttle's cargo compartment for the third time.

Sara had requisitioned the shuttle and two personalized Aetheric suits of armor from the UHFC, saying they were taking them out to field test some of her powers, away from the public eye. Word had traveled around of what she was, and the display on the beach the previous afternoon had convinced the requisitions officer that it was a good idea for them to leave the city.

The suits were printed up from the personalized scans in their files, and an hour later, they were ready to go.

"That's what Silva called it. Though when I asked for the exact location, she pointed me to the Azores," Sara said with a slight grin, adjusting her brown leather jacket.

They had changed back into their tee shirts and jeans, and Sara had printed them some jackets on the hotel's public printer to prepare them for the cooler temperatures they were bound to encounter. She never liked the way artificial leathers felt on her skin, but she was not about to drop the kind of money a real leather jacket would cost.

Silva, draping her skinny ferret body around Boon's neck, gave Sara a chittering rebuke, to which the captain threw up her hands. "Okay, it's Atlantis," she said with a light laugh.

"Wait, the Azores? The islands out in the Atlantic?" Boon asked, walking over to the controls and reaching for the button to close the ramp.

There was a metallic *clunk* that made her spin around in surprise.

A large man in full Aetheric armor had stepped onto the ramp, and was advancing on her. She held up her hands defensively as the armored man reached up and activated his faceplate to fold back into the helmet.

"You have room for one more? I've always wanted to go to the Azores," Baxter said, flashing a bright white smile.

Boon stood up, dropping her hands, her mouth hanging open. "Sergeant Major?"

"Baxter. What the hell are you doing here?" Sara demanded hotly, stepping around Boon to face off with the much bigger man.

Baxter gave her a shrug. "Colonel Grimms asked me to keep an eye on you. I think he just wanted someone watching your back," he said, the smile never leaving his face.

Shit. How are we supposed to talk with the pixies if he's tagging along? I can't even mention them around anyone that's not a War Mage; I don't know what would happen if we actually tried to bring him to their city.

Sara sighed, crossing her arms. "Are you serious? We're War Mages. I'm pretty sure we can protect ourselves."

Baxter's eyebrows crawled up his forehead, and he looked over Sara's shoulder at Boon, noticing the ferret for the first time. "Well, I'll be damned. How the hell did that happen?"

"It's a long story, but as you can see, we are fully capable of taking care of ourselves," Sara insisted with a little more anger than she actually felt. The fact that he was watching out for her made her go a little gooey inside, and she had to fight that part of herself down.

"I believe there is nothing on Earth that could stop the two of you, after what I saw one War Mage do on Colony 788, but I have my orders. Just think of me as a friend, catching a ride," he suggested, his smile coming back. "Or I could always catch a ride of my own."

Double shit. He knows where we're going, so there's nothing keeping him from following us.

Sara hung her head in defeat. "Fine. Stow your armor, we don't want to scare the locals by showing up in full battle rattle." She reached over and slapped the ramp controls, forcing Baxter to move quickly to avoid getting caught in the closing gap.

She stalked to the pilot's chair and started the engines. As soon as Boon was seated beside her, and Alister was safely in her lap, she punched the throttle, shooting off the landing pad at high acceleration.

An evil grin lit her face when a *bang* sounded from the floor of the cargo area, and she heard Baxter curse.

Boon wisely didn't look back to see if he was okay.

An hour later, Sara was making a wide, sweeping bank around the eastern most island of São Miguel. Baxter was strapped into one of the passenger seats between the cabin and the cargo area, far enough away that Sara was sure he couldn't hear them talking softly.

"Is this it?" she asked Alister and Silva, who were both standing on the dashboard, their faces pressed to the window, looking down at the island.

Silva turned and chattered excitedly, and Boon said, "Yeah, that's it."

"Okay. I'm supposed to aim for the volcanic crater on the west of the island, right?" Sara asked, just to be sure before she began their descent.

Silva chattered again, and this time Alister joined with a "Merp," not taking his face from the window.

Sara circled a few more times, bringing the shuttle lower with each revolution so they could better see the lay of the land from above. When they were only a few hundred meters from the ground, Silva turned and hopped into Boon's lap. She leaned over the navigation map and pressed a small paw to a location on the screen, leaving a navigational marker.

"Thanks," Sara said, giving her a look that said *'not bad'*.

She leveled out the shuttle and brought it down into a clearing that bordered a thickly wooded area. The gravitic engines kept the noise to a minimum, making the landing a quiet affair.

She cycled down the engines and put the shuttle in standby as Boon unstrapped and headed back toward the rear of the ship. Baxter undid his own lap belt and fell in behind her. After shutting down the craft, Sara slid out of her seat and joined them as Boon was lowering the ramp.

"Hold up, big boy, where do you think you're going?" Sara asked from behind Baxter.

"I'm going with you. That's why I'm here," he reminded her, smiling at her over his shoulder.

"Not right now. We are meeting with some very shy people, and I don't want you scaring them away. You're just going to have to wait here." She crossed her arms to let him know she was serious.

He didn't seem to take the hint.

"It'll be fine. I'll just keep back, out of the way."

Boon—with Silva around her neck, and Alister following

closely behind—escaped down the ramp before she could get sucked into the argument.

Sara sighed in impatience. She leaned in and put a hand to his chest. "Baxter, I know you want to help, and I appreciate that, I really do. But this is a delicate situation, and having you here is throwing a wrench into it. I really need you to stay here, otherwise I'm not going to get anywhere. I'm a War Mage, I can take care of myself," she assured him again. By decreasing the space between them, she had been hoping to elicit his feelings to her cause, but her own feelings were rearing their head.

Fuck. Why does he smell so good?

"Please?" she pressed on. "Just twenty minutes. I'll keep in contact the whole—"

"Uh, Sara?" came Boon's uncertain voice from outside.

Sara closed her eyes in frustration, dropping her hand from Baxter's chest. "Give me a minute, Boon. I'm kinda in the middle of something," she said, her voice rising an octave.

"You should probably come out here. Like, right now."

Boon's voice was artificially level, setting off warning bells for her and Baxter both. Together, they turned and ran out the back of the shuttle, their panic rising. Sara leapt from the side of the ramp toward Boon's voice, her hands coming up, ready for a fight.

She could see Boon standing stock-still, her hands held up in surrender. Silva and Alister were both on the ground, sitting at attention. All three had their backs to her and were staring into the woods.

Sara stumbled to a stop beside Boon, one of her eyebrows rising in confusion at the sight before her.

Standing at the edge of the clearing a few meters away were eleven pixies. Ten of them were standing in a semicircle around a central, female pixie. The ten were obviously guards, in their suits of Aetheric armor, holding coil-rifles. What was odd was that the armor and weapons were nearly identical to the equipment that Sara's group had stowed on the shuttle. The helmets were slightly different, to accommodate the pixies' long, pointed ears, but it was the same design otherwise. The weapons were small, but still looked like they could do some serious damage.

The central figure wore white robes, and her hood was thrown back to reveal a head of strawberry blonde hair with a tan face that was sporting a serious expression. She looked like a priestess to Sara, but the golden tiara she wore on her head suggested nobility.

Baxter slid to a stop on the other side of Boon, looking left and right. "What do you see?"

He was oblivious to the eleven tiny humanoids arrayed before them.

The priestess-or-noble cocked her head at Baxter and, in a deeper than expected voice, said, "He is not bound to one of you?"

"Bound?" Sara asked, looking from the pixie to Baxter, who hadn't heard either of them talking.

"He must be bound, if he is to proceed further. Otherwise we may not continue our conversation," she said, locking eyes with Sara.

So old. Her eyes are so old, Sara thought with a shiver.

"I have a few questions first," she answered.

CHAPTER 15

GRIMMS SAT in his command chair on the bridge, watching the view screen along with Dr. Hess, who stood beside him. The view was almost completely expanded once again, signaling the end of their journey. The science team had been busy, collating data from the jumps and taking readings and measurements of the warp field. Dr. Hess consulted his tablet, mumbling to himself in his usual fashion.

"We are coming out of warp in ten seconds, sir," Connors reported from the helm.

Dr. Hess dropped the tablet to his side and watched the final seconds of the voyage. "This is incredible, Cora. I don't know how you did it, but the compression on this Aether thread is beyond anything we Elif are capable of."

"It comes down to the core, Dr. Hess. It is able to translate my spellforms much more efficiently," Cora said cheerily.

"Dropping from warp in three, two, one," Connors counted down. There was a flash of blue Aetheric light, and the view screen displayed an entirely different set of stars.

"Mezner, confirm our location," Grimms ordered. He

stood from his chair, rolled the tightness from his shoulders, and made his way to the holo projector.

As he and Dr. Hess approached, the projector came to life, displaying a golden icon and not much of anything else.

"We are within a million kilometers of our target destination, sir," Mezner reported, after the computer calculated the positions of the stars around them.

Dr. Hess nodded. "Very good, Ms. Cora. A jump this distant is difficult to make accurately, even for our twin sets. That you've accomplished even this approximation without Captain Sara to guide you is incredible."

Cora laughed, "Thank you, doctor. To tell the truth, we may have gotten a little lucky, but I won't know 'til we do a few more warps for comparison. A data set of one is useless."

"Not 'useless,' just inconclusive. We now have a 'ballpark number', as you humans say, to start building our model for the next set of jumps," Dr. Hess said, typing furiously on his tablet. One of the human scientists on his team joined him, and they consulted quietly.

Grimms patted the edge of the holo projector and said, "Good work, Captain."

"Did you just pat me?" Cora asked in his comm unit.

Grimms felt his face flush; he had done just that. He cleared his throat. "Uh, no. I spilled some coffee on the projector earlier," he lied, hoping she'd buy it.

To his relief, she laughed in his ear. "Good to know you're keeping me clean, Commander."

Grimms smiled. "Just doing my part, ma'am."

"So, doctor, how did we do? Did you get some good data?" Cora asked over the bridge's speakers.

Dr. Hess lifted his head from the quiet conversation he was having with his colleague. "Oh yes, Ms. Cora. We have the final measurements on the Aether thread, and they are fascinating."

"You keep mentioning the thickness of the Aether thread, doctor. What does that have to do with our speed?" Grimms asked. *Does this have something to do with why Cora is more suited for controlling a ship than anyone else?*

"Do you understand fluid dynamics, Commander?" Dr. Hess asked.

Grimms shook his head. "Not any more than the layperson. What does flow dynamics have to do with warping through space?"

The doctor began flipping through screens on his tablet until he found what he was looking for, then turned it so Grimms could see. It was a 3-D model of a pipe with water flowing through it. The water started in a wide open pipe, six centimeters in diameter, and flowed at ten meters per second until it came to a flange that narrowed the pipe to three centimeters, and increased the speed of the water to forty meters per second.

"This is an example of flow rate. The same amount of water is flowing through each section of the pipe every second, but because the second section of the pipe is half as wide, and therefore has one fourth the area, the speed needs to be four times as fast to get the water out in the same amount of time. Do you understand?" Dr. Hess asked, raising his eyebrows.

Grimms nodded as visions of his physics classes at the academy flooded his memory. "Because the fluid can't compress, it is forced to move faster. What does this have to do with warping?"

Dr. Hess smiled as he lowered the tablet, obviously grateful he did not need to explain further. "The warp thread is like a pipe that the ship travels through. A warp bubble is formed around the ship and a small volume of space around it. The bubble is made of Aether, which creates a barrier between the reality inside the bubble and the one outside.

Then a 'pipe' is created between the starting position and the destination, and the reality inside the bubble flows through the thread. So, like in the example, the ship and the reality around it is the water, and the Aether thread is the pipe."

Grimms nodded. "So the thinner the pipe, the faster the water needs to flow." He rubbed his chin in thought. "How did you drop the rock out of warp in your final test, Captain? Wouldn't the rock need to travel through the barrier from one reality to the other?"

"I didn't actually push the rock out through the barrier; I just created a second barrier closer to the ship that didn't include the rock, as I dropped the larger one around it," Cora said.

Dr. Hess's eyes bulged at that. "You changed the shape of your warp bubble while in warp? How could you do that? You would need to cast two spells at once."

"I did cast two spells at once, but only for a split second, and they were almost exactly the same, so it wasn't all that hard. I couldn't cast two spells for much longer than a split second," Cora said modestly.

"You shouldn't have been able to do it at all!" he exclaimed. "And this was before you had the core? I've never heard of such a thing."

"Like I said, it was only for a split second, and I was basically casting a copy of the same spell. Sara and I did it all the time while practicing quick spellwork. It's like priming yourself for the next spell with the back of your mind."

Before Dr. Hess could continue what Grimms thought might be a long series of questions, Mezner spoke. "Sir? We have an Aether communication coming in." She double-checked her console. "It's coming from an Elif relay station close by."

Grimms frowned. "Is it being sent to us directly?"

"No, sir. It is being broadcast to any human or Elif ship

in the area. They are sending the signal wide, though, so it's not getting far," she said.

"Put it onscreen, Ensign," Grimms said, looking up as the image of the star field changed to the face of a particularly young looking Elif male.

Dr. Hess gasped in surprise, but the stranger began talking before he could comment.

"To any friendly ship in the area, this is High Prince Paelias DeSolin. I am in need of rescue. I have escaped the destruction of Effrit, and am currently aboard my private yacht *Empori*. Please respond to the private channel included in this message. Our vessel is damaged, and we are unable to maintain warp for a long jump. We are currently in deep space, but the ship is only minimally armed, and is therefore unable to defend itself from a Teifen attack. Please send a message as quickly as possible."

The prince's eyes were rimmed in red, as if he had been crying, and he tugged on his ear tip nearly the entire duration of the message.

"What do you think, Captain?" Grimms asked, his eyes narrow as he regarded the frozen image of the prince.

"We must save him," Dr. Hess demanded, nearly hysterical. "While the prince lives, the royal line is still in place. His presence would do much to rally my people."

Cora's voice was much more measured than the doctor's. "He's right. We need to save him. If for no other reason than the fact that he knows what is happening in the Elif's home system. This war is far too large for just us to fight; we need the Elif backing us. The return of their prince would go a long way for their morale."

Grimms nodded. "Mezner, forward this to the UHFC and include a request for instructions."

"You are not going now?" Dr. Hess looked as if he had been slapped.

"We will send them help, doctor, but I need clearance from UHF Command before I can put this ship in danger. I shouldn't need to remind you that we are fairly defenseless without Captain Sonders onboard. She shields us and maneuvers our offenses in battle," Grimms reminded him, running a hand over his short, white hair. "We are the only working ship with a tank system, and possess one of only two cores ever discovered. If the prince's message is a trap, we don't want to lose the *Raven*."

The doctor threw up his hands. "How could it possibly be a trap? The message was encoded. The Teifen can't receive it, so they have no idea he is out there, but you can be sure they are looking. The longer we wait, the more danger he is in."

"I understand your feelings on the matter, Dr. Hess, but the fact remains that this ship is far too valuable to risk without orders. My first concern is this ship and her crew. We wait," Grimms said with finality.

He returned to his seat with a scowl on his face as he thought through all the ways this could go terribly wrong.

"You think it's a trap?" Cora asked in his comm.

Grimms nodded and murmured, "What are the odds that message could have found us out here in the middle of nowhere?"

"Well, if they were passing it from relay to relay, then I suppose it's not that far-fetched," she said, her voice not all that convincing.

"Could be, but I just have a bad feeling about this. How did he escape a planet that, presumably, was surrounded by thousands of Teifen battleships? If their warp is damaged, how did they get so deep into space? It doesn't sit well with me," Grimms said.

"Fair enough. But remember that we are not completely

defenseless. We still have weapons, and the hull armor is rated for Aetheric cannon blasts," she said.

"Only one or two, and I'm sure the damage would be substantial."

"True, but I can always jump us away if it gets bad. I'm just saying it's not a suicide mission," she soothed, and Grimms could imagine her putting her hands on his with the comment.

He gave a grim smile. "We'll see what the UHFC says."

IT ONLY TOOK the UHFC an hour and a half to answer Grimms' request for further instructions. It was a text-only message, three words long.

[Retrieve the prince.]

"Connors, get me a heading and prepare for warp. It looks like we have a rescue mission to complete."

"Aye, sir. Heading imputed, awaiting Captain Cora," he replied.

"Warp in three, two, one," Cora said.

The screen smashed down to a point, and they were underway.

"I hope this goes better than I imagine," Grimms said quietly into his comm.

"Me too, Commander," Cora replied.

CHAPTER 16

THE PIXIE PRIESTESS bowed to Sara, then to Boon. "I am Nyx Morenna, Keeper of the Records. We felt your presence when you returned to Earth a few days ago, then yesterday we felt the birth of a second War Mage. We have been expecting you," Nyx said, in her deep and feminine voice.

Sara and Boon both bowed, copying Nyx's movements. "I am Sara Sonders, and this Alicia Boon." When Nyx looked to the familiars, Sara quickly continued, "And this is Alister Burke, my…" She wondered how best to refer to him. "Companion. And this is Silva August, Boon's companion." The familiars gave the best bows their animal forms would allow.

"A pleasure to meet you. Now, we must do something about your guest," Nyx said, indicating Baxter.

Since Sara and Nyx's conversation had begun, Baxter had gotten more and more dazed. He was now standing slack-jawed, with blank eyes.

"What's wrong with him?" Sara asked, concerned.

"He is under the influence of our protection spell. Alant and Altis provided us with a number of very efficient spellforms to keep this place safe from wandering humans. Even us pixies are able to provide enough Aether to power them comfortably. They were such craftsmen with spellforms," Nyx said dreamily.

"I'm sorry, who are Alant and Altis?" Sara asked, trying to place the names and failing.

Nyx smiled. "Forgive me, I forget that humans purged their knowledge of magic. Alant and Altis are the names of the War Mages that brought us to Earth. They built their city out here on the peninsula, which became known as Alantis. This was before the ice melted, and the land was claimed by the sea. All that remains of their once proud lands are these mountaintops we now stand on." She spread her arms to indicate the green fields and forest.

"Alantis. As in *At*lantis?" Boon asked, trying to clarify that the pixie was talking about the fabled lands of an advanced race that sank into the sea.

Nyx gave a smile. "Yes, the name has changed slightly over the years, but it is the same place. It was named after the War Mages."

"They were the ones who captained the dreadnought?" Sara asked.

"Yes. They are the ones that brought us to this world," she said with a half-smile. "I am guessing you have come for volunteers for your siblings?"

"Volunteers? To become familiars?" Sara asked to clarify.

Nyx gave a stately nod, "Yes. It is tradition that the second pairing of a War Mage twin set is chosen for their specialty. Mine, for example, is a specialty in history and controller systems."

Sara's eyes widened a bit at that. She knew Cora had the potential to become a War Mage, but she never guessed that there would be pixies who'd volunteer to be familiars.

"I am actually here to find the dreadnought that Alant

and Altis brought.," she admitted. "We need to find the machine that can make more cores for the fleet, and my sister's core pointed us to the dreadnoughts."

"I see," Nyx said. "We should go speak with the elders, in that case. You must first bond with your guard, if he is to be trusted with our secret," she gestured to Baxter, who was still slack-jawed and dazed.

"Right, so what does that entail?"

Nyx approached Alister, and held out her hand to him. "I will give the spellform to Alister so that he may provide it to you."

Alister reached out a paw and covered the pixie's smaller appendage. They both closed their eyes, and a moment of silence passed between them.

Nyx released his paw a few seconds later and said, "Now, the important part of the spell is that he must give back in equal measure. He will need to give you a portion of his Aether in return, using *you* as the spellform. Does he know your shape well enough to do this?"

Sara blinked at that. "When you say 'know' my shape, what are you talking about, exactly?"

"He must know your form; your body's shape. It is how one gives a portion of themselves to another. He will use you as a spellform, while you use him as a target for the spell," Nyx explained, her head cocked to the side, as if this were the most obvious thing in the world.

Sara considered that. It would be like when she had focused her Aether into Alister in order to complete the Familiar spell. Which meant he would need to know her in her purest form: naked.

Fuck.

"You know what? Let's just skip it for now. We can just leave him here," Sara said, flipping a hand at the slack-jawed man, her face burning with embarrassment at the thought of him studying her while she stood fully exposed to him.

It wouldn't be that bad. You've even fantasized about it a few times, she scolded herself, and her face burned all the brighter.

Nyx hesitated a moment before saying, "I would not advise that, if you care about him. Most people that enter our area of influence are turned away by the spell after a few minutes, wondering why they wanted to go into our woods at all. However, sometimes an individual becomes obsessed with entering, and will not be deterred. They come, and the spell cannot dissuade them, so they stay here, under its influence. Alant and Altis built a safety into the spell, in case individuals came that would not leave us in peace."

Sara had a bad feeling about what that safety was; considering a War Mage created it, she figured it wouldn't be good for Baxter. "Let me guess, it erases their mind or something?" she asked, a hand on her hip.

"Oh, no. Nothing so complicated as that. It simply kills them. If they stay in the area of influence for more than an hour, or return more than twice in one day, the security measure is activated, and the body is rapidly decomposed, leaving no trace."

Sara and Boon both stood with their mouths open in shock. "It *kills* them? Fuck, those guys were not messing around," Sara said.

"I get the feeling, from the fact that your friend has not tried to wander away, that he is rather stubborn about leaving you," Nyx said with an apologetic smile.

Sara took a deep breath and blew it out in a rush. "Yeah, he won't leave while I'm still in there." *God dammit. I can't just let the thing kill him...* "When he becomes bonded to me, will he be able to interact with you?"

"Yes. And your contract with Alister will extend to

your bonded guard. He will be able to mitigate some of the rage you feel when casting for long periods, as well as have an increased Aether reserve and an increased flow into his well. He will also feel your general direction and some of your emotions, like Alister does. The bonding is permanent, but unlike with Alister, you and your guard may travel apart without repercussions," Nyx helpfully explained.

"Great. Sounds… great," Sara said, shaking her head with her eyes closed as she processed what she was getting herself into. "Basically, I have to bond with him or he will die, because he is a stubborn son of a bitch." She blew out another breath. "I don't really have a choice, do I?"

No one said a word.

She stepped up to Baxter and gently turned him around. He stumbled along at her guiding hands, as she directed him back toward the shuttle.

When they were about halfway there, Baxter blinked a few times and looked around in confusion. "What? What happened?" he asked, shaking his head slightly as he continued up the ramp of the shuttle under Sara's prodding direction. Alister was right on her heels.

"Oh, so much. But that's not important for now. Right now we need to have a talk. Here, have a seat," she said, directing him to sit on a crate beside her Aetheric armor, which was strapped to a rack.

He sat, rubbing at his head. "Why does my head hurt? Did I hit it on something?"

Sara unlaced her boots and kicked them off as she pulled the light leather jacket from her shoulders. "Something like that. Listen, Baxter. I have a question for you." She sat on a crate opposite him in the small cargo area and pulled her socks off by the toes, tossing them on her crumpled jacket on the floor.

"Sure, what's up?" he asked, rubbing his temple with his eyes screwed shut.

"Turns out I do need someone to watch my back," she said, leaning forward with her hands on her knees, watching for his reaction.

Baxter's head popped up, one eyebrow higher than the other. "Really? That seems a little sudden, considering you just tried to convince me to stay in the shuttle."

"Would you have?"

"Not a chance. Grimms gave me an order, and I follow my commanding officer's orders. Especially when I agree with them," he added, catching her gaze and not looking away.

Sara sighed. "Yeah. That's what I thought. What would you say to becoming my guard, in an official capacity? It wouldn't keep you from your normal duties; it would just connect us in a similar way to me and Alister. Would you be willing to do that?"

Baxter gave her a hard look, trying to judge if she was being serious or not. "Absolutely. If I can help you out, I'll do whatever it takes."

"Even if the bond will last the rest of your life?"

He took a moment to consider, then his intense eyes met hers. "Absolutely."

Sara gave a smile. "One more question. Why? Why are you willing to do whatever it takes?"

Baxter gave a huff of a laugh. "Your power is what's going to save all of us. That's a heavy burden—one you shouldn't have to carry alone."

Tears suddenly welled in Sara's eyes at his nobility, but she fought them back. "Oh, that was unexpected. Um, okay. You're a good man, Baxter," she replied, trying to discreetly wipe her eyes.

"Why did you take your shoes off?" he asked, confused.

She smiled, then laughed and stood, undoing her pants. Rocking her hips, she pushed them past her thighs as she said, "We need to do a spell -- "

"Whoa!" Baxter yelled, throwing a hand up in front of his eyes as he turned away from her suddenly bare bottom half.

His obvious embarrassment at the situation emboldened her, making the next few minutes easier. *Thanks for being a decent guy, Baxter*, she thought, as she pulled her shirt off and dropped it to the side, then stepped out of the piled-up jeans around her ankles.

"Look at me, Baxter," she urged, leaning into his line of sight.

He crossed his legs and looked down at his lap, his eyes hooded behind his hand. "I'm actually good, Captain. I don't need to—what the hell, Captain!?" he exclaimed, as her crumpled panties slid across the deck and bumped up against his boot.

"Oh, now I'm 'Captain'? I guess that means I'm your commanding officer again?" she said, with a little heat. The cool, metal deck was sending shivers up her spine. "Look at me, Baxter. This is going to be as awkward for me as it is for you, trust me."

His foot began to bounce with nervous energy, making both legs shake in their crossed position. "I don't think that would be possible. This is about the most awkward situation I've ever been in, and that's including the time my pants caught on fire at a wedding."

Sara snorted a laugh at that. "How on Earth did you manage to catch... you know what? We'll save that story for later."

She stepped forward, her bare feet making no sound on the deck, and with a gentle finger, lifted his chin so he was forced to look at her.

To his credit, he skipped right past her exposed body and looked her right in the eye.

"I know you're a gentleman, but just this once, I'm going to need you to leer a little. You're going to have to use my body as a spellform, so take it all in, buster. This might be your only chance," she said with the warmest smile she could muster.

He took a deep breath and gave her a nod.

She stepped back and began explaining what he needed to do, while he slowly began looking her over.

His legs were still crossed.

CHAPTER 17

With a flash, they dropped out of warp.

"Get me a scan of the area, Mezner. Ensign Hon, power up weapons, and be ready for anything," Grimms ordered from his command chair. He was gripping the armrest with white knuckles, and made himself relax. *Don't let your people see your anxiety, Grimms. You know better.*

"Sir, I have one ship on scans, the prince's yacht, *Empori.* The sector is clear," Mezner reported. "It's three million kilometers out, and heading our way."

"Connors, get us over there," Grimms said, narrowing his eyes as he thought for the thousandth time of how this could go wrong.

The gravitic engines hummed to life, pushing them through the black. The golden icon and the green icon of the *Empori* began moving closer together in the holo projector.

"Six minutes till rendezvous, sir," Connors reported.

Everyone was on edge during the short journey, making the bridge unusually quiet as everyone focused on their consoles, watching for the slightest problem.

"Mezner, contact the pilot and be sure they know to

attach to the hard point as quickly as possible. If we need to run, I don't want to leave them behind," Cora said.

"Aye, ma'am," Mezner said, punching a few buttons on her console and speaking quietly into her comm.

"Thirty seconds to rendezvous," Connors updated.

Grimms watched as the icons closed until they were almost on top of one another. He caught himself gripping the arm of his chair again and relaxed his fingers.

"Fifteen sec—"

"Contact! A Teifen cruiser just jumped in, twenty two hundred kilometers to port. Firing gauss cannons," Hon reported, and quickly jabbed at the fire-control system.

The ship thrummed as twelve slugs, at a hundred kilos each, accelerated from its four large tri-barreled turrets. At the same time, Grimms could see another red icon appear on the holo projector. Then another, and another.

"Multiple contacts, sir. Three cruisers and a destroyer. A second destroyer. Sir, they keep coming," Mezner reported, as Hon targeted more ships, sending out slugs as fast as the auto loaders could feed them into the barrels.

"Charging the Aether cannons. I need a firing solution, Hon," Cora said, her voice calm despite the tension.

"Aye, ma'am. Taking aim at the first and second cruisers. Targeted," he said.

The ship shuddered, and two streaks of blue energy appeared on the view screen. They lasted a few seconds before blinking out.

"Direct hit on cruiser one; it looks like their shields are down. Yes! Direct hits with the gauss rounds. The ship is listing, sir. The second Aether bolt missed," Mezner reported.

"Connors, get us right on top of the yacht. As close as you can, and make it fast," Grimms ordered. "Cora, can you jump both ships if we're not connected?"

"Yes, it's just like the warp bubble."

"Good, as soon as you have them, jump us out of here. We can't take on this many ships without Sara," Grimms said, cursing under his breath.

"Several ships are powering Aether cannons," Mezner reported. Her eyes went wide, as her fingers danced across her console, confirming what she was seeing. "Sir, a dreadnought has jumped in."

Grimms looked to the projector, and saw a new red icon flashing. *A dreadnought means this is not just any fleet.* A dreadnought was not just a ship; it was a seat of government, a flying capital city, thirty kilometers long and powered by hundreds of mages. *It's the regional governor.*

The same governor who had just defeated the Elif in their own home system. They couldn't stand against the dreadnought even *with* Sara.

"Five seconds 'til the yacht is in range," Connors updated.

The ship bucked and rolled slightly to the left.

"We've been hit with an Aether bolt, port side armor is compromised," Mezner reported.

Connors rolled the ship over, exposing the undamaged side, in case of a second hit.

"Incoming gauss rounds."

"We are in range of the yacht, sir."

"Jumping," Cora announced, and the icons in the display disappeared. The projector zoomed out until they crept into view again.

"We've jumped six point four million kilometers, sir. They will be able to warp here in less than thirty seconds."

"Not if they can't see us, Connors," Cora said confidently. "I'm masking our gravity print with the engines. We should look like a small asteroid to their sensors. I was able to extend the effect to cover the yacht, as well. We need to get that ship attached to a hard point *now*."

"You can cloak us?" Grimms asked, surprised.

"Not very well with this yacht, but yes. I can change our gravity signature. The core is burning through calculations at an unbelievable rate, and making all the necessary microadjustments to the gravity drives. I haven't had a chance to try this method since learning about it from the core. I know it's working, though."

"How?" Grimms asked, not sure how she could take a sensor reading of their own ship.

"Look at the projector," Cora said.

The holo image no longer displayed a golden icon to indicate them, but it still contained the fleet, at a distance.

Then Grimms understood.

The sensors worked in the Aether, detecting things through the imprint they made with their gravity field. Everything had gravity, even if it was only a tiny amount, and that gravity pressed on space-time, causing it to warp. Cora was projecting the exact same signature they were making, and, like opposing sound waves, they were cancelling each other out.

"I've heard the theory, but I didn't think it was possible," Grimms said, watching as Connors guided the yacht to its docking point.

"It wasn't, 'til we found the cores."

"Sir, the dreadnought has gone to warp," Mezner noted with concern.

"Hon, keep those weapons primed. Connors, when will we have a lock?" Grimms barked.

"Thirty seconds, sir," Connors answered, his brow furrowed in concentration as he guided the yacht remotely.

"Contact. The dreadnought just dropped out of warp, three hundred kilometers starboard."

"Hon, get a solution for Cora, and open fire with the

gauss cannons. We're going to need to hit them hard and fast," Grimms said, leaning forward and not liking the odds.

"Belay that, Hon. I don't think they can see us on their scan, otherwise they would have opened fire right away. I think they know we're here, but not exactly where," Cora said.

Grimms bit his lip, hoping she was right, though he didn't understand how the Teifen could know to follow them here.

Unless someone told them.

"Mezner, has a signal gone out from us or the yacht since our jump?" Grimms asked urgently.

"Checking, sir," Mezner said, leaning into her console to check the log.

"They're firing gauss cannons, brace for impact," Hon reported, holding onto the edge of his console. After a few seconds, he double-checked his scans. "They missed. I think they are firing blind, sir; they are just peppering the area, hoping for a lucky hit."

"The yacht is locked onto the hard point, sir," Connors called out. "Warp coordinates Alpha set."

"Change to jump point Theta," Grimms ordered, a bad feeling in his gut.

"Theta set, sir."

"Warp in three, two, one," Cora quickly counted down.

The view compressed, and they were away, just as the area they had recently occupied was filled with hundreds of slugs.

Everyone took a breath, letting the nervous energy out in a rush—everyone but Grimms and Mezner, who were looking at each other from across the bridge.

"Mezner? Was there a signal?" Grimms asked again, his brow furrowed with anger.

"Yes, sir. There was an Aetheric burst right after we

jumped, then again before the dreadnought began firing on us," she reported, confirming his worst fears.

"Sir?" Connors asked, not understanding the significance of this.

"The prince's ship is signaling the Teifen, Ensign," Cora said, her voice dark.

"It was a trap," Grimms growled.

CHAPTER 18

S<small>ARA LACED UP HER BOOT</small>, her face still burning from having Baxter's eyes on her so intently. Though if his squirming was any indication, he hadn't enjoyed it much either. *We should try that under different circumstances. Stop, Sara. This is ridiculous, and not appropriate.*

Alister rubbed his head against her side in solidarity. "Mrow."

She smiled down at him, "Thanks, man. That means a lot."

He bunted her side again, and she gave a laugh. She noticed Baxter was smiling at the cat's antics as well.

It had taken him twenty minutes to feel confident enough to use her as a focus for his Aether, but the entire time, he had kept it professional. There was no leering, no comments, just focused determination. She appreciated his demeanor.

That didn't mean that it wasn't the most exposed she had ever felt in the presence of another person. But she realized that was the point, in a way. She had revealed her vulnerability to Baxter, linking them for life.

Now she could feel his Aether nestled in her well, its flavor slightly different than her own. She cherished the odd feel and what it meant.

"So, pixies?" Baxter asked, standing with his back to her.

He had turned around once the spell was done to give her some privacy. She said it was stupid, since he had just stared at her naked body for a full twenty minutes, but he insisted. Her heart fluttered a little at the gesture.

"Yes. Pixies," she said, finished tying her laces and throwing her jacket on.

She stood and put a hand on his back to let him know it was time to go. She felt his muscles tense under her hand, before he turned and gave her a bright smile.

"And Alister is one of them?" he asked, motioning for her to go down the ramp first.

Alister jumped to Sara's shoulder and gave a "Merp" in answer.

Baxter nodded. "Okay, good to know."

"So, this is going to be odd for you; I know, because it still is for me. Just try not to stare, okay?" Sara smiled over her shoulder at him.

She felt a small surge of trepidation and determination, and knew it was his. *Great. Now I have two people's emotions in my head, in addition to my own. I suppose it will take the guess work out of our relationship...*

They crossed the open, grassy area, headed toward Boon and the forest. Boon was sitting on the ground, cross-legged, with Silva wrapped around her neck like a too short scarf. Nyx was sitting in front of her in a similar position, but she was leaning over Boon's tablet, which was on the ground between them. The ten guards were still standing in a half circle behind her, but in much more relaxed positions than they'd been in when Sara had led Baxter away.

Sara looked back at Baxter to see how he was taking the sight of his first pixies, but his face was undisturbed, a half-smile etched into his dark features.

When they got closer, Sara could see that Boon and Nyx were playing a game of chess on the tablet. As she watched, the pixie slid three fingers across the screen, dragging a rook across the board. "Checkmate," Nyx said excitedly.

"Seriously? Again? Are you sure this is your first time?" Boon said skeptically, holding the tablet up to inspect the board.

Nyx held up her hand solemnly. "I swear, it's beginner's luck." She saw Sara and Baxter approaching, and stood to her full height, not even coming to Baxter's knee.

She held out a hand to shake with him, and he knelt down, taking her hand between his thumb and forefinger and shaking gently.

"Hello, Sergeant Major Baxter. My name is Nyx Morenna, Keeper of the Records. It is a pleasure to meet you. Our friend Boon here told me a lot about you while we played some chess," she said graciously with a half-bow.

Baxter, for his part, was much more composed than Sara would have been if she had been handed the same circumstances.

"A pleasure, ma'am," he said with a bow of his head. He noticed the ten guards and, standing, gave them all a salute. "Gentlemen."

The ten guards surprisingly snapped to attention and returned the salute.

Baxter smiled down at Nyx. "If you are ready, I believe Sara is eager to meet with the Elders."

Nyx leaned back, looking around Baxter's leg to give Sara a wink. "Good choice on your guard. He seems like a put-together fellow."

Sara just nodded, her mouth hanging open at the whole interaction.

"Come. The Elders await," Nyx said.

Then she turned and headed into the woods.

AFTER A KILOMETER and a half of pushing their way through dense woods, they stumbled out into a clearing that brought Sara, Boon, and Baxter up short.

In the center of the woods was an open prairie—or at least it had been at one time. Now a city in miniature, roughly a kilometer in diameter, filled the space. It was, in some ways, a modern city: there were the equivalent of high-rise buildings, fifty or sixty meters tall, and intricate parks, with fountains dotted throughout. But the city had cobbled streets, and the buildings were made of stone and adobe as often as wood and plaster.

Around the city was farmland, growing plants Sara had never seen. To her surprise, she saw a pixie on a small tractor in the distance, plowing a field. The design of the tractor was very unusual, and had the same glowing lines of Aether running across its surface that their Aetheric armor did when powered. She stood slack-jawed in wonder, and noticed a few pixies doing the same, as they noticed her and the others.

"Come, we must meet with the Elders in the town center. You will be able to sight-see when we are done," Nyx promised, beckoning them forward with a wave of her hand, as she and the guards stepped onto a well-maintained cobbled street between fields.

As they approached the city, Sara began to see that it was more modern than she had originally thought. The windows were all glass. The streets had electric lighting. There were tracks down the center of each road, conveying streetcars full of pixies who stared at the giants walking down their streets. They passed an open market full of pixies doing their shopping.

As they went further into the city, a crowd began to gather around and follow them. The pixies cleared a path for the guards and Nyx, but their eyes never left Sara, Boon, and Baxter. Alister and Silva rode on their companions' shoulders, their heads held high, as if riding parade floats.

Sara could tell they were headed for the center of the city, where the tallest building spiked into the sky. She guessed it was a hundred meters tall, and could see windows in twisting, irregular patterns, as if the floors were at random levels. Looking at the building beside them, which was three meters tall and had three floors, she guessed the central spire must be a hundred or more floors high.

They came to a plaza around the spire, and, to Sara's surprise, there was a fountain with two life-sized human statues standing in regal poses in the middle. Both humans were men; upon closer inspection, Sara could tell they were twins. They wore skin-tight suits, not unlike the battlesuit she would wear under her Aetheric armor.

"Alant and Altis?" Sara asked Nyx as they passed.

"Yes, this memorial was constructed after their deaths. Over the millennia, it has been rebuilt many times, not unlike this city." She pressed her hands together and bowed to two smaller figures at the base of the fountain.

Sara didn't see them at first, but she should have known to look for them. There was a fox-like creature, and a cat very similar to Alister, with odd, too large ears. They were statues of Alant and Altis's familiars; it seemed that the pixies showed them special respect.

"Come, the Elders await us in the meeting place," Nyx said, continuing on to the central spire.

There was a human-sized set of wooden doors set into the

front of the building, and two smaller doors built into them for easy pixie access.

Nyx indicated the larger doors, and said to Baxter, "Would you mind? We can open them, but it takes us a few minutes at the mechanical controls."

Baxter gave a slight bow. "Not a problem, allow me."

He pulled on the handle. The door didn't budge. He gave it another pull, and it screeched a little in the frame.

"It seems to be stuck. When was the last time they were opened?" he asked, giving another pull to no avail.

"Um, it's been a while. We usually open them on festivals, but the last festival was six months ago. Just give it a good yank. It should come loose," Nyx said, her face red with embarrassment.

Baxter set his feet and yanked hard on the door, rattling the whole frame, but not having any success with the door. He scratched his head and turned to Sara with a smile. "You mind giving me a hand?"

Sara noticed that a rather large crowd had gathered, and felt bad for poor Nyx. "Sure, step back, please."

She sent what she wanted to Alister, and the spellform appeared instantly in her mind. She poured a trickle of Aether into it, forming a small shield on the inside of the building, against the wooden door. Alister manipulated the shape of the form in her mind, as Sara continued to feed it.

The shield moved with inexorable force, pushing against the stuck door until, in a rush, it burst open, swinging so hard it slammed into the outside wall. The small shield spell continued to move out of the doorway at a steady pace until Sara dismissed it.

The bang of the door had made a large portion of the watching pixies duck or run for cover, and Sara mouthed 'sorry' to the crowd. Several of the guards had raised their rifles, but quickly lowered them.

Nyx had a hand over her heart, and was breathing heavy. "Oh, my. We really should have maintained that better. You'll have to forgive us, it has been nearly thirty thousand years since a human has needed to use these doors." She motioned for them to follow as she entered the building.

Sara was not surprised to see electric lights illuminating the interior as she stepped through the doorway. The architecture reminded her of somewhere she couldn't place, with stone tile flooring and rich wood accents. The first three floors of the building were centered around a single large room, with an intricate pattern inlaid in the floor's center. Small staircases wound around the walls, giving the pixies access to the upper levels.

In a semicircle on one half of the room was an ornate wooden structure that provided seating for seven pixies. They all wore robes similar to Nyx's, but they were much older than the Keeper of Records, some even showing wrinkles along with their white hair. There were four males and three females, seated alternately. Each wore a serious expression, and two smoked long pipes, causing a blue haze to settle over the room.

"War Mage, please, come," the female in the center said, her voice high and pleasant despite her obvious age.

Sara walked to the center of the room, with the others following close behind, and bowed, as seemed to be the custom among the pixies. "Greetings, I am Sara Sonders, a War Mage. This is Alicia Boon, also a War Mage. And this is Sergeant Major Baxter, my bonded guard. I am glad to be here; there is much to discuss."

"That there is, like the fact that you broke our door," the male to Sara's right said in a grumpy, gruff voice. Blue smoke puffed from him as if he were steam-powered.

Sara's eyebrows rose slowly. "Oh. Uh, sorry?"

"Oh, don't mind Trin, he's always bothered by something," the woman in the center said, throwing Trin a dirty look. Once Trin huffed and looked away, she turned back, all smiles. "It is a pleasure, my lady. I am Givis Hostern, elected High Elder. Welcome to Alantis, capital city of pixie-kind."

"Thank you, Givis. I must say, this is all a little unexpected. A hidden city full of pixies? It's amazing," Sara said in wonder.

"Oh, if this impresses you, you should visit Serit City in Luxembourg. Now *that* is a sight to behold," Givis chuckled.

"There are more cities like this?" Boon asked, gobsmacked.

"Of course there are! You think we could all fit in one city?" Trin gruffed.

Givis flashed him a look that could strip the paint from a barn, then smiled at the humans and said, "There are many cities across the world, though not nearly as many as you have. Most have been updated, but here, tradition keeps us a little behind the times. But I am guessing that your companions have brought you here for something more than chitchat about pixie culture. What can we do for you, my lady?"

Sara gathered her thoughts. This place, and what she'd had to do to bring Baxter to see it, was a little overwhelming. *There is an entire race that has been living just out of sight for as long as there have been humans.* She found the idea so far from her reality that she was distracted to the point of missing the High Elder's question.

Boon, seeing her captain freeze up, jumped in to cover for her. "Madam, we are seeking the War Mages Alant and Altis's dreadnought. There is technology onboard that we must recover to help us in the war with the Teifen."

"Ah, yes. The *Exitium,*" Givis said with a grave nod. "It has been preserved for ones such as yourselves. The Lords hid it well, knowing that the seas would rise to bury it, keeping it far from the grasp of mere mortals."

Sara blinked a few times. "It's at the bottom of the sea?"

Givis smiled. "Of course. What safer place is there?"

CHAPTER 19

"Commander, there is a Sir Reitus on the line for you. He says he is the captain of the prince's guard," Mezner said from her station, as Grimms studied the holo projection of the surrounding systems.

They had picked a warp point that would take them deeper into Elif territory, but it was a relatively short jump—only an hour, even without Cora pushing the speed past their normal capabilities. The captain wanted to give everyone some time to think out their next move. Ambassador Foss and Dr. Hess had joined the crew on the bridge, and they were debating how to deal with the *Empori*.

Grimms pushed off from the projector table and crossed his arms. "Put it on the main screen," he told Mezner.

The image of compressed space was replaced with that of a handsome Elif man, his black hair pulled back in a pony-tail. He had sharp features and intense green eyes that did not look happy. "Colonel Grimms, I am Sir Reitus, head of Prince Paelias DeSolin's head of security. Why has the prince not been allowed to board your ship? The *Empori* is rather crowded and, with the damage we have received, not suitable for his Highness."

Grimms recognized the question for what it was. This guard was not asking because *he* wanted to know, but because his lord had ordered him to. He felt an immediate sympathy for the soldier, but he could not endanger his own ship for the whims of a childish lordling.

"Sir Reitus, I apologize for the delay, but we are working on a problem that will need some care to solve. Would the prince not be more comfortable aboard his own ship for now?"

Sir Reitus began to answer, but cut off before the first word escaped his lips, and looked to the side, obviously listening to someone. He gave a nod then turned back to Grimms. "I apologize, but the prince wants you to know that this treatment is far from what he would expect from humanity."

Ambassador Foss leaned in and spoke privately to Grimms. "Colonel, I suggest that we at least bring his Highness aboard. Our peoples will need to work closely together in the future, and if the reports are true, he will be the emperor."

Grimms gave a nod. "I understand the politics, but there is a signal originating from that yacht, and we don't know if it is coming from an Aetheric device attached to the ship, or if it's is being sent by someone onboard."

In his comm, Cora spoke up. "Tell them we will be in contact in one minute. Say we are making arrangements for the transfer."

Grimms looked back at the screen. "We are preparing accommodations. Please allow us a few minutes; we will contact you shortly."

Sir Reitus bowed his head. "I thank you, Colonel. My

prince will be relieved." The communication was ended, and the view returned to normal.

"I assume you have a plan, Captain?" Grimms asked, looking to the ceiling, as he did when talking with Cora.

"We need to determine where the signal is coming from, and use that to our advantage, if we can," Cora said.

"Yes, but if the signal is coming from a traitor onboard the yacht, then we are just bringing that problem with us," Grimms retorted.

"There would never be a traitor in the prince's guard," Foss scoffed. "Royal guards are the most vetted soldiers in the empire. It is preposterous to think that one could have slipped through the rigorous testing." Dr. Hess nodded in agreement.

"That may be, but I'm not going to risk my homeworld on the Elif's reputation. If you remember, that did not work in our favor in the last war," Grimms said, feeling cornered.

Cora interjected. "It's not a matter of trust, Commander. This is simple elimination; if we can rule out one or the other, we can mitigate the danger. We have been ordered to retrieve him, so now we just need to figure out how to lose the Teifen."

"Sir? I have an idea," Ensign Hon piped up from his station.

Grimms turned in surprise, but gestured for him to continue.

"I've been going over the tactical data sent to us from the Elif communications networks over the last few weeks. In the data are last known ships' positions and strong points. We could use that information to set up an ambush," he said, turning a little red at all the scrutiny.

"What good are ship locations, if the information is weeks old, Ensign?" Grimms asked. He realized the young man must have an idea, but he was not seeing it.

"Well, ship *locations* would not be much use," he admitted, becoming animated as he sent information to the holo projector. "But take a look—this is a Galvox shipyard. The system is uninhabitable, but there are a large number of asteroids and planets, and the Galvox have been using them for resources to build their fleets. In addition to serving as a shipyard, the site is used as a training ground for the crews. All the reports say that the Teifen don't know about the system; that if they did, they would have attacked years ago. The Elif have a satellite in orbit, out in the system's Oort cloud, so the info is fairly up to date. They've found that the Galvox have hundreds of finished ships in the system, with thousands more under construction."

Grimms zoomed in on the system, getting a good look at the most recent images from the Elif satellite. The system was crawling with Galvox ships and installations. There was a huge shipyard orbiting the swollen star, soaking up the energy that poured off it as it burned the last of its hydrogen. Hon was right; there were *thousands* of ships in various stages of completion.

The Galvox were not as magically inclined as the rest of the sentient races, but they made up for that by having a population that dwarfed all three races by a factor of five. They fought by overwhelming the enemy in ships that were unshielded but agile, and bristling with weapons.

If he zoomed in far enough, he could see swarms of the little beings crawling all over the ships in spacesuits. At first, Grimms was confused as to what they were doing, then he realized they were putting the ships together by hand. He watched as five of the short bastards wrestled an armor plate into place, and a sixth stepped up with a handheld welder.

I suppose when there are hundreds of trillions of them, manpower becomes cheaper than automation.

"This is perfect!" Cora said excitedly. "The Galvox don't have the best sensors, so I can hide us right on top of them with the gravity manipulation trick I used before the jump. We can warp insystem, detach the empty yacht, and jump back out to the edge of the system. I'll monitor for any transmissions, which will tell us where the signal is coming from, and then the Galvox will attack the Teifen when they jump in!"

"It won't be that easy. We'll need to get the Galvox interested before the Teifen arrive; otherwise the Teifen will be able to jump away before any damage is done. We also don't know how long it will take the Teifen to arrive," Grimms said, scratching his beard.

"Sir, I just picked up another transmission from the yacht," Mezner interrupted.

"They can send messages while in warp?" Grimms asked.

"It's more of a locater signal. If I had to guess, I would say that the Teifen at least know what direction we're headed in, if not our destination," Mezner said.

Grimms thought it over for a minute as the rest looked on. Eventually, he gave a nod. "Okay, here's the plan…"

THEY DROPPED out of warp at Theta coordinates, and waited.

The prince and two of his guards had been moved to a private room aboard the *Raven*, while the rest of his crew and guards, forty-four in all, were being kept in the hangar for the time being. Sir Reitus was brought to the bridge, and introductions were made.

The guard was still in his Aetheric armor, and stood much taller than a normal Elif—which was tall, considering the average height of the Elif was a few centimeters over two meters. He was pleasant and cordial, and when asked to, he stepped out of his armor and stowed it in the hall.

After ten minutes of the humans and Elif waiting together, the first Teifen ship warped in.

"Warping in three, two, one," Cora counted down, as soon as the ship appeared.

They were once again in the warp field, traveling on a direct line to the Galvox system, before the second Teifen ship had arrived.

"Warp time is six hours, twenty-three minutes," Connors reported.

"Good. The trap is set, now we just need to cover our bases," Grimms said, turning to Sir Reitus. "We have a problem. I'm going to need your help."

Sir Reitus bowed ever so slightly. "I am at your disposal, Colonel."

"We need to make sure no one from your ship is sending signals to the Teifen."

Sir Reitus was taken aback. "I find it very unlikely that that is possible, sir."

"I understand your reluctance to believe that one of your own could be feeding the enemy information, but we need to be sure."

Cora spoke up, seeing the aggravation on the soldier's face and deciding on another tact. "Sir Reitus, I am Captain Cora Sonders. We would be most appreciative, and better able to assist your prince, if we were able to eliminate some possible sources of the transmissions. This is just a precaution, and in no way are we accusing you or your people of foul play."

Sir Reitus looked around the room for the owner of the voice, and was confused when he didn't find her. "Is this the new ship the emperor spoke of? With the ancient tech?"

"You're a quick one, Sir Reitus. Yes, this is the *Raven.* Welcome aboard."

CHAPTER 20

SARA STRIPPED DOWN NAKED in the cargo area of the shuttle, as it hovered over the water. She pulled her battlesuit out of her backpack and began putting it on. Boon was doing the same, but with more conservative movements as she threw glances toward the cockpit, checking to make sure that Baxter was still up there, and not sneaking a peek at her.

"Boon, he's not going to look. Will you just relax?" Sara said, sealing her skin-tight suit closed. She began unstrapping her armor, before remembering she would need to help Alister into his suit. "Shit, we didn't get a suit for Silva," she realized, smacking her forehead. "How could I forget that?"

"Oh. Should we just stay up here then?" Boon asked, pulling her hair out of the back of the battlesuit and sealing it up.

Sara shook her head. "No. I think you guys should come. We're going to learn quite a bit, and having you there will save me from having to explain it to you after the fact. I'll just take us down in a shield bubble."

Boon thought about that. "Won't you need to use your hands? I mean, we'll have to get in the ship somehow; we don't want to cause a hull breach, and I don't think battle-suits are rated for pressure. I know they are used in vacuum, but pressure is way different. Alister will be exposed, as well."

Sara cursed. Of course they weren't rated for pressure; the armor was, but not the suits. So far, this was the worst diving party she'd ever put together. Granted, it was the *only* one she'd ever put together, but oh-for-one was no way to start.

"Baxter. We're decent, come on back," Sara yelled to the front of the shuttle. "We have a problem."

Baxter stepped out from the cockpit, still in his battlesuit from earlier. "What's up?"

Sara waved a hand at Alister and Silva, curled up on a chair together. "We need to protect them from the crushing depths, and I can't make a shield bubble, because I will need to gain entrance to the ship when we get there."

Baxter didn't even think for a second before saying, "Just have Boon keep them in a small bubble with her. Alister just needs to be near you, right?"

Sara and Boon stared at him until he felt self-conscious and asked, "What?"

"Why the fuck didn't I think of that?" Sara rolled her eyes and opened up her armor.

The suit opened up like a blooming flower, exposing its padded interior. She turned and stepped backward into it, and it closed around her. She shot a small amount of Aether into the spellform that was recessed in the interior of the faceplate, bringing the suit to life. The faceplate became clear to her eyes, giving her an unobstructed view. She could see Boon's suit closing up, and Baxter just getting his open.

Sara stepped to the wall controls and opened the ramp. The shuttle was hovering a few meters above rolling waves of deep blue. She held onto the edge of the opening and walked out onto the ramp, then turned back to the others.

"Okay. Boon, you keep them safe and follow close; I

don't want to lose my powers because Alister and I are too far apart," Sara warned, as Baxter stepped close and attached a rope with a carabiner, then did the same to Boon and himself.

"Don't need to worry about us getting separated this way," he explained, his black faceplate hiding the smile Sara knew he wore.

She rolled her eyes again. "Good thinking, Baxter. Boon, grab the kids; we're off to the pool."

Boon scooped up the two waiting familiars and, with a toss, launched them into the air. A shield bubble half a meter in diameter popped into existence around them, then floated to her side. She gave a thumbs-up. "Ready."

Sara knew that, while the spell seemed simple enough, Silva was having to constantly change it to keep the bubble moving along beside Boon. It was a spell a human mind would not have been able to perform, but it took barely any thought for the pixie.

Sara nodded, turning to the end of the ramp as the others stepped up beside her. "Ready?" They nodded in response. "Jump!" she yelled, hopping off the ramp, and the others came a heartbeat behind her.

They fell the few meters, crossing their arms to their chests as they were taught in diving school at the Academy. They plunged into the waves and sank like bricks.

Sara watched as the blackness engulfed them, and her heart began to speed up with every meter they sank. She was in the Navy, but she and the ocean had never gotten along too well. She was fine with the beach and swimming, but the depths were the last place on Earth she'd yet to explore. In a lot of ways, space was easier. With the arrival of the Elif and their tech, a lot of research had been conducted, but only on a very small scale. They learned that the Aetheric armor could withstand any depth that Earth could throw at it, but she still found it disconcerting to be free falling in open water.

Sara felt a spike of nervousness from both Alister and Baxter, and turned to see how they were doing. She panicked for a second when she couldn't see them, then realized that they had fallen far enough that the light from the sun was no longer reaching them. If she remembered correctly, that was around two hundred meters. According to the map Givis had provided them, the location of the dreadnought was at a depth of just over two thousand meters.

Sara sent a mental command to her headlamps, and the area around her bloomed to life. She caught sight of Boon's and Baxter's suits switching on their lights, and was finally able to see Alister and Silva in their shield bubble. They were curled around one another, their eyes large as they took in the hostile environment. Sara sent calming feelings to Alister as she mentally wrestled her fear away for his sake. She watched as he calmed, his grip on Silva loosening.

"Boon, be sure to keep calm. Silva is getting your nervous energy, and it's putting her on edge," Sara said over their comms.

She barely caught Boon's nod in the dark waters. "Right. Sorry, Silva."

Sara saw the ferret relax a little, and felt better. The last thing they needed was for Silva to lose concentration and collapse the shield bubble.

Sara turned back to the job at hand, and began cycling her faceplate's view. She set it to a wire overlay of a sonar pulse. The pulse took a while to get back to her, but once it did, the onboard computer updated the information in real time.

The wire frame view was a little less daunting, but only slightly. It looked like they were still over a thousand meters from the seafloor, but falling fast. She could pick out several anomalies that the computer interpreted as fish, as well as other living things that gave her the creeps. She highlighted on her view the exact location of where Givis had said the entrance would be. She could see it was pointing to the base of a large mountain, situated on a flat area that eventually fell to deeper depths beyond its edges.

They were a little over two hundred meters from the supposed entrance, when Sara sent another sonar pulse for a more detailed image. The flecks of stuff that flew past her faceplate made it look like they were speeding through a snowfall, but she didn't want to know what the flakes were; she guessed they were something gross.

The mountain loomed before them, their lights only illuminating a small section of its sheer side. Sara sent Alister what she wanted, and a spellform immediately appeared in her mind. She powered it, and a flat shield appeared under her feet, catching her as she fell onto it. She almost lost her balance, but Baxter landed beside her and, with a hand to her shoulder, kept her upright. Boon landed last, and Sara caught her around the waist to steady her.

"Everyone okay?" the captain asked, looking at the others for signs of damage or panic.

"I'm good. After the first five hundred meters, it actually got a little boring," Boon said, reaching out and grabbing the shield bubble with the pixies in it. "Are you guys okay?" she yelled, pressing her faceplate to the shield to transfer the sound, like they had been taught to do when someone's radio went out.

Alister opened his mouth in what Sara recognized as a "Merow," even if she couldn't hear it, and Silva just gave a nod and rested her head on Alister's back.

"I'm good, Captain. Why did we stop?" Baxter asked, looking at the dimly lit wall of rock.

"According to the directions, we're here," she answered, waving a hand through the heavy water.

"It's in the mountain?" he asked.

"I guess so. It wouldn't be much of a hiding place if it were out in the open. The marker says it's right there, but I don't see an opening," Sara said, double-checking the location with the map. *We're right where we are supposed to be...*

"Maybe it moved? The ocean floor is always resettling, and this area is full of volcanic activity," Boon said, shrugging.

"She said they map it regularly. I'm guessing the entrance just got covered up with sediment. Hang on, I'm going to try something," Sara said, stepping forward.

She had Alister provide a second spellform, and sent a spike of power into it. A section of rock blasted up off the rock wall, clouding the water with a thick, white dust.

"What the fuck was that?" Baxter asked, stumbling as the shock wave hit them.

"Force blast. I started it inside the rock, and shot it upward. Sorry, I should have warned you," she said, trying to make out the wall in the cloudy water, but seeing nothing as the cloud enveloped them. She sent out another sonar pulse, and the hole finally revealed itself. "There it is. I'm going to move us closer; don't fall off the shield," she cautioned as Alister morphed the spellform, sending it forward at a walking pace.

Boon stumbled back a step, but Baxter steadied her with a hand and a nod. They moved through the cloudy water, toward a circular opening that was far from natural. It was several meters wide, allowing the shield to slip easily inside.

"These walls aren't organic," Baxter noted, shining his lights on the smooth surface. "I think it's the same composite material we use as paneling on the *Raven*."

"I think you're right. How has it stayed so clean?" Boon asked.

"If I had to bet, I would say that this passage has been sealed the entire time," Sara mused. "There's no chance anyone could have stumbled upon it, if it was covered. Hey, I think we're coming up on the ship." She squinted through the gloom and saw a dim reflection of the light. The passage suddenly ended in an airlock that was the same design used on the *Raven*.

"Yeah, I think this is it," Baxter agreed, stepping forward. He brushed sediment from a control pad cover that was attached to the hull, beside the door. "It's dead. How are we going to get in?"

"We don't want to flood the ship, so we can't force the door. We can try the manual override," Sara suggested.

Baxter knelt down and found the small door the contained the pumping mechanism. He cleaned it off as best he could and, after a few power-assisted tugs, popped it open. Inside was a handle that looked a lot like an emergency brake; it even had the button on the end. He reached in and depressed the button, pumping the handle, but Sara could tell it was moving far too easily.

"It's been disabled," he said, looking over his shoulder at Sara.

"Boon, I'm going to need you to create a shield around us and seal it tight to the hull of the ship. I have a feeling this is like the core; inaccessible to anyone but a War Mage. If I'm right, I'll need to touch the control panel with my bare skin," Sara said, stepping up to it.

"Okay, give me a second. I haven't cast two spells at once before." Boon set her shoulders, but then stood up straight and said, "Oh. Well, that's pretty easy. Thanks, Silva."

Sara laughed. "Yeah, the pixies are pretty good at this. Okay, keep the shield powered. I'm going to start creating breathable air, and I need you to open a small hole in the bottom of the shield bubble so I can push the water out. Got it?"

Boon nodded. "Got it."

Sara began feeding the spellform that Alister formed in her mind. The act of creating something from pure Aether took a lot of power, but she had plenty. After nearly thirty seconds, the water began to boil, as the air content overcame the water's ability to absorb it. Sara pushed harder, burning through her well of Aether at a rate that would have scared her before becoming a War Mage.

Soon, the level of water began to lower, as the top of the shield bubble filled with compressed air. Sara poured more and more power into the form, surprised at how much it was taking to move the volume of water. After nearly three minutes, the level was below the shield platform they stood on.

"Okay, wow. That took a lot. Go ahead and seal up the shield bubble so I can bring the pressure back down."

"Sealed," Boon reported from behind her.

"Okay, I'm going to reclaim enough air to get us back to one atmosphere," Sara said, bringing up a pressure reading from her suit's sensors. Her eyes widened when she saw the number. "Holy shit. We're at two hundred atmospheres. That's incredible."

"Yeah, decompression at that level would rip the flesh from your bones if you opened up your suit. Be careful, ma'am," Baxter said nervously.

"Don't worry, I will be," Sara assured him, smiling at his concern.

She began feeding a new spellform from Alister, converting the compressed air back into Aether. The process was much easier than creating the air, but still used a bit of power. Sara kept an eye on the pressure meter, as it fell much faster than it had risen.

A minute later, she sent a mental command to her glove, and it clam-shelled open, filling her suit with a strong smell of ocean and rot. "Oh, god. The smell." She gagged, then held her breath to keep from dry heaving as Boon laughed. She threw a dirty look Boon's way, and reached out, touching the control panel. She pulled her hand away quickly, shocked at how cold it was. She was surprised there was no ice on it; the panel must have been only just above freezing.

Taking a breath to prepare for the cold, she began to choke at the smell. She mentally chided herself for the stupid move. *Dumb ass.* She pressed her fingers to the panel and waited, fighting the cold and hoping her hunch was right.

After a few seconds of doubt, she had begun to run through other ideas on how to get in when the panel came to life. Instead of the usual controls that would appear on the *Raven*'s airlock, a green line slid down the panel, like the scanner on the cores' boxes, and she smiled.

She pulled her hand away and closed the glove, then waited a minute for the air to recycle in her suit before taking another breath. The smell was still there, but much less so now that the filters were working in a closed environment again.

A set of lights burst to life around the airlock, causing the crew's faceplates to dim in response, to keep them from being blinded. A *ka-chunk* reverberated through the hull, causing them to stumble back a little. The center of the airlock began to spin, causing a thick crust of sediment to crumble and shower down onto the shield platform. The center stopped spinning, and a split appeared, bisecting the door horizontally, and began sliding open, scraping sediment from its surface as it slid into the hull.

The interior of the airlock was exactly the same design as

the *Raven*'s, with soft blue light filling a compartment large enough for twenty people.

Sara turned to the other two and shrugged. "Easy peasy," she said, laughing. "They definitely made access impossible for anyone but a War Mage. Next time, we should come down in a shield bubble from the start. That took way too much power."

Boon turned and looked back the way they had come. The corridor through the mountain was lit by the powerful lights around the airlock, but fell to blackness a few meters out into the ocean. "This is insane. How did they bury this ship?"

"One thing you will learn is just how much one War Mage can do. Imagine what two could do together," Sara mused, cocking her head to the side. "Come on. Let's see what they left for us."

Boon turned back, the small shield bubble containing the familiars in her hands. They sat curled together, but alert.

Sara pointed at Alister, catching his attention, then gave him a thumbs-up while sending him a questioning feeling. He opened his mouth, and she recognized him saying "Merp." She gave the 'okay' hand gesture and stepped into the airlock.

The others followed, and she flipped the switch on the wall to cycle the airlock. The outer door slid closed, and the wall monitor flashed a red message. She activated the translation program in her suit, and the message changed from ancient human script to English in her view.

"Just waiting for it to cycle," she told the others, translating the words for them. "You can drop the shield outside, Boon."

"Right," she said, a second before a crashing *BOOM* shook the ship. "What the fuck?" she screamed, looking around for the danger.

"I think it was the water collapsing against the hull," Baxter said with more calm than Sara thought was possible after hearing that.

"Maybe next time we collapse the shield in increments," Sara suggested, giving a nervous laugh.

The flashing red changed to green, and the inner door *ka-chunked* and split open, revealing the wall of a darkened corridor that looked brand new, if not a little dusty. They stepped into the corridor, looking left then right, the light of their suits falling to darkness in both directions.

"Be sure to keep those two in there," Sara instructed, gesturing to the familiars. "The air is no good in here."

"Got it. Which way?" Boon asked, then jumped when a strip of blue light in the floor of the center of the corridor lit up, leading to the right.

It began to pulse in a wave.

"To the right, I think," Sara said, stepping past Boon and following the pulsing light.

CHAPTER 21

"Prepare to detach the yacht," Grimms ordered, watching the countdown of the warp. They were twenty seconds away from arriving in a heavily populated Galvox system. The plan was to detach the yacht and jump away, leaving the yacht as bait. They needed to jump in close enough that the Galvox would send ships, but not so close that they could be detected as well. Cora was getting ready to cloak them, but it would take her a second to calibrate the engines, and they would not be able to change direction once she was manipulating the gravity field, so they would be exposed for the first thirty seconds or so of the operation.

"Hon, power weapons. Mezner, I want a pulse scan of the system as soon as we are out. Send it with some power behind it to grab the little bastards' attention."

"Aye, sir," Mezner acknowledged, her hands hanging over her console in preparation.

Both Ambassador Foss and Dr. Hess were strapped into the visitors' couch at the back of the bridge. Sir Reitus was standing beside Grimms at the holo projection table, held in place by powering small spellforms that were embedded into the table's edges.

"The Galvox will try to swarm us. We will need to quickly put some distance between us and the *Empori*," the prince's guard said, his nervousness slipping through his hard demeanor.

"Don't worry about that, Sir Reitus. I have a few tricks you haven't seen before," Cora said confidently. "Dropping warp in three, two, one."

The view flashed blue, and several things happened at once. Mezner pulsed the system with an Aetheric blast that populated the holo projection in an instant. Connors detached the yacht with a shuddering *thud* that reverberated through the ship; he then engaged the gravitic drive, pushing them to starboard, away from the yacht.

But the thing that put everyone on edge was Hon yelling, "Contacts!"

Grimms saw that they had warped directly into a large formation of Galvox ships. The ships were all the same and on the smaller side, being less than two hundred meters in length. But there were at least twenty of them, and they bristled with weapons. The closest ship was less than fifty kilometers away; practically right on top of them in space terms.

"Open fire; we need to keep them from destroying the yacht before it can send the signal to the Teifen," Grimms ordered, gripping the table's edge with white knuckles.

There was a buzzing through the deck as all twenty-four PDCs opened up, auto-targeting the enemy ships. The gauss cannons fired in rapid succession, each turret aiming for a different ship.

"Evasive maneuvers, Connors. Keep us clear but close," Grimms said, leaning in to study the rest of the system, and leaving the immediate battle to his people for the moment.

He barely noticed the four explosions, Galvox ships being

incinerated by gauss rounds. He was watching the inner system for any sign of reaction, knowing they were going to need the rest of the Galvox to start heading their way, if they were going to do some damage to the dreadnought that was hot on their heels.

Another shoddily made Galvox ship was ripped apart by concentrated PDC fire. Then the Galvox seemed to catch up to the situation, as they scattered in haphazard fashion, making targeting difficult.

Difficult, but not impossible at the close range.

Another ship was disabled by the PDCs.

"Connors, activate the yacht's preloaded course," Grimms ordered calmly; just then, the *Raven* bucked from a hit to the armor plating. "Damage report," he yelled.

"Glancing blow to the bow. Nanites are already en route," Cora replied before Mezner could read the report coming up on her console. "Hull integrity is at seventy percent from the earlier Aether blast, so try to keep that side from exposure, Connors."

"Aye, ma'am," he answered, his finger flying across his controls, sending them in a spiraling dive away from incoming fire.

Another shudder told them they had been hit a second time, and Connors changed direction. He began shifting course quickly, not giving the agile Galvox more opportunities than was necessary. Despite the shoddy construction and haphazard design of their craft, the Galvox were quick, dodging and juking at a much faster rate than the *Raven* could hope to match.

Grimms noted the green icon of the yacht speeding away from the battle, juking left and right to avoid being targeted, and heading insystem at maximum acceleration. Luckily, it looked like the Galvox were ignoring it for the larger threat of the *Raven*.

Another Galvox ship was ripped open as Hon fired another volley of gauss rounds, but the three remaining turrets missed their targets.

The *Raven* was hit again, this time causing the lights to flicker.

"They got a lucky shot. Reactor three is damaged. Repairs are underway," Cora said. "Firing Aether cannons."

Two beams of brilliant blue appeared in the holo display, and another ship exploded, though the second beam missed its target. The remaining Galvox seemed to become frantic, and the space they occupied became filled with hyper-velocity slugs.

"Jump!" Grimms yelled, and the view on the main screen changed.

He saw that they had jumped a short distance of a few hundred thousand kilometers. The Galvox flew in circles for a beat, before turning their way and pouring on the speed. Grimms was surprised at the acceleration they could achieve; they were nearly as quick as the *Raven.*

"The *Empori* has just sent out the signal, Sir," Mezner reported.

The Galvox let loose a volley of gauss rounds, but they were still a distance away, though closing fast.

"Jumping," Cora said, and again they were a distance away from their original location. "Cloaking."

The golden icon disappeared from the holo display, and Grimms watched the Galvox closely. They seemed unable to find them and, after a few seconds, changed course for the yacht.

"Contact. The Teifen fleet is emerging from warp," Mezner said excitedly. "They're right on top of the yacht."

By now, several hundred Galvox ships were closing in on the yacht, and they immediately opened fire on the first Teifen ship, ripping through its unshielded hull. Then the next Teifen ship arrived, and was peppered with slugs and Aether bolts as the Galvox began using their Aether cannons. By the time the first two Teifen ships were expanding balls of fire and debris, the rest of the Teifen armada had arrived, including the monstrous dreadnought.

Grimms watched as it became all-out war between their enemies. Hundreds of fighters began to pour from the dreadnought and two carriers that had come late to the party. The dreadnought let loose with hundreds of cannons and PDCs, filling the area with a hail of fire that made Grimms shudder.

The Galvox were not backing down, however, and their quick movements kept most of the ships intact after the initial volley. They began taking heavy losses when the Teifen fighters entered range with the small Galvox warships, and began ship to ship battle. Soon, sections of the dreadnought were being blown apart, but the ship was so huge that Grimms was having trouble telling if the damage was serious, or superficial.

"Incredible, I've never see the Teifen take such a beating. They have already lost a dozen ships, and several more will not survive the minute," Sir Reitus said with awe. He turned to Grimms. "We jumped position instantly in that battle. How is that possible?"

"I told you I had a few surprises up my sleeve," Cora said —rather smugly, to Grimms' ears.

"There is a lot happening, Sir Reitus. Humanity is returning to the galaxy, and we plan on making that fact a tough pill for our enemies to swallow."

Sir Reitus turned back to the holo display, his face full of wonder. Grimms watched as two more Teifen cruisers were destroyed. The dreadnought was taking serious damage, but so were the Galvox. They were throwing everything they had at the dwindling armada, and Grimms hoped it would be enough—though, deep down, he feared it would not.

Still, this was a blow that would cripple the Teifen's hold on this section of the galaxy.

"Let's get out of here. Connors, warp point Beta," Grimms said, watching another Teifen fall to the never-ending barrage of Galvox.

"Warp in three, two, one," Cora counted.

The image on the holo projector froze with the last data from the battle. A large plume of flame was jetting from the fore of the dreadnought.

Grimms smiled.

CHAPTER 22

Sᴀʀᴀ ᴡᴀs ɢᴇᴛᴛɪɴɢ ғʀᴜsᴛʀᴀᴛᴇᴅ. They had been following the light strip for over ten minutes, and had passed several closed doors. They had tried to open a few, but the entrances were locked and unresponsive. Sara decided they needed to stick to the light instead of getting sidetracked trying to access doors that could very well be supply closets. They'd been led through a number of turns, which would have left them lost, if not for the auto mapping feature of their armor.

"How big is this ship? We've walked far enough to make two trips up and down the *Raven* by now," Boon commented.

Sara checked her HUD; sure enough, they had walked over a kilometer, and still had not seen anything but corridors. "I have no idea. But the light seems to be leading us somewhere. It disappears as we walk, so it knows where we are. Maybe it's heading to the bridge."

They turned a corner, and the light led to a large double door, like the ones that led to the cargo bays on the *Raven*. When they approached, the power indicator came to life, and the doors slid open. Stepping through, they entered a room so large that the lights on their suits couldn't reach the other side, just fading after several hundred meters.

"Okay. This has got to be the largest ship ever built," Sara said, tilting her head back, trying to see the ceiling.

"The light leads out toward the center. Should we follow it? There won't be any cover out there," Baxter warned, always thinking tactically.

Sara snorted a laugh. "Cover from what? If you haven't noticed, the place is deserted."

Baxter turned to her and put his hands on his hips. "So was the crashed ship we found Dr. Hess studying, but it still had active automated defenses."

Sara was glad he couldn't see her flush of embarrassment. "Good point. I kind of forgot about that."

"No worries, Captain. That's what I'm here for." She could hear the smile in his voice.

Sara rolled her eyes. "We're still going out there. Unlike that derelict, this ship invited us in and is providing helpful directions," she pointed out, holding her head high and walking past him.

She still had Alister prepare a shield, just in case, and she assumed Baxter was doing the same as he trailed behind Boon, who was in the middle.

They followed the line as it pulsed, happily leading them who knew where. The uniform deck plates gave way to mounds of dark material. The light continued down a path between the low mounds, and when Sara knelt to examine them, she realized it was dirt. Very *dry* dirt, as if grass used to grow from it but had dried up and left the cracked soil underneath.

Baxter knelt next to her, scooping up a handful of the stuff and crumbling it between his fingers.

"I think this was a park," Sara said, standing and shining

her light over the large patch of soil that stretched out into the darkness.

"I think you're right. Why would there be a park on a spaceship?" Baxter asked.

"Well, if the ship is as large as I think, the occupants would need a place for leisure time. Plus, a taste of home would make long journeys more bearable," Boon said, holding the shield bubble under her arm like a beach ball.

"I think she's right," Baxter said, nodding at Boon's small armored figure. "By all accounts, the dreadnought was a city, with enough people on it to populate Earth after a few generations."

"Come on. Let's get to wherever this light is taking us so we can start searching for answers," Sara said, stepping past Baxter and continuing deeper into the desecrated park.

After another five minutes' walking, Sara could see that the light ended a few hundred meters ahead. She saw the outline of something like a pyramid with the top cut off, in an open area of deck, between patches of dirt. As they got closer, she saw that the structure had a control panel on the side, and a smaller print scanner, exactly like the core boxes. When they were a meter or two away, the light in the floor went out completely.

"Well, I guess I should turn it on?" Sara inferred, shrugging.

"Be careful, the air is not breathable. Don't leave your suit open for long," Baxter reminded her, making her grin and shake her head.

"Yes, Mom. I'll be careful," she said.

She sent a command to her glove, and it opened with a hiss. She upped her air production to increase the pressure in the suit, keeping a positive airflow and filtering out any foreign bodies. Reaching out, she pressed her thumb to the scanner and waited. After a three count, the familiar green line rolled down the pad, scanning her thumb. She closed the glove and stood back, waiting for whatever was about to happen to happen.

The panel on the side of the podium came to life, obviously going through a boot sequence, then went blank. They stood there waiting, but nothing happened.

Sara turned to look at the others. Boon shrugged, while Baxter looked around in the dark for any threats.

"Maybe it doesn't have enough power?" Boon asked.

"Maybe…" Sara began, but was cut off by a rumbling, deep within the ship.

A shield popped up around them. Baxter was holding out a hand, powering it, and watching for danger. Sara thought the sound was familiar somehow. Then the rumbling subsided to a hum that was more felt than heard, and it hit her.

"Those are reactors coming online," Sara said, cocking her head to the side to hear better. "It's what the simulation at the Academy sounded like when we practiced emergency shutdown and restart procedures."

"Maybe, but how will we—" Baxter was cut off when the lights came on.

The room, if you could call it that, filled with light as panels in the ceiling came to life, projecting the image of a blue sky with white fluffy clouds. Sara stumbled back a few steps as she took it all in.

The space was easily a kilometer long, and half as wide and tall. The artificial sky made the dead and dried patches of dirt look ominous in their desolation. There were structures dotting the landscape that looked like facilities for the old park, along with depressions that were obviously dried up ponds and lakes.

"This is incredible," she said, spinning around to see it all. "How can this ship be this big?"

"It was designed as a colony ship, and only later re-engineered as a warship," a friendly male voice said.

Sara, Baxter, and Boon all spun at once, each throwing up shields, so that there was a barrier three shields thick between them and the podium. Standing in the center of the podium was a man wearing a battlesuit and an open, hooded robe; he had a small, large-eared, cat sitting regally next him.

"Alant?" Sara asked, confusion raising her voice an octave.

The figure took a bow. "At your service, War Mage."

CHAPTER 23

Grimms walked down the corridor, his face tight with concern. He had his hands clasped behind his back, and his shoulders were stiff as he mulled privately. Sir Reitus walked beside him, keeping quiet as Grimms swam through the muddy thoughts of his next action.

"Will the prince be amenable to answering questions?" Grimms asked the tall Elif suddenly, after a few minutes of walking in silence.

"Yes, he wants to help," Sir Reitus said, then added, "but be aware that my prince is very young, despite his appearance. He is not yet twenty of your years old. In my people's time, that is barely out of childhood."

Grimms nodded. "Thank you for the warning. After the interview, I would like to talk with you again."

"I am at your disposal, Colonel," he said, bowing slightly as they walked.

Grimms had spoken with Cora earlier, in the ready room, once the *Raven* had escaped into warp. So far, they had not detected any Aether bursts to give away their location, or direction of travel. However, both he and Cora agreed that it was rather suspicious that the prince had been able to escape at all. The entire planet of Effrit, including the space above it, was crawling with Teifen at the time, and the yacht had no means of defense or evasion, beyond a few PDCs.

Cora decided she would not make her presence known to the prince, instead staying silent. That way she could monitor him and his guards to see if they let anything slip. Grimms planned on having Sir Reitus with him after the interview to be sure the prince stayed unaware of Cora's monitoring.

They turned at the next corridor intersection, coming to the room they had set aside for the prince. Two Elif soldiers stood guard outside the door, both in battlesuits after having been told they must leave their Aetheric armor in the cargo bay. Grimms and Cora didn't want an armored force not under their control freely roaming their ship. Grimms had gone so far as to have a squad of his Marines, led by Specialist Gonders, fully kitted for battle and placed on standby, just in case.

The soldiers slapped their fists to their hearts, coming to attention. Sir Reitus saluted them back with a tap of his fist to his own heart. "We will see the prince. Stay out here and make sure we are not disturbed."

"Yes, sir," the one on the left said, his voice much more sing-song than Grimms would have guessed from his imposing stature.

The door slid open, revealing a small guest cabin, where the prince was pacing back and forth and vigorously tugging at his ear tip—a sure sign of nervousness. He spun to the door as Sir Reitus and Grimms stepped into the room.

The prince was short for an Elif, maybe only a few centimeters taller than Grimms' stocky build. He had golden blonde hair that hung to his shoulders, and blue eyes that were red and puffy from crying. If Grimms were to guess, he would put the prince's age at fifteen human years, though the white robes that hung open over a golden battlesuit made him look older.

When the prince saw who had entered, he rushed to embrace the head of his guard, wrapping his arms around Sir Reitus's waist and pulling him in tight. A tear slipped from the youth, but his face was hidden before he could begin crying in earnest.

Grimms was taken aback at the gesture until he remembered that Elif tended to be much more communal, often embracing in place of a handshake. He tended to forget that the Elif he was closest to, Dr. Hess and Ambassador Foss, had studied human cultures extensively, and refrained from the traditional contact when in public.

"Reitus, I am glad to see you. This isolation is not to my liking," the prince said, his face buried in the much larger Elif's chest.

"My apologies, your Highness. In the heat of battle, I forgot to assign you companions. I will have Sareet and Fromin join you after we are done speaking with Colonel Grimms," Sir Reitus said, stroking the prince's hair in a familiar way.

The two were obviously close; at least, the guard *acted* close to his charge. Grimms could not tell if it was genuine, or simply part of protecting the prince.

Protection comes in many forms, the colonel considered. *I need to become more familiar with the Elif's culture, if we are to be working this closely with them.*

The prince finally released Sir Reitus, and stood tall in as regal a pose he could muster, then faced Grimms. "I thank you, Colonel Grimms, for the assistance. I fear what could have happened to me if you were not close by."

Grimms, not knowing what else to do, gave a half-bow. "It was no trouble, your Highness. We ended up dealing the Teifen a grand blow, so I consider the task well worth the effort." He cringed inwardly, realizing his words could be taken badly, but pushed forward in hopes it would slide. "Your Highness, I have a few questions I'm hoping you can answer for me."

The prince stepped back and sat on the edge of the bunk, the only seating surface in the cabin, and reached up to tug at his ear, but stopped himself. He wiped his eyes with the back of his sleeve instead, and put on a brave face. "Of course, Colonel. What can I answer for you?"

Grimms crossed his arms, his default posture when processing information. "We don't have any direct intel on the attack on Effrit. Can you tell me what happened, from your perspective?"

The prince swallowed, staring off into the distance for a few seconds before beginning. "I was with my magic tutor when the alarms went off. I didn't know what was happening until a servant came and told us that the Teifen had warped their entire fleet into the system, and that the Navy was under attack. He said he would take me to my ship, so I followed him to my family's dock." He fell silent, as if considering saying more on the subject, then rushed on just as the pause became obvious. "Then Sir Reitus showed up with a bunch of the guard, and they took me onboard the *Empori*. We took off and were attacked once we were in orbit, but we were able to go to warp and escape. Then you found us," he said, smiling sheepishly up at Grimms' gruff expression.

He was lying about something, or at least leaving something out, Grimms was sure. "The servant that brought you to the *Empori*, is he here with you?"

The prince's face flushed at the question. "No. He said he would stay behind to help protect the palace."

Grimms scratched his beard, considering, then gave the prince a warm smile. "I thank you, your Highness. I hope your stay with us is not too troublesome. We should be arriving at Earth soon, and you will be delivered to your embassy there."

The young Elif stood. "Thank you, Colonel. I shall let them know that you treated me kindly," he said with a bow of his head.

Sir Reitus bowed at the waist, and Grimms followed suit, not knowing the proper etiquette but figuring a bow never hurt.

"I will send you companions soon, your Highness," Sir Reitus promised, then he opened the door, allowing Grimms to exit first.

Back in the corridor, Grimms walked in silence while Sir Reitus made arrangements for the prince's companions. The servant was key, but Grimms was having trouble guessing how. The problem was that he had no perspective of Elif politics.

"What can you tell me about the events?" Grimms asked Sir Reitus, when he had finished with his orders.

Sir Reitus took a breath. "I was alerted of the attack just before the palace alarms went off. We had a training exercise in the yard, so I was on the other side of the palace from the prince. We track all the royal family members with devices implanted in their wrists, and I could see that he was heading for the dock, so I grabbed the men on the practice field, and we rushed to meet him. When I got there, he was standing at the base of the yacht's ramp, and a servant was rushing out through another door. The rest happened just like he said; we took some damage, but were able to escape with a well-timed warp."

They came to the bridge, and Grimms led him to the ready room, closing the door behind them.

"Did you recognize the servant?" Grimms asked, pouring coffee for himself, and tea for the Elif.

Sir Reitus thanked him and took a sip of the tea before answering. "Now that you mention it, I did not. However, I was not paying that much attention to him, and there are a lot of servants in the palace. You think the servant may have placed the tracking device?"

Grimms blew out a breath. "Someone did. And by both your accounts, the prince was off-planet before the Teifen got into the palace." He paused, figuring out how to best word his next question. "You'll have to forgive my lack of knowledge on the subject, I mean no offense, but are there Elif that would help the Teifen take over Effrit?"

Sir Reitus's eyes became hard. "Elif and Teifen relations are difficult to comprehend sometimes. The first thing you need to consider is that both empires are vast, covering several hundred star systems, in the case of the Elif, and several thousand in the case of the Teifen. When you have that many people, the edges of the empires begin to get…" He considered his words. "Blurry."

"So the systems on the edge are less loyal?" Grimms asked to clarify.

"I suppose you could call it that, but I would argue that it's more a question of survival than loyalty. On the edges, things don't come as easily; it's a hard life out there. The Elif and Teifen empires share borders where star systems held by each side are close in proximity. Those systems will trade with one another for survival."

Grimms raised an eyebrow. "They trade? As in, they have professional relationships with each other?"

"Yes. Despite the highly aggressive nature of the Teifen, they are still a people that need to survive, just like you or I. Most of their aggression is concentrated in the armed forces, or closer to the governors and emperor. For the most part, they are just people, trying to make it to the next day. I say all of this to make it clear that there is not a hard line between our people. It is possible that a Teifen sympathizer could have gained entrance to the palace."

"Interesting," Grimms said, sipping his coffee.

After a minute, Sir Reitus said, "You told the prince we were heading to Earth. It was my understanding that we were first stopping in a system to make sure the Teifen were not following us."

"Yes. I was just letting him know that it wouldn't be long," Grimms said, not wanting to reveal his and Cora's plan to find out if there was a traitor onboard.

"Very well. If there is nothing else?" Sir Reitus said, standing to go.

Grimms glanced at the clock, noting there was still half an hour before they'd reach their destination. "Actually, if you wouldn't mind, I would like to hear more about this edge culture of Teifen and Elif."

Sir Reitus sat back down. "Of course, Colonel."

CHAPTER 24

"What is this?" Boon asked, waving a hand through Alant's figure, making it warp and blur where her hand interfered.

Alant didn't answer. In fact, he didn't seem to react to Boon in any way.

Sara stepped forward and saw that his eyes followed her. "What are you?"

"I am all that is left of Alant. A program, built to transfer knowledge to the next generation." He waved a hand at Sara. "And here you are."

"So, you're an artificial intelligence?" Boon asked; again, Alant didn't answer.

Sara rolled her eyes for what seemed like the hundredth time that day. "I think it only responds to the one that activated it," she said to the others.

"That is correct. This program will only recognize its user," Alant confirmed, answering her unasked question.

"Okay, this isn't going to be annoying," Sara grumbled, but continued before he could make a comment. "Are you an artificial intelligence?" she asked, echoing Boon's query.

"No. The Sentience Act of 638, following the Artificial War, forbade the creation of artificial sentience or programs that are able to act independently."

Sara's mouth dropped open. "Holy shit. The machines really did try to take over."

"Correct. The Artificial War started when several super intelligences were created, and gained independence of manufacturing in the year 612. The—"

She cut him off with a hand gesture. "Stop. While that sounds like it will be incredibly interesting, we don't exactly have time for a history lesson right now." She looked around at the piles of dirt and abandoned park buildings. "Can you refresh the air in the ship? It would be good to get out of these suits."

"Of course," Alant said, giving her a smile that creeped her out a little.

The air began to stir, starting as a soft breeze that quickly intensified. Dirt and dust was kicked up into swirling clouds, only to be sucked upward into unseen vents.

Sara stumbled back a step as a hard gust of wind hit her, knocking her off balance. "What the fuck are you doing?" she yelled over the howling wind.

"Refreshing the air to be breathable, as you asked," Alant said, cocking his head to the side. "Do you wish me to stop?"

Sara checked on Boon, Baxter, and the familiars, but they seemed to be dealing with the winds without too much problem. "No it's fine. How long will it take?"

The wind died as she asked, and returned to a soft breeze. "I am finished. The air will continue to recycle till the *Exitium* is shut down again. Would you like the rest of the systems brought back online?"

Sara checked her suit's readout and saw that the air was now breathable. She blinked a few times to be sure her eyes were not tricking her. "How did you convert the air in here so quickly? There must be millions of tons of it to exchange."

"The ship was designed to re-pressurize after a breach in the shortest amount of time possible. Exchanging the air is part of the same process. The *Exitium* was designed to be efficient in times of trouble."

Sara double-checked the readout on her suit, and decided to give it a try. She sent a mental command, and the faceplate opened with a hiss and slid to the top of her head. She took a few deep breaths; the air was crisp and clean, if not smelling a little of dust. She sent a second command, and the whole suit opened up, letting her step out. She stretched, reveling in the feeling of freedom.

Boon did the same, stepping out of her suit to stretch her arms above her head with a squeal. She lowered the shield bubble and let it fade when it touched the ground, freeing the familiars. Alister immediately jumped to Sara's shoulder and rubbed his face on her cheek. She gave him a scratch under the chin.

"Aren't you coming out, Baxter?" Boon asked, pushing her hips side to side, stretching them.

"No. One of us should stay suited, just in case," he said, still checking the rest of the area for danger.

Sara chuckled to herself quietly, but he had a point, so she didn't give him any shit. Besides, she could feel his concern for her and Boon's safety, and it warmed her heart to know he cared so much.

"Go ahead and get the rest of the systems online, Alant. While you're doing that, maybe you can answer some questions," Sara ventured, stepping up to the podium.

"That is why I am here; to answer your questions," he said helpfully.

Sara considered her questions and ordered them in her mind. "First, how did this ship end up on Earth, and where did the humans that were already here come from?" Ever since she and Cora had discussed this ship, the fact that there were already humans here had intrigued her.

"We knew that the Elif were going to betray us to the Teifen—there was far too much pressure for them not to—so we prepared in stages. The first stage was to outfit four of the dreadnoughts for colonization. This ship and three others were selected. We selected four planets we knew were unknown to any of the other races, far from their spheres of influence. But before we could even re-outfit the ships, the Elif struck.

"Two of the dreadnoughts were caught in the battle, unable to escape to their new homes, while the *Exitium,* and *Clipeum* were successful in their retreat. However, we did not have the resources onboard to provide for an advanced colony. We arrived here on Earth and found that it had been colonized by our ancestors, long before faster than light travel had been discovered; the people who had come before us were from a sect of humanity that, for religious reasons, forsook magic and their connection to the Aether.

"Upon our arrival, it was decided that integrating with our now primitive human ancestors was our best course of action. It let us hide ourselves from the Aether and therefore become more difficult to detect. We built our society out here on this peninsula, and called it Alantis, after me and my brother.

"We soon discovered that a meteor shower was coming that would influence the climate and start melting the great ice floes. We calculated that Alantis would sink into the ocean, and we took this as a sign to abandon the old ways and merge with the human societies that had established themselves here. So we edited our genome to repress our Aether receptors, and went out to live amongst our prede-cessors."

Boon had stepped up next to Sara during the tale. "Holy shit, Captain. Atlantis was real? This is too much."

Sara laughed. "Really? We're mages who are able to fight off starships, and *this* is too much for you?"

Boon shrugged. "I mean, *Atlantis*? Come on."

"Look around, Boon. This had to get here somehow. Why not call it Atlantis?" Sara asked.

"I guess," Boon said, shrugging. Then she hopped up and down a few times in excitement. "Does that mean we're Atlantians?"

Sara frowned. "I don't think so. If we are, then so is everyone else, at this point."

Boon frowned, then grinned. "Fuck it. I'm calling myself an Atlantian."

"You do you, Boon," Sara chuckled.

CHAPTER 25

"WE HAVE ARRIVED in the Sol System. We ask that our Elif guests prepare for departure to the embassy," Cora announced over the ship's intercom.

Several Marines were stationed throughout the ship, watching their guests—not interfering, but being sure to catch any odd behavior. Grimms had ordered them to look for any Elif that sought out privacy when they reached their destination. The crew had been informed that they were going to make a decoy stop, to test if any of the Elif were sending signals to the Teifen.

On the bridge, Grimms sat in his command chair looking at a view of the Sol System, faked for the sake of their guest, Sir Reitus. The view swung around to show that they were in a high Earth orbit. They went through the motions of approaching the orbital space station that served as the launch point of all Navy personnel.

"How long has it been since you were home?" Sir Reitus asked, making small talk with Grimms as the crew went through the motions. He was standing beside the colonel in a parade rest stance, his hands clasped behind his back.

"Only a day or so. We were testing a few new systems when we picked up your signal. In truth, we still have a few tests to run after we drop you and your people off," Grimms said, having trouble with the deception.

While he and Sir Reitus were talking in the ready room, Cora had contacted him through his comm, letting him know her plan in detail. She was going to drop them out of warp in the uninhabited system they were currently headed for and fake the readings to show they had arrived in Sol. She had informed the Marines and the bridge crew of the deception, and told them to look for any transmissions or odd behavior from the Elif. She was not convinced the tracking device on the prince's yacht was the only thing the Teifen had planted.

Grimms agreed, but had to keep a straight face as he and Sir Reitus continued their conversation. Grimms knew he was a terrible actor, but was relying on the fact that Sir Reitus had never met a human, and therefore wouldn't know how to recognize one's odd behavior.

"Anything, Mezner?" Grimms asked, wanting this to all be over.

Mezner looked a little surprised at his question, and flicked a glance in Sir Reitus's direction before saying, "No, sir. Nothing yet."

Grimms stroked his beard distractedly, watching the faked image of his home begin to grow as they 'approached'.

"It is a beautiful planet, Colonel. It reminds me of Effrit long ago, before the city began to cover the continents," Sir Reitus said, seeing the way the blue and green planet reflected the sun.

"It's a good planet. We want to keep it. Other than three small colonies, this is our entire presence in the galaxy. It's a vulnerable place, protected by its anonymity more than its Navy," Grimms said. He worried he might be laying it on a little thick, but he also believed what he was saying, more than he liked to admit.

Sir Reitus nodded. "I understand the feeling. Losing Effrit was a blow the Elif may not recover from, and we have a thousand worlds to fall back on."

Grimms thought about what a thousand planets would mean for a fighting force. "How can there be no Elif ships left? If there are a thousand worlds in the empire, shouldn't there be the makings of a fleet? They were not all in the Effrit system, surely."

"They were not, but the leadership was. The Teifen governor that was leading the war on behalf of his emperor must have been monitoring us much closer than we thought; they waited to strike until there was a meeting of the High Council and the admirals. We had nearly ten thousand fighters in the system when they attacked, but the Teifen flooded in with three times our number. Though they took heavy losses, in the end, they were too many and far too aggressive for us to stop them. There are still small Elif fleets that were on other missions throughout the empire, but their home leadership is smashed. The garrison of ships the Teifen left behind will take a large force to defeat, though, and it will take time for the remnants of the Elif navy to organize," Sir Reitus said, his eyes hard, and his slim jaw set.

Grimms knew the anger of impotence, of not being able to do the right thing because of circumstance. He felt for the knight. "We will do what we can to reestablish the throne. Getting the prince to safety is our first priority."

Sir Reitus gave a curt nod. "Thank you, Colonel."

They waited in silence for another five minutes before anyone spoke.

"I have a signal, sir," Mezner reported with disappointment. "It just went out."

"I caught it, too. It was weaker than the transmission

from the yacht, which suggests a mage without amplification, but the message will still get back to the Teifen," Cora said, surprising Sir Reitus, who was obviously having a hard time remembering she was watching.

The view of Earth disappeared and was replaced with open space. The holo projector switched its display from the Sol System to a view of an unidentified system with a much smaller and brighter star.

"What is happening? Did we jump again?" Sir Reitus asked.

"Gonders, a transmission went out thirty seconds ago. Did you or your men see anything?" Grimms asked into his comm, ignoring the Elif's question.

"Yes, sir. One of the soldiers slipped away a few minutes ago. I had Deej follow him, and he just reported that the soldier was hiding in a supply room. I had him arrest the soldier, sir," Gonders replied.

"Cora, do you have any video of the supply room in question?" Grimms asked, sure they had their man.

"Yep. Give me a second, I'm reviewing it now... Oh, yeah. That's him. The time matches perfectly with the message. We have him." Cora announced this last over the bridge speaker.

Sir Reitus looked around in confusion. "Have who? What is happening, Colonel?"

"Sir Reitus, I'm sorry to say you had a traitor in your midst. Captain Cora and I were concerned that the Teifen may have put a second system in place to track the yacht; now we know they did. We have your man in custody, and I would like you to go down and meet Specialist Gonders in the brig. Maybe you can shed some light on the situation," Grimms said, standing and motioning toward the door.

"Are you not coming?" Sir Reitus asked, his eyebrows raised.

"No, I've arranged for a Marine to escort you, and Captain Cora will be able to monitor the situation. I have to wait and see who shows up. Hopefully the Galvox took care of our problem, but I doubt it."

Sir Reitus bowed. "Very well, Colonel. I shall get to the bottom of this, you can trust in that."

"I hope so. This is not something we will take lightly. That soldier's actions put my planet at risk. I cannot allow that," Grimms decided seriously.

AN HOUR and thirteen minutes later, a fleet of Teifen ships warped into the system. At first, it was one… then two, but they just kept coming until there were well over a hundred drifting through the abandoned system. Grimms watched as his worst fears were realized.

"They're after us," he said, leaning over the projection table and watching the swarm of Teifen circle like sharks.

They had positioned themselves next to a large asteroid, and Cora was masking their presence with the engines.

"They could just be after the prince," she said hopefully.

"No. He was the bait. They let him go, knowing he would call for help. They knew humans were out here, but had no way of finding us except through the Elif. This was a trap for humanity from the start," Grimms growled.

"Sir, we've received word back from the UHFC. They are ordering us to return to Earth immediately, now that we've arrested the traitor," Mezner said, relaying the message.

"Great. Now they want us to bring the whole mess home. What if we didn't get them all? There could be another traitor," Cora said.

Grimms shook his head. "I don't think that's likely. It must have been incredibly difficult just to get one in."

"But it could happen," Cora argued.

"It doesn't matter, the UHFC ordered us back. It's their problem now," Grimms said, shaking his head. "Connors, plot me a course for home. Captain, let's make this trip a short one; how do you feel about pumping a little extra Aether into the engines?"

"Sounds good. I'll take off as soon as the coordinates are loaded."

"Sir. There is a new contact. It's the dreadnought," Mezner said, looking up from her console, her eyes wide.

Grimms zoomed in on the behemoth. It was damaged badly, but seemed to be mostly in one piece. There were several places where it was burnt, and large sections of armor had been blown off, but it still looked like it could take on the entire fleet back home.

He wondered how it survived the Galvox so well. The last they had seen of the dreadnought, it was under heavy fire, and there were more reinforcements coming.

"Let's get out of here," Grimms said darkly.

"Warp in three, two, one."

CHAPTER 26

"ME AND BOON here are the only War Mages modern humans have, so far," Sara told the image of Alant. "We don't know the limits of casting yet, but Boon's familiar, Silva, told us that we can mitigate the rage that fighting for too long produces. Is there anything else we can do to protect ourselves and those around us?" she asked. *While we're here, I may as well learn some tricks of the trade from an actual War Mage.*

Alant nodded. "Your twin will be able to absorb some of the feedback and lessen the effects of overcasting. You may also bond guards that will do the same, though to a much lesser extent. The most effective form of mitigating the rage is your familiar, since they have ultimate say on whether a spell is cast. It takes training and a thorough understanding of their Mage's emotions, but it is a skill they will hone with time. However, even they can become overwhelmed easily, so it is important that you recognize your own limits."

The ship had been coming online slowly over the past few minutes, with clangs and humming thumps deep within the structure. Alant had told them that it would be prepared for travel in a few days, after the reactors were trimmed, and maintenance was performed by the core. When asked how they were supposed to get the ship out from under the mountain it was currently encased in, he laughed and said they just needed to take off, insisting that a mountain was not nearly enough to stop the *Exitium*.

While the ship did its thing, Sara had been asking questions about control of her and Boon's powers, trying to get a feel for what a War Mage was capable of, and what they were missing.

"What if you don't have a twin?" Sara asked, looking to Boon, who gave her an appreciative smile.

"It is exceedingly rare for a War Mage not to have a twin, but it has happened over the millennia. In that case, it is imperative that the single bond with a guard who will stay close to them. The stronger the emotional link, the more effectively their rage will be siphoned. This puts much pressure on the guard, though, and they will start to decline along with their Mage, so the War Mage needs to split their abilities between constructive and destructive magic to give them both more time. As their bodies become more and more sensitive to the Aether flowing through them, there will come a point when one spell will be enough to push them over the edge," Alant said, folding his hands into his robe's sleeves in a way Sara thought was rather pretentious.

"How long can a War Mage go without any checks?" she asked, trying to determine the baseline.

The image of Alant shrugged. "That depends on the War Mage. We are not all created equal; some are more powerful than others, and some are able to fight off the effects of Aether fatigue better than others."

"So we need to test ourselves without making the mistake of going too far. Great, that sounds safe," Sara muttered.

"It is not as dangerous as you might guess. There are

tactics you can use in your training that will let you push the limits without spilling over." Alant gestured to the base of the podium he stood on. A section slid open, revealing a row of headbands whose design Sara recognized from the dampeners she had used in her final exam back on Earth. She didn't realize at the time that the tech was of ancient human origin. "With these, you will be able to use your powers to their fullest extent, without channeling so much Aether that endanger yourself. There are physical indicators that you're going too far, and you must recognize these in yourself before testing those abilities in a real-world situation."

Sara reached down and picked up three of the devices, handing one to Boon and, beckoning Baxter closer, handing him the third.

"Why do you want me to have one? I'm not a War Mage," Baxter asked through his armor's speakers.

"True, but you're my bonded guard. So my abilities are going to affect you; plus, in a real battle, you will be adding to the overall effect by using your own Aether. So I want you to do a little practice with us." Sara smiled up at the black faceplate.

"You would like to practice now?" Alant asked, not surprised.

"I was thinking we could just cast 'til we start feeling whatever it is we're supposed to feel. Why, do you have something in mind?" she asked the projection.

"It is much more efficient to practice in a simulation. Real-world objectives are a better stress test," Alant explained.

"True, and if we had a holo room, I would use that," she agreed, then gestured to the desolate park. "But I don't see one, so—"

She was cut off, as the entire park changed from the barren, dusty landscape to a city street.

"This park was a multi-use room. It provided a place for

the pixie travelers to hide, along with an open area for relaxation and entertainment. In addition, it was used as a training ground for the legions onboard," Alant said, waving a hand at the near-perfect holo projection all around them.

"Okay. This is pretty cool," Boon said, taking in the alien street.

They were standing in an intersection in a metropolis. Looking up, some of the buildings disappeared into the clouds overhead. The construction was mostly of glass and polymers that reflected the light of the sun down into the canyons between the towering buildings. Sara could see vehicles parked on the street, but unlike most street vehicles, they did not have wheels, instead hovering over the metal-like pavement. The design of the buildings had the impression of natural formations, with sweeping twists and lines. There were skybridges made of glass, letting the pedestrians see down to the street below. There were shops full of alien wares lining the ground level, but the city was abandoned, frozen in time; even leaves and the little litter there was hung suspended in the air.

"Where is this city?" Sara asked, trying to take everything in at once.

"This is an intersection in the capital on the planet Asgard, our homeworld."

Sara wrinkled her brow, and turned to Alant. "Asgard? As in the home of the Norse gods?"

He gave her a blank stare, trying to understand what she was referring to. "I am sorry. I do not understand the question. Who are the Norse?"

She waved a hand. "We can come back to that. So what are these physical tells we should be looking for?"

"The first sign that you are pushing yourself too far will be a buzzing in the head, similar to something vibrating lightly against the base of your skull. If that is ignored, the second sign will be a loss of hearing; not complete, but enough that it will sound as though there is a plug in your ear. The third will be hallucinations. You will see things as you wish them to be, not how they are. For example, when looking for the enemy, if none are to be found, you may replace them in your mind with your own men, seeing *them* as the enemy. By the time you are this far gone, it is usually too late for you to recognize the danger you are in, and you will be lost to the rage," Alant said with a frown.

Sara shuddered. She had experienced all three of those on Colony 788. If it were not for Alister, and their then weak, empathic connection, she would have been too far gone, lost to her rage.

"Right. So I guess we just need some enemies to battle," she said, stepping back into her armor and letting it close around her.

Alant smiled all too cheerily. "They are already on their way."

CHAPTER 27

BAXTER THREW UP A SHIELD, falling to one knee, and gave Boon and Sara a clear shot over the barrier and himself. Sara stepped close, her thigh bumping up against his shoulder, and took aim at the twelve Teifen soldiers leaping over a burning vehicle. She sent a blast of raw force, razor thin, and sliced through their armor as if it were tissue paper, splashing blue blood and guts across the dull gray metallic pavement with a *sploosh* that made her own guts twist in disgust.

"I'll get the right," Boon shouted, sliding on one knee and slamming her shoulder into Baxter's shield, then popping up and extending her arm, sending a blast of Aether to super-chill the air in a tight cone.

There were three Teifen running from behind a vehicle, trying to take cover behind a concrete pillar. She caught the last one fully, freezing him solid in his armor, and the back leg of the one in front of him. The two Teifen kept moving forward with their momentum, falling to the ground. The one in the back shattered to small pieces, sending shards skittering across the ground to pile up against his comrade's prone form. The leg shattered with the impact as well, but the Teifen was not dead; his screams of pain were loud enough to be heard through his armor. The third made it to cover and, in an impressive show of speed, raised his coilgun and began sending slivers of metal at them on full auto.

Sara dropped behind the shield along with Boon, as it flared with the unending barrage of shards.

"You holding up okay?" she asked Baxter, scanning the area in front of them through the sparking shield.

"This is nothing. Even before we bonded, I had enough power to hold off one rifle. How are you doing? We've been going at this for an hour, and I'm getting some strange feelings from you." He wasn't looking her way, but scanning the field himself.

"I'm starting to get the buzz Alant was talking about, but it's pretty faint. What about you, Boon? You hanging in there?" Sara asked the small figure beside Baxter.

"Yeah, but I have the buzz for sure. And my ears are starting to get a little fuzzy." She checked behind them, throwing up a shield with a yell.

Sara spun and saw the shield that Boon had thrown up sparking with several rifles' worth of ammo. They had been so focused on the front that they had let the enemy get behind them.

"I'm calling it. Boon is already starting to feel the second effect. Alant, end program!" Sara shouted the last through her speaker.

The gunfire stopped instantly, and the cityscape fell deathly quiet. Then the city itself faded out, leaving them kneeling on a dirt patch a hundred meters from the podium where Alant was standing.

Sara stood, brushing dust from her armor. "Let's take a break. I wish we'd brought some food with us, I'm starving."

"Yeah, I could eat," Baxter said, dropping his shield and standing along with Boon. "I could really go for a turkey melt right about now," he added, noisily taking a sip of water from the straw in his helmet.

They made their way back to the podium and sat down on the relatively clean deck plates, resting quietly for a few minutes. They all had their helmets folded back to get some fresh air. Alister and Silva crawled out of Sara's and Boon's hip pouches, where they had been kept during the simulated battle, and met between the two women to curl into a mutual ball and promptly began to nap. Eventually, Sara started the conversation she knew she and Boon needed to have.

"We need to get you a guard. You were way more susceptible to the effects of that amount of Aether than I was—at a lot faster rate, too," Sara said, leaning back on her extended arms and crossing her ankles.

Boon was sitting cross-legged, and hung her head. "I know. I wasn't casting half as many spells as you were, either. I think the fact that my sister is gone is going to make this a much more difficult prospect."

"I don't know about that. I think you're just going to have to get creative," Baxter said, leaning back in a similar pose as Sara.

"What do you mean?" Boon asked, looking up at his smiling face.

Baxter waved a hand at the still figure of Alant. "You heard what he said. I know you're new to this whole mage thing, but trust someone who went through the academy; magic is more than the sum of its parts. If you can start using creation magic along with destructive, you'll be better balanced, and able to fight longer. Maybe take the chance to heal others while in battle, or mend stuff."

Boon thought about that. "How would I use mending in battle?"

Baxter shrugged. "I don't know, repairing armor? It was

just an example. If you want, we can work on a game plan? I'm sure Gonders would be willing to work with you; she's pretty good at the constructive uses of Aether."

Boon's cheeks flushed red at the mention of Gonders, and she looked down at her hands.

Sara raised an eyebrow. "You okay?"

Boon nodded rather vigorously. "Yeah. I'm good. It would be nice if she could help me out."

Sara cocked her head. "Of course she would."

"Maybe…" Boon started, but broke off to bite her lip before continuing. "Maybe, she would be my guard?"

Baxter scratched at his buzzed, white hair. "You could ask her. She's a good choice to have by your side."

Boon smiled, her face half hidden as she watched her hands wringing together "Yeah, she is," she said dreamily.

Sara's eyes widened. "Really? *Gonders*?"

Boon's head snapped up, a shocked look on her face.

Sara laughed lightly. "Boon, I had no idea you liked her. You seem so…" She waved her hand around in a nebulous way. "Conservative. I figured with your religious background, you wouldn't swing that way."

Boon frowned. "Not having pretty dresses wasn't the only reason I left, you know."

Sara held up her hands in surrender. "Hey, I didn't mean anything by it. You've just never mentioned it before."

"Why would I?" Boon asked, making Baxter laugh.

"She's got you there, Captain. It's not like you've ever said you like men," he pointed out, his eyes bright with mirth. Then a look of concern flashed across his face. "You *do* like men, right?"

Now it was Boon's turn to laugh.

"Okay, okay. Sorry. For what it's worth, Gonders is a pretty good catch; you couldn't do much better." Sara waggled her eyebrows suggestively. "And I mean that as a guard *or* a lover."

"That would be awesome," Boon said, her eyes glazing with unspoken thoughts.

Baxter smiled and gave Sara a wink. "I'll be sure to put you two together every chance I get, then."

Boon blushed crimson, sending both Sara and Baxter into giggles.

CHAPTER 28

"How long do you plan on staying down here?" Baxter asked, pushing himself to his feet.

They had been sitting and planning out battle strategies for Boon and Sara for the last twenty or thirty minutes, but the sound of growling bellies had interrupted them several times. Now that they knew where the ship was, though, and knew how to get aboard with little difficulty, they could come back when they were better prepared.

"I suppose we should resupply. The shuttle will be fine in hover mode for a while, but I didn't really think about having to stay out here for any length of time," Sara said, extending a hand for Baxter to help her up. "Alant, you said the ship would be ready to move in a few days; do we need to be here for it to keep preparing?"

"Not at all. Now that there is a War Mage to take control of her, the *Exitium* will prepare on her own. When her captains are ready, they can take over. They will need a day to properly bond with the core, but they would be able to perform basic maneuvers until a full integration can happen," he assured her.

His statement about the core reminded Sara that they needed to find the machine to make them. "Alant, where are the cores made? We need more for the new fleet."

Alant tilted his head to the side. "I do not understand the question. They are made where they are made."

Now it was Sara's turn to be confused. She looked over at Baxter and Boon, but they just shrugged. "What does that mean?" Sara asked Alant.

"I do not understand the question. Are you asking what my words mean?" Alant asked.

Sara waved her hands back and forth in a 'stop' gesture. "Wait. I think we've started down the wrong path here. Let me start over." She put her hands on her hips, trying to decide how to get what she wanted from the program. "How are cores made?" she began.

The Alant program stood straighter, and looked her in the eye more intently. "The secret of core creation is what separates us technologically from the rest of the galaxy. It is a closely held process that is never to be told to any who are not War Mages. Please ensure the room is free of those who could divulge the information, including bonded guards."

Sara looked from the still figure to Baxter. "Does he know you're here? He doesn't acknowledge you when you talk to him."

"Yeah, but in the simulation, the enemies targeted me, so I assume it knows there are others here," Baxter said, looking to the door they had entered from. "Tell you what, I'll go explore some of the rooms we passed while you talk. I don't want to cause any trouble."

Sara bit her lip, not wanting him to leave, but knowing it was probably for the best. If the War Mages of old were that secretive about the process, there must have been a reason.

"Okay, but keep your tracking beacon on. I don't want to lose you on this ship," she said with a smile.

A spike of fondness came from him, and he winked at her. "Don't worry, Captain. I'll be careful." He turned and jogged off across the dusty floor.

Sara watched until the big double doors slid open at his approach, and he disappeared, turning down the corridor beyond. Then she looked back up at Alant. "Okay, buddy. It's just us War Mages. How do you make a core?"

For the first time, the Alant program looked at Boon. "Please identify yourself with the scanner."

Boon looked to Sara with questioning eyes, and Sara gave a nod. Boon stepped up and pressed her thumb to the pad that Sara had used to activate his program. The familiar green line rolled down, and after a moment, the projection bowed slightly, "Thank you, Mage."

"Oh, now you see me," Boon said, uncharacteristically sarcastic.

"Of course. Now that we are alone, are you sure you wish the words to be spoken out loud?" Alant asked.

"Why is it such a secret? I understand the pixies being hidden; there is a race of people at stake. But why so secretive with the cores?" Sara asked, suddenly unsure.

"Because unlike with the pixies, this knowledge can be spoken to anyone; there is no compulsion or contract keeping the words secret. Therefore, it is imperative that few people know the secret, and it is nearly impossible to make a War Mage give up information they do not wish to."

Sara thought about that, but it was Boon who figured it out. "It's important because the other races could create them, if they knew the secret?" she guessed.

Alant gave her a nod. "That is correct. The majority of our advancements could be copied by the Teifen, Elif, or Galvox. Without those advantages, we would be overrun immediately. Therefore, the secret can be trusted to no one, save us."

"Okay, that makes sense. So, what's the secret?" Sara asked, crossing her arms in sudden nervousness.

"A core is an artifact of pure Aether. They are not *made*, but *created*. Traditionally, twin War Mages cast four spells at once, focusing their power until the core is complete," Alant said, making it sound simple.

Boon held up a hand. "Wait, you said that other races could make them if they knew the secret, but then you just said that it took two War Mages; the other races don't have War Mages. How could they make them?"

Alant smiled. "We use two War Mages so that the secret is kept safe. For as long as we have known the technique, only War Mages have practiced it. However, it was not a War Mage that figured out the original process. A core can be made by any four mages, as long as the four spellforms are used. It does not take a large amount of Aether, or time."

"Oh. Okay, that makes sense then," Boon said, slightly chagrined.

Sara reached out and squeezed her shoulder. "I'm glad you asked. It saved me from looking like the dumb-dumb," she said seriously. Then she laughed.

When Boon gave her a dead fish look, Sara focused again on Alant. "What are the spellforms?"

Four spellforms appeared in front of them, rotating slowly. "Have your familiars memorize them."

Alister and Silva were already sitting at their feet; as soon as the forms appeared, the pixies began to study them closely.

After a minute or two, Alister looked up at her and said, "Merp."

"You got it?" Sara asked, and he nodded. She turned to the ferret. "What about you, Silva?"

Silva chattered, ran up Boon's leg in a flash, and disappeared behind her back, only to reappear over her shoulder and wrap herself around Boon's neck.

"She's got it," Boon interpreted.

The spellforms vanished, and Alant continued. "You must focus all four spells on the same spot, and feed them with power until the core is complete."

"What happens if we stop before the spell is done?" Sara asked.

"The released Aether will saturate you and everything around you for hundreds of kilometers. So much Aether will be absorbed that the objects in question will be pulled into the Aetheric plain to drift outside of time and space for all eternity. The spells do not provide the Aether used to create the core—they only open space-time and let the pure Aether flow into this reality from the Aetheric plain. The amount of Aether that is used is far beyond anything two War Mages could ever hope to channel in a lifetime," Alant said helpfully.

"Holy shit," Boon said, her eyes wide.

"Yeah. Let's not fuck this up," Sara said, a little over-whelmed herself. She had a thought. "Just to be clear, the two War Mages don't have to be twins to do the spell, right?"

"That is correct. Any two War Mages may perform the spell together. The importance is not in *who* is doing the casting, but *what* is being cast. That is why this secret is guarded so closely," Alant said gravely.

Sara turned to Boon. "Okay, let's give it a try. Remember, don't stop 'til it's done. I want to walk away from this."

"Don't worry about that; I want to get back home too."

"Is it your Spanish lover? You want to get back to see her?" Sara asked, straight-faced.

Boon cocked an eyebrow in confusion before turning crimson and stammering, "Gonders is not my 'Spanish lover'!"

Sara looked up, as if trying to remember something. "No, I'm pretty sure she was born in Spain."

"I mean she's not my lover!" Boon said, hopping slightly with frustration.

Sara just winked at the blonde girl, making her growl cutely. "God, you're adorable. Gonders is going to eat you up when she finds out."

Boon hung her head in defeat. "Can we please just get on with this?"

Sara smiled and nodded, then took a deep breath, closing her eyes to focus. She was so out of sorts from the last few days. *I desperately need a nice long yoga session.* Hanging out with Alicia would do in the meantime.

She reached her hands out, and Boon found them with her own small, warm ones. They clasped hands and centered themselves.

"I'm ready," Sara said.

"Me too. Silva?" Boon queried, and the ferret chattered softly.

"Alister, you take the two forms from the left, and Silva, you take the ones on the right," Sara instructed.

She sent a mental request to Alister, and a spellform appeared in her mind. Then a second one materialized next to it. Sara began gently at first, knowing the spellform would tell her how much it needed. She kept her focus on the two spellforms, steadily increasing the Aether flow until it felt like the right amount. She slowly opened her eyes, and nearly lost focus at what she saw.

Between her and Boon, a point in space seemed to warp and bend in a circular pattern. The center was the blackest black she had ever seen, reflecting no light. Upon closer inspection, she could see that everything behind the black ball was still visible to her, just scrunched up into the space around the ball, folded on itself. It was as if she had poked a hole in some spandex, and then forced a thick rod through the hole; all the same material was there around the rod, but it was warped and stretched. This was the same, but instead of spandex, the material was space-time.

The black ball grew in size while she watched, stretching the reality around it. Sara looked up and saw Boon staring at the spot with a dazed look of wonder, her mouth open slightly.

Sara began to worry when the black ball was the size of a basketball. That was much larger than the core on the *Raven*, but she knew she couldn't stop the spell before it finished on its own. She felt a spike of panic run up her spine. She opened her mouth to ask Alant if it was supposed to be this big, when the ball stopped growing.

The black surface became hazy, like a thin layer of clouds was forming on the surface of a planet, and was being viewed from far off. The cloud thickened, changing from a haze to a gray, roiling mass. The now gray ball began to shrink, and Sara realized it was being compressed by the gray mist on the surface. As it contracted, the gray mist began to thicken, and reflect more light. It compressed further and faster the longer it went on, until in the last instant, it snapped to the size of a softball, and the thick, now whitish mist became the solid mirrored surface she was familiar with.

The spells in her head stopped drawing Aether from her, and the core fell from the air to hit the deck with a *thud*.

The two women stared at each other in shock.

"Did we just make a black hole?"

CHAPTER 29

THE *RAVEN* DROPPED out of warp in the outer Sol System. The auto repair function had been busy the last few warps, repairing damage as they traveled. By the time they made two long jumps on approach to Earth, the ship was good as new.

They were given permission to dock at the orbital station and wait for an escort for the prince. The station was called 'Xanadu', even though its official name was John Glenn Space Research… Something or Other. To tell the truth, Grimms couldn't remember the official name, because even on written orders, the station was referred to as 'Xanadu'.

Connors brought them in the last few thousand kilometers, swinging around the huge, cylindrical station in low Earth orbit. There were a large number of warships attached to the station, their long, wedge-like hulls sticking out like thorns.

Once docked, Grimms and Sir Reitus made their way through the ship's corridors to meet Prince DeSolin and his guards in the docking bay.

"Have you made any progress with the prisoner?" Grimms asked the brooding Elif as they walked.

Sir Reitus shook his head. "Not yet. He is keeping his mouth shut. I don't understand; he has been a loyal guard for years... I find it hard to believe that he is a traitor."

"Have you tried truth serum or other drugs? I know your people don't like to use them, but I feel like this may be an exception," Grimms said, stepping through the double doors of the bay.

The bay was mostly empty, with only a few Marines at post in their armor, and a tightly packed group of Elif in their battlesuits. Their armor was broken down for travel, the plates folded over one another to create a tight package that could be loaded onto small carts.

In the center of the Elif guards was the small figure of the prince. He stood with his arms crossed, but his eyes were wide with worry.

"I have considered drugs, but for now he is restrained and fitted with an Aether dampener. I regret that I was not able to get the information from him," Sir Reitus said darkly.

The prince saw them approaching and, to Grimms' surprise, looked worried at his head of guard's expression, as if the thunderstorm brewing there was for him. The guards surrounding the prince parted, allowing the two men to approach.

Sir Reitus bowed at the waist. "My prince, I have been interrogating the traitor, but have not been able to gain any knowledge; I apologize."

The prince nearly flinched at the bow. "Oh. That's quite all right, Reitus. It is of no concern; we have arrived and, against all odds, we have survived."

"Your Highness, I request that I be allowed to stay aboard the *Raven* so that I might ferret out the traitor's motives. I feel he represents a danger to you and the empire that needs to be addressed," he pressed, head still bowed.

The prince didn't seem to know what to do with that, and started and stopped several times before saying, "I suppose that would be for the best. The embassy is well-guarded. However, I wish for you to return as soon as you have any information. Don't take too long."

Grimms felt like the prince was not being quite as princely as he should be. Before his suspicions got out of control, he reminded himself that, even though he looked like a young adult, the prince was basically a child, and would not be great at decisive action.

"I thank you, my Prince. I shall endeavor to protect the empire in whatever way I can," Sir Reitus said solemnly, while slapping his fist to his heart in salute.

The bay door slid open to show a breathtaking view of Earth and the space beyond, while the plasma shielding held in the atmosphere. A large Elif shuttle rose over the lip of the bay and, with practiced ease, slipped through the shielding. The contrast of silence to the chest-thumping thrum of gravitic engines as the shuttle entered the sudden atmosphere of the bay was enough to make the prince take a half step back in fear. None of his guards seemed to notice—or at least, they acted as such for his sake.

Obviously, this child prince has not spent much time in a ship. He's probably been cloistered in his palace his entire life. I should cut him some slack, considering how terrifying this all is to him…

The shuttle landed, the belly opened up, and a ramp was extended. An Elif female hurried down the ramp first, followed closely by a male. They both wore robes of office, and Grimms recognized the woman as Effrit's ambassador to Earth. She was the one always on the news feeds, singing the praises of the Elif and their great union with humanity.

She seems to have forgotten her ancient history, Grimms thought bitterly, then admonished himself. *It was not* these *Elif; it was their ancestors. Still, they knew the truth, and led us on. But there are those like Sir Reitus; honorable men who fight for the good of all. I can get behind Elif like him.*

"My Lord," the ambassador said in a pleasant, melodic voice, bowing low. "I am Deria Hestis, Ambassador to Earth. I am honored, and relieved that you have made it here. Please let us keep you safe so that you may rise to your throne and lead us all to victory."

The prince stepped forward and embraced the ambassador, as was the Elif's customary greeting. "I thank you for your diligent service to the empire. I gladly accept your offer," he said in what Grimms recognized as a formal exchange of sorts.

The prince turned back to Colonel Grimms. "I thank you for my rescue. The empire is indebted to you," he said with a slight bow of his head.

Grimms gave him a smile and a salute. "It was our pleasure to help, Prince DeSolin."

Then the prince and his retinue turned and boarded the shuttle. They were out of the bay in less than a minute, the shuttle burning hard for Earth.

"I thank you for letting me continue my investigation with the traitor. I wish to find the answers, for our sake and yours," Sir Reitus said, turning and bowing to Grimms.

In truth, Grimms had no idea that he'd want to stay, and it irked him slightly that the knight had not let him know ahead of time, but he knew it was for the best. His crew was not prepared to deal with the Elif traitor at the moment.

"It is not a problem. Please, don't let me keep you; my crew is returning from leave, and there is a resupply shuttle on the way," Grimms said with a tight smile.

"Thank you, I shall return to my duties at once,

Colonel." He sketched another bow before turning and marching from the bay.

On his way out, he passed by Gonders coming in. They exchanged quick greetings, and then she saw Grimms and hurried over. Unlike Grimms, in his uniform, she was dressed in her black, form-fitting battlesuit.

She gave him a salute. "Sir, I'm glad I caught you."

Grimms returned the salute. "What can I do for you, Specialist?"

Gonders checked her arm tablet. "There is an inbound shuttle carrying some special ordnance from UHF Command, along with our supplies. They just sent me a message, wondering where they should store them. I'm guessing they will message you as well, but I didn't know how to answer."

Grimms frowned; he hadn't heard anything, but he had been busy this morning. He checked his messages, saw the one in question, and opened it up to read the specs. His eyebrows rose higher with every word.

"Is this correct? These are unbelievable," he said excitedly, forgetting momentarily that he was talking to a specialist.

"Oh, um, I guess, sir. I don't know why they would lie about them," Gonders said. She was unsure how to respond, and her light brown skin flushed to a light maroon. She decided now was a good time to become busy with something. As Grimms continued to read, she redid her ponytail, pulling back her long, black hair.

Grimms smiled at her embarrassment of his excitement, and said, "Sorry, but with something this powerful, we might stand a chance against the Teifen. When did the R&D guys come up with this?" he wondered out loud, not expecting an answer.

"I heard that the plans came from the core that Captain Sara took with her to the debriefings. The word is the molecular printers are churning out all kinds of new things; I guess the Elif only had the plans for a few artifacts from the old days," Gonders said with bright smile. "With these, we could take out a cruiser in a few shots."

"Hmm, yeah. This says they can be fitted in a special slug for the gauss cannons, or used as a warhead on a missile. We don't have missiles, so slugs it is." A thought hit him, and he activated his comm. "Captain Cora, are you there?"

Cora's voice came over his comm instantly. "Where else would I be, Grimms?"

"Well, I wouldn't want to interrupt your television viewing time," he teased, making Gonders raise an eyebrow at the familiar tone he used.

"Har har. What can I do for you?" she replied dryly.

"Have you seen the specs on these new ordnances the fleet is sending us?" he asked, as Gonders stood watching the bay door for the incoming shuttle.

"Yes. I just got the message. These weapons are vicious," she said.

"If they are supposed to be used in the gauss slugs, is there a place to store them for the auto loaders?" he asked, making Gonders tilt her head in consideration before nodding.

"Hang on," Cora said, going quiet for a few beats. "Well, I'll be damned. There sure is. We need to fit them in the slugs first, but those should be a quick print."

"So where should Gonders put the ordinance?"

"I'll let her know, and then I'll start manufacturing the slugs," Cora said.

A message beeped on Gonders' tablet, and she gave it a quick read, "I've got it, sir. Cora wants me to take them to the printer. Thank you, sir."

Grimms gave her a nod and started for the door, but

before he got three steps, his comm buzzed. With a sigh he answered, "This is Grimms."

"Sir, we have a communication from the UHFC. They are trying to contact Captain Sara, but are unable to raise her. They want to know if we know of her location, or if we are able to contact her," Mezner said through the comm channel.

"I'll see what I can do," Cora said, still listening in.

Mezner sounded surprised. "Oh, Captain. Thank you. They said they had a few questions about the Familiar spell."

"I'll try and raise her, but maybe I can help them out in the meantime. Send me the channel, Mezner," Cora said.

"Do you still need me on this, Captain?" Grimms asked, taking a steadying breath. *It's always something.*

"I've got this, Grimms," Cora answered.

Grimms closed the channel, and took a breath. *Finally, I can get some lunch.*

His comm buzzed again, and he hung his head slightly as he stepped out into the corridor.

"This is Grimms…"

CHAPTER 30

"THERE IS a core attempting to contact this ship," Alant said, surprising the two women.

They were inspecting the core they had created, and trying to figure out what each of the spellforms did individually. Alister and Silva were just as interested in the conversation, trilling and meowing along from their perches on their Mages' shoulders. Sara wished Cora were there; with her knowledge of spell theory, she would be a great help.

So far, they'd figured out that there was a binding spell, a shield spell, and a creation spell, but the final spell was unlike anything they had ever seen. In some ways, it reminded Sara of the spellform used to warp a ship, but only vaguely. They were getting ready to attempt each spell on its own to see its effects, when Alant had interrupted them.

"A core?" Sara parroted him, looking at the one in her hand. "This one?"

"No. That core is not in an active state. The core attempting to contact the *Exitium* is designated as the *Raven,*" he said.

Boon and Sara perked up at that.

"Can you put it through?" Sara asked.

In answer, there was a crackling of a speaker coming to life, and then Cora's voice came out. "Hello? Sara? Are you there?"

"Cora! How did you contact this ship?" she asked, then, "Why didn't you just contact me?"

"There you are. You're somehow out of range. Where are you?" Cora said with relief.

"We're on the *Exitium*. It's a dreadnought class human ship. You are not going to believe what we've found here," Sara said excitedly.

"It's still in working order?" her sister asked, amazed.

"Yeah. It's powering up now and doing maintenance. I'm told it will be ready to take off in a few days' time. But that's not the best news... We learned how to make cores!"

There was silence on the line for a second. "That is so good to hear. I was worried we were going to be fucked. This whole war is stressing me the hell out," Cora said. "That reminds me, the UHFC was trying to contact you about the Familiar project. I handled it, but we have a bigger problem."

Cora then relayed the events of the last two days, including the ship's new abilities, and the prince's being whisked away on a shuttle with his men.

At the end of her account, she let Sara in on what was bothering her. "The UHFC is convinced that there was only the one traitor; they are not seeing the larger problem beyond the politics. There could very easily be a *second* traitor. In fact, I'm sure of it," Cora finished.

"Why do you think there's a second traitor?" Sara asked, her face hardening with concern. Her sister didn't make huge jumps in logic, like she tended to do herself.

"It was too easy. The Teifen have thousands of years of experience in war and deception. There is no way they gambled on an obvious tracking device and one guard. There is something else happening here," Cora said, grinding her teeth the way she did when she couldn't find the proper answer to a question, when she thought it should be obvious.

"You think we're going to come under attack?" Sara said, worried that Cora was right.

"I do. It's just a gut feeling right now, but I need you back on the *Raven* and ready for the worst. We could easily be the turning point for the Navy. I need you," Cora said, sending a shiver down Sara's spine.

That was the first time her sister had ever said that.

"We're on our way," Sara said simply.

The channel cut off, and she contacted Baxter. "Meet us at the airlock. We're heading back to the *Raven*. There might be a Teifen attack force on its way."

Sara felt a spike of fear and determination vibrating through her and Baxter's new connection. It was faint, like talking between two tin cans attached with a string, but it was still there. *This is going to take some getting used to.*

"Yes, ma'am. On my way."

Next, Sara turned to Alant. "We need to go, but we will be back in a few days when the ship is ready. We can talk again then."

"Would you like me to make a copy of this program on the core you have?" Alant volunteered.

Sara hadn't even considered that as an option, but agreed right away. She would be able to give the core to Fleet Command, and they would have a teacher for the new War Mages, when they came along. With the program's built-in safeties, the secrets would stay safe.

A panel opened on the podium, revealing a half-sphere indentation where a core could be attached. "Insert the core, and I shall copy it over," Alant instructed, indicating the open panel.

Sara pressed the core in, and it fit perfectly. There was a hum as it spun up for a few seconds, then it stopped.

"The copy is complete. We shall talk again soon. It was a pleasure, War Mage," he said with a slight bow, then returned to his standby pose, falling still.

Sara grabbed the core and slipped it into her hip pouch. "Come on, We need to get back up to the ship."

Boon nodded and followed her at a jog across the park. She looked around one last time, wondering what the place would have looked like when it was filled with vegetation. Then she had a random thought that unsettled her slightly.

Who's going to fly this thing?

CHAPTER 31

GRIMMS WAS FINALLY SITTING in the ready room, about to take a bite of his sandwich, when Cora broke in over the speakers. "I don't like it, Grimms. This was all too easy. The Teifen have a backup plan, I know it."

Grimms sighed, putting the sandwich down, and took a quick sip of coffee. "I don't disagree, but there is not much we can do about it. The UHFC has the prince and his men, and we have given our warnings."

"It's not good enough. The whole system is at stake. The entire race. I've been monitoring the Elif embassy, but there is so much comm traffic, I can't discern if a signal is being sent to the Teifen," Cora growled.

Grimms' comm buzzed, and it was all he could do not to roll his eyes. *All I want is to eat my damn sandwich.* "This is Grimms," he greeted.

"Sir, Sir Reitus is here to see you. Should I send him in, or do you still need a few minutes?" Mezner asked, knowing he was eating lunch—or trying to—and got cranky if he missed a meal.

"Send him in, Mezner. Thank you," he said, finishing off

the coffee and giving the sandwich a long look before pushing it to the side.

Sir Reitus came in and gave a bow. "Colonel, I've made a development with the prisoner. I thought you should know right away."

Grimms indicated the chair on the other side of the desk. "Please, have a seat. What have you learned?"

Sir Reitus sat, and Grimms noticed the deep frown lines around his scowl. "I normally would not put any credence to this information, as it was retrieved by using drugs, as you suggested. Though given a very small dosage, the prisoner could not resist revealing what he knew. His information fits with what I've observed since our escape from Effrit."

Grimms nodded. "You made the right decision, I think. I understand your concern, but we are pressed for time. What did you find?"

Sir Reitus took a breath and, for the first time that Grimms had seen, tugged on the tip of an ear before continuing, "When pressed, the traitor admitted that he had been ordered to send our location. He was not aware of what the message meant, but he said that Prince DeSolin had ordered him to send it."

"The prince? Why would he tell the Teifen where he was?" Cora asked, surprising the knight, though he recovered quickly.

"Captain, I wondered the same, so I put the question to the prisoner. He said that the prince promised him it was for the good of the empire. I honestly don't think the prisoner knows more," Sir Reitus said. He hung his head in shame at his next words. "Normally I would not believe such a story, but the prince has been acting strangely ever since we left Effrit. It is as if he thinks this is all a game, and he will simply be returned home after. The prince is young, so it could be that he is being manipulated."

"If the prince is sending those messages, we could be too late! The guards are all being watched, but the prince was sent directly to the embassy, where I'm sure no one will suspect a thing. He could be sending the messages *now*! We need to get in there and stop him!" Cora was nearly shouting, she was so angry.

Grimms slammed his fist down on the desk. "Cora! This is not the time. We need to get in contact with the embassy, and prevent the prince from sending anything more out. They have an Aether dampening room; we need to have him moved there."

"If they will listen to us at all. That's their *prince*, the next *emperor*; I doubt they are going to lock him up on the word of a drugged up prisoner and the hunches of a starship captain and a guard," Cora spat back.

"I agree that the embassy will do little to help us in this, Colonel. They will take the word of their lord over our word. I will have to go talk with him directly. He may listen to me, as I have served him faithfully all his life," Sir Reitus reasoned.

Cora took an audible breath, which Grimms found odd, considering she was projecting her voice with her mind, and not actually speaking the words. "That may work, but it would be too late by the time you got down there. I have another idea. You're not going to like it..." she said, her tone defeated.

Grimms sighed. "Sara?"

"Sara."

THE SURFACE of the ocean bulged upward for a second before bursting in a foamy spray, as Sara shot the five of them out of the water in a shield bubble that she had formed while in the airlock leaving the *Exitium*. She figured the group bubble would be much easier than trying to get to the surface individually, and, as a bonus, there was no pressure difference that they had to take into account.

The shield hovered above the waves while Sara turned in a circle, looking for the shuttle. She found the hovering craft a little ways off, its back ramp still open. She'd begun moving her group toward it when her comm buzzed.

"This is Sara," she said, guiding the shield bubble into the open cargo bay, and letting the spell fade. There was a *clang* as all three armored mages landed on the deck. The shuttle swayed at the sudden weight, but righted itself almost immediately.

"Sara, it's Cora." There was a slight hesitation. "We have some news. It looks like the Elif prince is the one that's been sending messages to the Teifen."

Now it was Sara's turn to hesitate. "Are you sure? Why would he do that?"

"We're pretty sure. The traitor started talking, but the details are fuzzy. If it is the prince, though, he's currently in the Elif embassy without supervision, and we can't monitor all the messages going out from there," Cora said. She took a breath before continuing. "We need you to get there and keep him from getting a message out. They have a dampening room you can put him in, but I don't think they are going to just let you walk in…"

Sara's face hardened. "You need me to force my way in? How sure are you that he's the culprit?"

There was silence on the line, and Sara imagined Cora talking it over with Grimms one more time. "We're sure enough to ask you to do this. Don't hurt anybody, and they can't complain too much. I mean, they will, but we need to be sure. The UHFC is not acting on this, afraid it will cause an incident."

"Oh, it'll cause an incident, all right. I don't know if I can do this without hurting anybody, but I can be sure not to *kill* anybody," Sara qualified. She closed the cargo ramp and tromped to the front of the craft to squeeze into the pilot's seat. "Cora. You're sure about this? You know it's going to be a shit-show."

"I know. I just can't think of a way to get this done quickly enough. Every minute could be a minute too late. We cannot let the Teifen know where Earth is."

"Right. Okay, see you back on the *Raven*." Sara ended the call and grabbed the control sticks. She took a breath and looked over at Boon as the girl slid into the seat next to her. "Hang on, everybody. Turns out we're in a hurry." She slammed the throttle open, rocketing the ship to supersonic speed in less than a second.

The internal dampeners compensated for the acceleration, so they weren't turned to paste by the sudden thrust, but they were still thrown back in their seats. Sara pulled up on the stick, and they were soon above the clouds, where she pushed the limit of the engines. The nose of the shuttle was a dull orange as they plowed through the upper atmosphere.

"What's going on? Who was that?" Baxter said from the back of the ship.

"It was Cora. Evidently, the Elif are going to try and betray us again, and we're the only ones who'll stop it."

"How are we supposed to do that?" Boon asked, her eyes wide.

"We need to go scare the shit out of a prince," Sara said, gritting her teeth.

CHAPTER 32

"THIS IS Captain Sara Sonders of the UHS *Raven*, I am requesting assistance in preventing a potential attack on the Sol System," Sara shouted into the comm.

She had been yelling her way up through the command structure of the UHFC for the last five minutes, as the shuttle screamed across North America, heading for Hawaii. She was finally talking to the base commander.

"You are to stand down, Captain. We cannot risk the political fallout. We need the Elif if we are going to win this war. The embassy is Effrit ground; we have no authority there. We are attempting to contact the ambassador, and we will deal with this diplomatically," the commander said for the third time.

"That is not good enough. There is a very real chance that the Elif prince is the one communicating with the Teifen fleet that attacked my ship. If he tells them where Earth is, what kind of chance do we have?" Sara argued. She wanted to rage and scream at their stupidity.

The commander's voice took on an annoyed edge. "Captain, you cannot just go to the embassy and speak on humanity's behalf. It is not the way things are done."

Sara ground her teeth. "I will not stand by and let some child lead the enemy to our door. I am going to stop this, and you can *help*, or you can get out of the way, but it is going to happen."

"Captain, you will not invade Elif airspace. That is an order," he stated sternly.

Sara took a deep breath, trying to calm herself. *God, I really need to do some yoga and work out this rage; it can't be good for my heart,* she thought.

She cleared her throat, and spoke as calmly as she could. "Commander, I cannot help that you are too stubborn to see the real danger. There is a person who, at any time, could send a message that will spell the destruction of everyone you know. I have the ability to stop him, so I will."

The commander gave a gruff laugh. "This is your final warning; you will not attempt to land at that embassy. If you do, you will be shot down."

Sara cut off the comm channel, and screamed with rage. Boon was watching with wide eyes, her hand over her mouth in surprise.

Baxter stuck his head through the cockpit's door, a look of concern on his face. "So, that seemed intense. What are you planning on doing?"

"Just what I said I would. I'm going in there and stopping the little shit from contacting the Teifen fleet. But more importantly, I'm going to find out why he's doing this in the first place," Sara declared, gripping the controls white-knuckled.

"What about them trying to shoot us down?" Boon asked, reaching up and scratching Silva's chin.

"The two of us will handle anything they throw at us."

TEN MINUTES LATER, Sara pushed the stick forward, diving from the upper atmosphere toward the big island. She highlighted the Elif embassy on the cockpit window with the navigation feature, and an icon appeared above a set of buildings inside the city. She made straight for them, slowing the shuttle now that the atmosphere was thickening again.

An alarm began to wail, and Boon reached up to flip a switch, dropping the wail to a drone. "They have us targeted," she reported, then made room on her lap for Alister to join Silva. The two familiars curled together and hunkered down for the fight.

"I'm not worried. I'm going to need you to take care of the defenses at the embassy. Try not to get too out of hand, and for god's sake, don't kill anyone. I'll provide cover and clear our path," Sara ordered, diving through the scattered cloud cover.

They closed in fast, and Sara waited until the last minute to pull up, screaming over the buildings and streets at just under Mach 1. She pulled the throttle back, and they slowed to a crawl, just outside the Elif embassy.

The building was in the Elif style, with bulbous towers and high arches. The embassy almost looked like a mix of Russian style onion domes, and a cathedral from the dark ages, but the whole thing was painted with metallic coatings in bright greens and blues. There was a wall surrounding the compound, with turrets along its top in armored boxes. A group of Elif in Aetheric armor were surrounding the landing zone, and each of them was pointing a rifle at the shuttle.

Sara was circling the courtyard to bring the shuttle in for a landing, when Boon yelled, "Oh, shit! We have inbound missiles."

The projectiles hit before Boon was done warning Sara

about them. They had come from the capital's defense grid, and were hypersonic when they hit, having had a flight time of less than a second from the launcher to the shuttle. The warheads were designed to explode after penetrating the hull of their target, that way they concentrated the destruction inside of the target itself, instead of spending energy on the armored hull.

The timing was extremely precise, and there was a failsafe built in, in the off-chance that the armor was able to withstand the impact of the hardened tip of the missile. The crushing of the tip would set off the explosion early, doing maximum damage to the armor, so that the next missile would have a better chance of penetrating. The missiles were smart, and judged the best course of action in a split second.

Sara knew all of this about ground-to-air missiles. She had taken classes on them at the academy. Even in *that* class, she tended to daydream once she'd grasped the material. However, one of the things she'd daydreamed about was how she would deal with such a weapon.

Back then, she'd lacked the power and control to actually carry out her plan, but that was then.

This is now.

Sara had been prepared for the strike even before she was diving from high atmosphere. She had Alister construct a thick, gelatinous shield. The idea was that the missiles would hit the gel and slow to a stop before they could get close.

It worked like a dream.

Sara could see the two missiles suspended a hundred meters off to their left, their rockets still burning at full blast, but not able to move through her and Alister's construction. With a second form, she wrapped each missile in a force spell and flung them out over the ocean, then crushed their tips, making them explode.

The detonation of the missiles served as the signal for

attack. All the auto turrets on the embassy walls opened up, spitting metal slugs out in curtains of steel. The guns were similar to the PDCs on the Naval ships, but with a smaller caliber of slug. The Elif in the landing zone began firing their rifles, though Sara guessed it was more for effect than any thought of actually damaging them.

She had already dismissed the gel-shield for a hardened one, and the slugs and slivers of metal ricocheted off, peppering the ground around the shuttle as she sank lower and lower.

Right before they touched down, two mages let loose with fireballs. They aimed for the cockpit, but the fire splashed across her shield with no effect, though they did turn the golden color a brighter yellow for a second.

Sara extended the landing legs, and the shuttle rocked slightly as it touched down. She smiled cruelly through the glass at the armored troops while they fired with everything they had.

A soldier stepped out from behind a pillar and, swinging a rocket launcher to his shoulder, let one fly. Sara caught the rocket with a force spell before it was halfway to the shuttle; with a complicated change, Alister morphed the spell into a shield bubble, and collapsed it around the rocket. The explosion was contained in the rapidly shrinking bubble, so that when Sara released the tiny shield, a ball of mangled steel and carbon fell to the courtyard to bounce once, and then lay still as it smoked.

"Boon, let's take out those turrets," Sara pitched, watching the soldiers as they looked at the small, smoking ball that used to be a rocket.

The women got up and made their way to the back of the shuttle with Baxter, and Alister and Silva rode on their Mage's shoulders. Sara activated the ramp controls, opening the back door and lowering the ramp. They stepped out and saw that the shuttle was surrounded. Further, the shield around the shuttle was taking a beating, making it hard to see past the sparks and flashes of golden color as every attack was repelled with ease.

Boon and Baxter began targeting turrets, crushing them with a force spell, and sending sparks and showers of broken parts to the ground.

"Lower your weapons," Sara shouted as the last of the turrets crumbled.

To her surprise, the soldiers stopped shooting… but they did not lower their rifles. Instead, a section of the soldiers encircling them shifted to the side, allowing a woman in robes of office to step forward.

The woman held up a hand. "Please, stop. There must be a way we can come to a resolution," she said, and Sara recognized her as the Elif ambassador.

"Ambassador, there most certainly is. Bring the prince to your dampening room, and allow me to speak to him," Sara said.

"That is out of the question. The prince shall be protected, for he is the new empire. We cannot allow you to see him; not after what you have done to our defenses. This is highly—"

She was cut off as a new set of guards pressed their way to the front. In the center of the newcomers was a young Elif in white robes.

"It is all right. I have nothing to hide from this Mage," the young Elif said. "I shall do what I must to protect my people."

Sara pointed directly at him. "This is the prince?"

The ambassador nearly choked. "This is His Highness, Prince Paelias DeSolin. You shall show him the proper respect—"

"We know you sent messages to the Teifen, and I'm here

to make sure you don't do it again," Sara told him. As she stalked to the edge of the shield, a small opening appeared for her to walk through. The shield was closed again before anyone could think to raise a weapon.

"That is preposterous. The prince was the only royal to escape the attack on our homeworld! Why would he want the Teifen to know where he has gone?" the ambassador asked, stepping in front of Sara to block her path.

The guards closed in tighter around the prince, obviously wanting to take him back inside. The prince however, stepped forward, and waved back the guards.

"I had no choice," he admitted, to the gasps of his soldiers and the ambassador. "The governor has my father and mother. He told me that he would release them if I led him to the humans' homeworld. I did it for the good of all Elif-kind."

The ambassador took a step back in horror. "My Lord. The Teifen are treacherous; you cannot take them at their word."

Sara grimaced. "It seems that is something the Elif and Teifen have in common, if the old histories are correct. Once again, your people will sell out humanity for your own personal gain, no matter how shortsighted that gain may be."

The ambassador knew exactly what she was referring to, and seemed surprised that she had any clue about the ancient history between their people.

Sara took a breath and blew it out in frustration. "How do you even know the emperor and empress still live?" she asked the boy.

"I spoke to my father. He is being held on the governor's dreadnought," he said defiantly.

Sara bit her lip, thinking of what that would mean, if the emperor was still alive. The prince may be a symbol of their empire, but he was far too young to actually rule. The still-living emperor, however, could mean a workable alliance between the humans and Elif. From everything she had heard, Emperor DeSolin was a good leader, if not a little mired in tradition.

The ambassador was talking frantically with the prince, but Sara interrupted them. "You're sure it was your father? Not just a trick?"

"I am. We have a passphrase to verify our identities in just such an occasion," the prince assured her.

"Well that's something, at least. We have some time to come up with a plan," Sara said, crossing her arms, and beginning to think up a strategy.

"Will you save my father?" the boy asked, and Sara noted that his eyes were filling with tears.

"If the options are to save him, or have you rule the Elif? Yeah, I'm going to do whatever I can to save him," Sara said, regretting the jab immediately.

The prince seemed unaffected by this, as he already appeared to be pretty miserable. "Then you should know that the Teifen are on their way. I sent the message an hour ago," he confessed, hanging his head, as tears dripped from his nose.

Sara closed her eyes. "Fuck. Me."

CHAPTER 33

THE MOOD HAD CHANGED DRAMATICALLY in the embassy courtyard following the prince's admission.

Their lord had betrayed an ally, and had publicly admitted to it. The fight had left them, and confusion and anger were fighting for the lead in their emotions. Sara didn't blame them. She would be beside herself, if her president had done the same to the Elif.

Sara turned to Boon and Baxter, and opened a comm channel through their armor. "Get back on the shuttle, and get Grimms on the line. He needs to know what's happening. I'll be back in a minute."

Boon gave a nod, and she and Baxter jogged back up the ramp. Sara had Alister form a bubble shield around her, and she lifted them off the ground and glided to the top of the embassy's wall. As she suspected, the place was surrounded by UHF troops.

As soon as she crested the wall, they all took aim at her, but held their fire. She scanned the ranks until she found an officer, then floated over to her as nonthreateningly as she could. She settled the bubble down in front of the colonel, and gave a salute.

The befuddled colonel returned the gesture. "Captain, you mind telling me what the hell is going on? I have orders to arrest you. Unfortunately, I know who you are, and what you're capable of, so I don't know that I can actually take you in without a lot of people getting hurt. And if it's all the same to you, I would not like to see anyone in the infirmary later."

"My sentiments exactly, Colonel," Sara said with a smile that she realized couldn't be seen through her black faceplate. "I need you to do something for me," she said, unstrapping her hip pouch and handing it to the woman. "There is a core in this bag that I need you to get to the admirals. On it is a program that will help them tremendously; it will also answer a lot of questions that they have. Be sure you don't touch it, though, 'cause it'll knock you out with a zap that your mother will feel. The admirals will know how to handle it. Lastly, I need you to tell them, 'Cora was right; the Teifen are on their way'."

The colonel's eyes went wide. "The Teifen know where Earth is?"

Sara nodded. "I'm afraid it's going to be a rough afternoon."

She turned, and the colonel cleared her throat. Sara turned back, and the woman said, "I'll just let them know that you were unavailable for questioning, then?"

Sara smiled and rolled her eyes, then remembered the damn helmet. She felt amusement coming from Alister. "Sounds good to me, Colonel," she said, before lifting off in the shield bubble to return to the shuttle.

The colonel watched her go. *Why did that cat look like it was snickering?*

CHAPTER 34

SARA HAD Baxter fly them back to the *Raven*, while she sat in the copilot's seat, on the comm with the UHFC. The arguments became circular before they had even exited the atmosphere.

Command argued that Sara had broken the law, and needed to turn herself in; she argued that if she hadn't gone in and confronted the Elif, the Teifen would have arrived and decimated the system before they could have mounted a defense. The UHFC agreed that the warning was what was going to save them, but nonetheless determined that she had broken the law, and they could not let that slide. She then argued that they could not win this battle without the *Raven*, and the *Raven* was not a warship unless she was on it.

This went round and round until a compromise was reached: Sara would return to the *Raven*, but turn herself in after the day had been saved. She agreed mostly to shut them up and get on with the preparations. Whether she would actually do it, she didn't know.

They entered the *Raven*'s docking bay while the ship was still attached to the station, being resupplied. Baxter settled the small shuttle into an auxiliary bay beside the three much larger dropships, and shut the engines down.

"You're going to try and rescue the emperor, aren't you?" Baxter said, turning in the pilot's chair to face Sara.

She nodded. "I have to. We can't let that boy take over, if we want to win this war."

"And how exactly do you plan on doing that? If you didn't hear Grimms' description, the emperor is being held on a *dreadnought*. You remember what those are like, right? We just spent a few hours on one, if you're foggy," he said, his voice dripping with sarcasm.

She gave him a disapproving face. "I remember. But in case *you* forgot, we have two War Mages to throw at it," she said, sticking out her thumb and pinky, and rocking them between herself and Boon, who had just stuck her head in the cockpit's open door.

"Actually, only one that can go on a rescue mission," Baxter corrected. "You have to stay on the ship. We're going to be in a naval battle; you can't leave in the middle of it," he argued.

She had to concede his point, but he wasn't done yet. "And Boon isn't exactly able to handle the amount of Aether you are. She doesn't have anyone to share the burden with; if the exercises on the *Exitium* are any indication, she would be in trouble pretty quickly."

Boon gave a cheerful wave. "You know I'm right here, don't you?"

Silva chittered her agreement from around the girl's neck.

Sara ignored them, biting her lip in thought. "You're right. She needs a guard. Do you think Gonders would be willing?"

Boon's face turned red, and she began waving her hands back and forth. "Oh, no. We don't have to go there. I'll be fine. I wouldn't want to freak her out or anything."

"She would do it if you asked, Captain. After that mission on Colony 788, she would do anything for you. She won't shut up about it," Baxter said, ignoring the blonde woman's objections.

Sara nodded and smiled. "That was a pretty good trick, blowing up the dome from underneath. Okay, so we get Boon on board the dreadnought, with you, Gonders, and the Marines. The *Raven* will keep the dreadnought busy from the outside, while you find the prison and break the emperor out."

"Hello? Don't I have a say in this?" Boon whined to deaf ears.

"If that ship is as big as the one we were on, it could take forever to find him. Not to mention there will be thousands of Teifen aboard," Baxter said.

"True, but they will mostly be busy with the battle. There can only be so many troops in one area; if we hit them hard and fast, you should be able to get in and get out before you're overwhelmed."

Baxter gave a short, barking laugh. "Easy for you to say. You won't be in the trenches."

Sara raised an eyebrow. "Are you saying that you and your special forces won't be able to handle it? You'll have Boon to back you up—she's an army all on her own."

"I guess were invading a dreadnought, Silva," Boon said, leaning hard against the doorframe.

"We can do it, but it's going to be tough. Our biggest problem is that we don't know the layout of the ship," Baxter said, scratching his chin.

"Maybe the Elif spy network has the plans for it? We can ask this Sir Reitus, and Ambassador Foss."

Baxter nodded. "It's a start. Let's get out there, it's starting to smell like animals in here," he said. He held up a hand in surrender toward the glaring eyes of Silva and Alister. "No offense."

Sara gave a laugh, and opened a comm channel. "Gonders, come meet us in the docking bay."

"I'm already here, ma'am. The commander wanted me to get you up to speed on the fleet's plans," she replied.

"Good, we'll be right out."

Baxter slid out of the pilot's seat and, with a smile, squeezed past Boon, who stood and turned to follow.

Sara reached out and grabbed her arm, turning her back. "Boon, I know you want to take your time with Gonders, but we don't have that luxury. She is a good woman and, arguably, a better mage than anyone else aboard besides you and me. Baxter's told me on several occasions that she would beat him in a straight up duel. You need someone to cover your back, and she really is the best choice.

"But I'm not going to ask her to be your bonded guard if it's going to make you so uncomfortable that you can't perform," she said, giving the blushing woman a warm smile. "Will you be able to do this? I need to know now. Honestly, putting all your personal feelings to the side, she *is* the best option."

Boon looked to the back of the shuttle to make sure Baxter was out of earshot. He was lowering the ramp, not paying them any mind.

"I would love for her to be my guard, and I couldn't ask for better backup. It's just that…" She bit her lip and turned a little redder. "The bonding lets you feel the emotions of one another. She's going to know I like her, and not in the 'let's be best friends' kind of way. What if she's not okay with that? Or worse, what if she hates me for it? Plus, I know she strives to be the best mage in the fleet; what if she hates me for skipping past her?"

Sara stood and put a hand on her shoulder. "Love is a

weird thing, Alicia. It can show itself in many ways, and not all of them obvious," she admitted, looking past Boon's shoulder to watch Baxter as he walked down the ramp to the waiting Gonders. "Sometimes it starts as admiration, or respect of someone's abilities, and sometimes it starts as a rivalry or jealousy. But it never starts at all if neither one of you starts the conversation. We have a little time before you and Gonders are going to be needed for this assault—I suggest you two have a nice, long conversation about what the bond does, and what each of you expects. I think you'll find she's amenable to your particular orientation. The world has moved on from when your parents and their cult tried to stop time." On impulse, she leaned down and kissed Boon's forehead. "You're a good soul, Alicia. Anyone would be lucky to have your affections."

Silva affectionately rubbed her cheek on Sara's hand, still resting on Boon's shoulder. That made her smile.

"Thank you, Captain," Boon said, and wrapped her arms around Sara, squeezing her in a tight embrace.

They walked down the ramp together toward where Gonders was waiting, standing at attention in her black battlesuit.

Sara gave her a salute in greeting. "Where did Baxter go?"

Gonders returned the salute and said, "He is returning his armor to the storage locker, ma'am." She looked over at Boon, and her mouth dropped open at the sight of Silva draped around her neck. "You have a familiar? How?"

Boon smiled shyly. "It sort of happened when we were on leave," she said, then mentally kicked herself for such an obvious and vague answer. She tried again. "Captain Sara taught me the spell on the way back from Colony 788. I practiced it for days before I finally got it right. This is Silva. Silva, this is Isabella." Boon turned bright red before amending, "I mean, Specialist Gonders."

Gonders, in a completely un-Gonders way, gave a laugh and a bright smile.

Damn, she really is beautiful. Good eye, Boon, Sara thought with a smile of her own.

Sara slipped an arm around Gonders' compactly muscled shoulders. "Walk with us, Gonders, we have something to ask you," she began.

She led them toward the locker dispensers, where Baxter was just shutting the door on his armor. He turned and headed for the door before they were halfway there.

"Let's talk, just us girls for a minute..." Sara said, watching Baxter's retreating backside a little longer than was appropriate. Alister gave her cheek a lick, snapping her back to the present. "Right, just us girls."

"Um, okay. What can I do for you... ladies?" Gonders asked, trying to play along, but feeling somewhat lost.

"Are you dating anyone, Isabella?" Sara asked, and there was a strangled choke from Boon, who was trailing behind the two women.

"Oh, you really meant a 'just us girls' kind of talk. Okay. Uh, no, I haven't found the right... person yet. I'm usually too busy with training to get close with anyone," she said, then threw a quick look back at Boon. "I like my morning runs, though."

Sara caught the look, and raised an eyebrow. "Boon, you run in the mornings, don't you?"

"Yes, ma'am," she squeaked.

"It's 'Sara'. We're just some girls, having a conversation. I'm not 'ma'am' right now, got it?"

"Yes, ma'am... er, Sara," she said, hanging her head in mortification.

"Isabella, how would you feel about being attached to Alicia in a long-term sort of way?" Sara asked, and Boon choked again.

"I'm sorry, uh, Sara, but what is this all about?" Gonders asked, taking a step back and looking at them both in confusion.

Sara pressed her thumb to the locker door, and it popped open. She turned and stepped into the armor cradle, opened her armor up, and stepped back out. "Alicia is a twin, but her sister died when they were very young," she explained, closing the armor and then the locker door, and turning back to Gonders.

"Okay, I'm sorry about that, but what does it have to do with me?"

Boon opened another locker and began the process of storing her armor, while Sara continued. "When someone becomes a War Mage, they need to be careful, or their power will overwhelm them. Almost all War Mages in the past were twins, and as twins, they shared the burden—but Alicia doesn't have anyone. There is a way she can do this, but it means bonding with another mage. That mage would then become her guard and, as a side benefit, *they* would become more powerful, as well."

Gonders knitted her eyebrows in thought. "Okay, but what does that have to do with me dating anyone?"

Boon stepped up, having finished with her armor, and spoke before Sara could continue. "Because the guard and the War Mage are not only attached in name, but they are also intimately linked through the Aether. As far as we know, it's a permanent arrangement."

Sara was impressed with Boon's courage. She was still flaming red, but pushing on despite her fear.

"I assume you want me to bond with you?" Gonders said, putting a hand on her hip and raising an eyebrow at Boon.

The girl nodded quickly. "But you should know that we

would share emotions, along with knowing the other's general location and condition."

That surprised Gonders. "We could read each other's minds?"

Boon shook her head stiffly, still exuding nervousness. "Not so much read each other's exact thoughts, as more... general feelings. Would you say that's right?" This last she asked of Sara.

Sara nodded. "I only get the occasional emotions form Baxter, usually because he wants me to feel them, or because it's so strong."

"You and the Sergeant Major are bonded?" Gonders asked in surprise. "But I thought you had Captain Cora."

"It's a long story, but yes. Baxter and I are bonded," Sara said.

Gonders was quiet for a minute, chewing on her lip as she considered their words.

Finally, she smiled and looked at Boon. "I would be honored to be your guard."

Boon smiled so hard, Sara thought she was going to tear her cheeks open. Then her face dropped, and she said, "Before you agree, you should know something..." Boon bit her lip, her anxiety a mirror image of the specialist's. "I may have feelings that you won't like," she said guardedly, her head down.

Gonders smiled. "I doubt that," she said, stepping up and lifting Boon's chin with a finger so they were looking each other in the eye. "Why do you think I run in the gym every morning?"

Boon blinked a few times. "To stay in shape?" she guessed quietly.

Gonders laughed. "That, but there's also a certain ensign I like to see, who comes like clockwork."

Boon blinked again. "Who?"

"Oh, for crying out loud, Boon. She means you, you dummy. She likes you. Now, you two get out of here. Go to my quarters. You can perform the bonding there, and have a little time to talk, or whatever," Sara said, gently pushing the two toward the door.

They thanked her and began walking side by side. Silva slipped from Boon's neck and hopped onto Gonders' shoulder, where she began rubbing her face on the woman affectionately.

Watching the two walk away, Sara was hit by the realization that they were nearly opposite in appearance. Gonders had light brown skin, and black hair with brown eyes, showing off her Spanish heritage, where Boon was pale white, with blonde hair and blue eyes, as if she had just walked out of the pages of a Nordic fairytale.

Same with me and Baxter. That's just got to be coincidence, right? She shrugged, and headed after the two women, keeping some distance to give them a little privacy. *Fuck. I forgot to get the update that Gonders was supposed to deliver,* she realized. *Oh, well. What's the point of having an all-seeing sister if not to ask for information?*

"Hey, Cora. What's happening?" she said into her comm, as if she were greeting a drinking buddy.

"So, Boon's a War Mage too, huh?" Cora greeted dryly.

Sara grimaced. "Oh, right. So, I have some good news; Boon finished the spell."

Cora sighed. "You don't say."

CHAPTER 35

Two hundred and fifty-six ships waited in formation close to Earth, ready to warp into battle at the first sign of the Teifen's arrival. The complete first fleet made up the bulk of the ships at two hundred vessels, and the remaining fifty-six ships were all that had been completed of the second fleet. They sat in fighting formations of ten ships per group, each ship able to cover their companions in the heat of battle.

Admiral Deitrik Johansen was in overall command of the fleet, and had given his orders and speech an hour before. The speech was rousing, but ultimately uninspired. 'We shall not fall; fight on and with pride,' etc. The orders, however, had Sara seeing spots, she was so angry.

"How can he not see what an asset we are to this fight?" she raged to Grimms and Cora, while pacing the small ready room.

"Captain, I think the problem is that he does see what an asset we are, and is afraid to lose it. He is working under the assumption that the governor's fleet is damaged and in need of resupply. Their numbers are close to our own—we even have the advantage there by a slight margin. He is making the call that best suits the situation," Grimms said in an entirely too reasonable a tone for Sara.

"If the battle is going badly, then we step in. We're support, just like the rest of the second fleet. That is not the reason I am upset," Cora said, her voice becoming hard. "The fact that he does not want us to even attempt a rescue of the emperor is beyond foolish, if you ask me."

Grimms again played the voice of reason. "The prince has proven himself unreliable, and the UHF Command thinks a rescue mission is a waste of time and manpower during the battle. They would rather disable the dreadnought and attack in force, when we control the battlefield."

"The emperor could be dead by then. Our only chance to save him is if we hit the Teifen fast and hard; they're not going to sit around and wait for us to pick them apart," Sara said, crossing her arms.

"I agree, Captain," Grimms said, drawing a shocked look from Sara. "Command has sent word that they have developed a few new toys from the plans on the core we delivered. We already have some impressive warheads loaded into the gauss cannons, as do the rest of the fleet. We can hit a lot harder than the Teifen are used to. We are even able to prevent the enemy from warping away, but the higher-ups don't want to use that device until it becomes absolutely necessary. It will disrupt not only the Teifen's capabilities, but also our own."

"So, we wait? Just stand by while the battle takes place?" Sara inferred flatly.

"Captain, you're already in a lot of trouble with Command. I don't want to see you compound the problem by disobeying orders during an engagement. Despite the fleet not having actual combat experience with the Teifen, they are trained well, and will perform to the best of their abilities. I think we should follow their lead," Grimms said, holding up a hand before Sara could interrupt. "That being said, I agree with you that the emperor should be a top priority. It seems that the Admiralty is split on this issue, as well. Admiral Franklin has sent a message requesting we carry out an attempt at rescue, if the chance presents itself."

"Wait, the admiral is ordering us to go in?" Cora asked.

"Not ordering, just making a strong suggestion. He will cover for us if the need arises."

The alarm for battlestations went off, sending a wail through the ship. Sara and Grimms ran out of the ready room, and onto the bridge.

"One Teifen carrier has warped in. The fleet is engaging, ma'am," Mezner reported.

Sara and Grimms bellied up to the holo projector to observe the battle.

"Cora, jump us to the designated support area," Sara ordered, marking the location on the holo projector. Admiral Johansen had sent the second fleet the coordinates as soon as the enemy was spotted.

They slipped into the Aether and back out again a few million kilometers from the battlefield. Sara settled in to study the battle as it unfolded.

A red icon appeared, twenty-six light minutes from Earth. As they watched, the first fleet began warping in formation, their green icons disappearing, and then, a few seconds later, reappearing on top of the new icon. Sara zoomed in to view the engagement area. The first formation of ten ships had warped in almost on top of the Teifen carrier, at less than five hundred kilometers, and opened up with gauss cannons. A thin line of orange showed the path of gauss slugs, and blue lines showed the Aether cannons. Two blue lines shot out from each of the cruisers, hitting the Teifen carrier broadside, followed by thirty or more gauss rounds. The carrier was still spilling fighters out of its bays when the overwhelming attack ripped the ship in half.

A cheer went up from the bridge crew at first blood, but the fight was far from over. A second Teifen ship warped in, followed closely by a third, then a fourth. The number of warships grew rapidly, until the space was filled with them; then the battle was on in earnest. Fire was being exchanged at incredible rates.

The human forces fought in formations of ten ships: one carrier, two cruisers, three destroyers, and four corvettes. The carriers quickly dumped their fifty fighters, then took a defensive position, providing cover fire for their heavier hitters. The cruisers focused on damage, having two Aether cannons, and ten of the large, tri-barrel, gauss turrets. The destroyers provided cover with their heavy armor and mage-supplemented shield generators, similar to what the Teifen themselves used. And finally, the corvettes would use their mobility to warp in and out of the battle, hitting soft spots in the enemy, before jumping out again. The entire dance took close communication and organization, as the group would make moves in unison, dodging incoming fire as best they could.

The tactics worked well, until the formation was broken. When a destroyer went down, it would open the rest of the formation to attack until a reserve could be called up from the second fleet, which was on standby. Those few seconds it took for the reserve to get to the line could cost another ship, creating a chain reaction that would end with several ships disabled or destroyed.

The Teifen fought in packs rather than formations. The carriers would spill their fighters out as close as they could to the human ship formations, then warp away, leaving the small, fast fighters to fend for themselves. Each of the fighters were armed with heavy torpedoes that they would only fire when right on top of their targets, giving the defenders less of a chance to shoot them down. The torpedoes were not all that powerful, but the Teifen were good at timing their strikes, and would wait for their targets to take several hits before letting the ordnance drop. On more than one occasion, a cruiser or carrier had succumbed to this blitz technique.

To make things more complicated, packs of Teifen cruisers and destroyers would take turns firing on a formation, before warping to another and coming at them from an unseen angle. No one pack would look for the kill shot, instead wearing the enemy down one volley at a time, in a relentless torrent.

After twenty minutes, it was obvious that the Teifen—while having slightly fewer ships, and being already damaged from their engagement with the Galvox—were keeping the battle in balance. Their superior tactics and highly aggressive natures made them far more dangerous than the UHFC had anticipated.

A ship icon appeared outside the battleground, behind human lines. It was the dreadnought, still badly damaged from its engagement with the Galvox. Despite its wounds, it began pouring fire into the rear guard of the human formations.

Sara gasped at the size of the dreadnought. It dwarfed anything humanity had built thus far; it could easily hold a city's worth of people, and probably needed them to power the thing.

Twenty Aether cannons blasted from its broadside, along with hundreds of gauss rounds. A full fifth of the United Human Fleet was torn to flaming shreds in the first surprise volley before they scattered.

"Prepare for battle, we're going in," Sara barked, not waiting for the orders she knew were coming. She slipped into the command ring at the center of the bridge and shot some Aether into its small spellform. A bubble formed around her, giving her a view of space from the ship's perspective. She brought up the 3D image of the battlefield in front of her, and marked a location with the swipe of a finger.

"Cora, power the Aether cannons and prepare to jump. Ensign Hon, you're weapons free once we engage, but send your initial burst here," she said, marking a spot on the dreadnought. "And use those new warheads; I want to split this thing open. Mezner, let Baxter know we're heading in and tell him to be prepared for a quick departure. Connors, give me fifty *g* acceleration for five seconds."

There was a flurry of activity as everyone carried out her orders. The ship shot forward, pushing the limits of its acceleration, and leaving the rest of the second fleet behind. At the five-second mark, Mezner spoke up. "Ma'am, the admiral is ordering the second fleet to engage."

Sara smiled. "I guessed as much. Hon, prepare to fire. Cora, time your Aether bolts to hit right before the gauss rounds. I want their shield down before the rounds get there."

Cora and Hon said, "Aye, ma'am," in unison.

Sara checked their speed: two point five kilometers per second.

That should get us deep enough. I hope. She looked over at Alister, who was sitting on her shoulder. "You ready for this?"

He locked his yellow eyes on hers. "Merp."

She smiled. "Yeah. Me too."

He licked her cheek, then hopped to the floor and stood tall next to her, prepared for battle.

She looked out through her view bubble, at the battle

happening millions of kilometers away. From where they were, it was just some barely visible flashes of light in a tiny speck of the vast sky, but she knew the fate of the world rested on the victory of the right specks of light.

"Fire."

CHAPTER 36

TWELVE SLUGS with the new warheads nestled in their centers shot out at nearly the speed of light, and streaked toward the lumbering target. A few seconds later, Cora let loose with the Aether cannons, and two brilliant blue lines of pure magic lanced through the dreadnought's shielding, quickly burning the section down to a deep red before the beams winked out. A split second later, the gauss rounds slammed into the thick, armored hull. Each slug burst with brilliant energy as the warheads ignited. The rapid explosions tore chunks of the ship free, and a white geyser of atmosphere shot out of the resulting rupture.

"Jump," Sara ordered, and powered a specialized shield that Alister provided.

The view changed from near empty space to the looming side of the dreadnought, as they instantly jumped a couple million kilometers. Sara had placed them only two kilometers from the damaged side of the dreadnought, and at their speed, they'd covered that distance in under a second.

The shield form Alister had provided formed a spike of golden energy that extended in front of the *Raven* for several hundred meters, growing larger like a cone as it swept back to surround the rest of the ship. The tip of the shield easily pierced the damaged hull section, spreading the hole wider the deeper they went. The internal gravity compensated for the sudden deceleration, as the shield punctured deeper and deeper into the side of the beast.

Sara pushed more and more Aether into the shield, assuring its integrity. It was a costly move, but in the end, they had decided it would be the quickest way to get their troops onboard the dreadnought. Sara felt her well draining, but at a much slower rate than she would have guessed.

Baxter must be providing me with more power. Good to know the tank is a little larger, she thought with a smile.

The ship slammed to a stop, lodged deep within the dreadnought's belly. Sara turned and looked behind herself in the viewing bubble, and could see half a kilometer of ruined ship, exposed to the vacuum of space where the *Raven* had plowed through.

They were close to the prison level, according to the plans provided by Sir Reitus. He had contacted the Elif Spy network, and ordered everything they had on the governor's dreadnought be sent to the *Raven.* A plan was made to storm the complex quickly from the inside, reasoning that the mass majority of Teifen soldiers would be guarding the docking bays and airlocks against boarders; no one in their right mind would guess that the enemy would dive into their massive ship with their own—a feat that was only possible with a War Mage's power.

"Baxter, we're in. Get your men to the prison, quickly," Sara said into her comm.

She could hear the smile in his voice. "Yes, ma'am. One emperor, coming up. Give 'em hell."

"Baxter?" She hesitated. "Be careful. I can't afford to lose you."

His reply was slightly more somber. "Yes, ma'am. This time you'll owe me a beer."

Sara laughed. "There will be a cold one waiting for you— the real stuff this time, not that non-alcoholic crap you gave me."

"Looking forward to it. Baxter out," he said, cutting off the channel.

Sara looked to her side in the viewing bubble and saw the troopers running across a shield bridge from the *Raven*'s docking bay to the ruined edge of the dreadnought's interior. She dropped the shield around the ship, letting them pass through. After a minute or two, all five hundred Marines, plus Boon and Sir Reitus, were aboard the dreadnought. A figure Sara recognized as Baxter, despite the distance and identical black armor of his compatriots, turned and gave a wave to the ship before following the troops through a broken doorway.

"Ma'am, there are fighters coming around behind us. They know we're here," Hon reported from fire control.

"Connors, give me a hard reverse out of this heap. Hon, we're going to be doing our best to disable this hulk, so target any and all gravity drives you can. Cora, we're going to be doing a lot of jumping, but I'm going to need those Aether blasts as soon as you can recharge; coordinate with Hon on shot placements. Set all PDCs to auto, for the fighters." Sara's face split into an evil smile, "Let's show these horned bastards who they're dealing with."

She powered a tight shield around them, exposing only the barrels of the *Raven*'s numerous guns, as Connors backed the ship out at high speed. As soon as they were clear of the dreadnought, the PDCs began spitting fire at the closing fighters, taking several by surprise, and splitting their unshielded hulls open with hundreds of high velocity slugs. The five surviving small fighters banked hard to avoid the guns, but the gun's tracking ability at this close a range was more than the pilots could handle, and they were soon nothing but tightly packed scrap, hurtling through space.

Hon began firing the gauss cannons, targeting shield projectors and gun emplacements on the dreadnought's hull. A dozen or more sensitive spots on the hull were torn to shreds, before the rest of the guns began returning fire.

"Aim for the shield projectors. We want this section unprotected for our return," Sara ordered, pumping more power into the shield, and shrugging off the return fire as best she could.

"Aye, ma'am," Hon replied, readjusting his aim.

While the *Raven*'s shields were produced by magic, they needed to be amplified and directed through shield projectors. Unlike the *Raven,* the Teifen used normal troopers to power their shields. A dozen or more people could pour their Aether into the spellform, which would redirect that power out through the projectors. This produced a shield, but one that could not be modulated for specific damage, and therefore was much more costly to maintain. If the projectors were damaged or destroyed, it left that section without the ability to use a normal trooper. Mages could be called in to produce shields directly, but they were much less powerful than the amplified versions, because they needed to cover such a large area.

The human ships used troops to power the shields as well, but instead of powering the rigid spellforms like the Teifen did, they powered an Aether accumulator that the captain could use as a sort of short-term battery in their own spellforms—though this made the process sluggish compared to what the smaller corvette class ships did. The *Raven* and other small warships didn't use the inefficient accumulator, instead relying on the captain to use the amplifiers directly. The small size of the ship was easier for one mage to cover, and because they had direct control of the Aether, they were able to manipulate the spellform quickly to fit the situation. This made them able to deflect relatively large amounts of fire for short times during their quick assaults.

The *Raven*, however, was powering her shields with a War Mage, who could channel enough Aether to rival a destroyer, while her entire crew powered the shield accumulator.

But even a War Mage has their limits.

After thirty seconds of direct fire, Sara was beginning to strain to maintain her shield.

"The fleet is in trouble, ma'am. We need to get out there and start taking out some of that firepower," Grimms updated her from his position at the holo table.

Sara took a quick look, and decided on a target. She swiped a finger indicating a location and direction for Cora. "How are we doing, Hon? You about done with those projectors?"

"Aye, ma'am. That was the last in the immediate area," he reported, before switching his guns to fire on the dread-nought's hull directly.

"Jump," Sara ordered, as her shield began to turn orange.

They disappeared, leaving the Teifen gun operators confused at their suddenly missing target.

CHAPTER 37

THE BATTLE WAS TURNING in a very slow and costly way.

After the dreadnought's initial appearance and subsequent devastating artillery volley to the rear line of the UHF, the lumbering ship became less of a problem. The human fleet had executed emergency jumps to the opposite side of the battlefield, putting the Teifen fleet between themselves and the dreadnought. This cut down the direct fire from the capital ship, but it was still able to saturate areas with gauss and Aether fire, once cleared of its own ships.

However, the improved ordnance of the UHF, in the form of the warheads, was hitting much harder than the Teifen had expected. In addition to the increased firepower, humans were good at shield magic, making them as tough a target as the Elif, with their exceptional shielding. But where the Teifen were at a loss was with the highly aggressive tactics humans used, which were on par with their own.

The Teifen had become used to fighting the Elif; while the humans used the same formation tactics as the less aggressive race, they used them to much more devastating effects. Where the Elif focused on protection and escape from naval battles, human forces attacked and pressed their advantages, hitting targets harder when they became damaged, in order to eliminate them completely—not satisfied that they were merely out of the fight.

It soon became apparent that even with the humans' devastating losses, they were not giving up. On the contrary, they became more aggressive, even taking a page from the *Raven*'s playbook and ramming the smaller of the Teifen ships. This sometimes proved too much for the human ships, and they were left either damaged beyond functionality, or shieldless, open to enemy fire. The tactic was used only in moments of desperation, but was still a tactic that left the Teifen horrified.

By the time the *Raven* was freed from the dreadnought's belly, the battle had reached balance once again, and was slowly turning in the humans' favor.

THE *RAVEN* APPEARED beside a damaged Teifen destroyer. The huge ship had been trading blows with Admiral Johansen's flagship, and both were damaged nearly to uselessness. The Teifen destroyer still had its front shield powered, and was heading directly for the admiral, firing everything it had.

"Admiral, warp out of here. We can take this one. You need to get your people to safety," Sara said to the flagship over the open channel.

Not waiting for an answer, Hon began pummeling the unprotected rear of the destroyer. A full volley of gauss rounds tore at the armored aft of the ship. Cora sent an Aether blast as a follow-up to the gauss rounds, punching a hole through the weakened armor and causing the destroyer to buck and begin to drift sideways. Hon followed up with several rounds of the warheads, which punched deeply into the ship before detonating. The resulting explosion blew off the rear quarter of the ship, ripping the reactor away from the main body. The hulk went dark, and several explosions tore through the remaining sections.

Sara noted that the admiral had warped when she gave him the chance, allowing the ship the opportunity to recover, and letting him replace personnel on the Aether accumulators.

"I thank you for the assist, *Raven*. The battle is turning, but we are picking up on a cruiser that is attempting to run. As soon as it clears the debris field, it will warp away. We cannot let that happen. I need you to stop it before it escapes," Admiral Johansen said over their comm link.

"Aye, sir. We're on it," Sara said, marking the location on her map. "Cora, jump."

They slipped through the Aether, appearing directly behind a damaged ship that was maneuvering around a spinning hulk that was once a UHF destroyer.

"Hon, light it up," Sara ordered, scanning the battlefield for any more runners. To her horror, there seemed to be quite a few.

It seemed, after the first Teifen ship broke away, that several of the enemy took it as a cue that the battle was to be fought another day.

"Admiral, I'm seeing several ships trying to flee. We need to activate the warp dampener," she said, knowing what that would mean for the fleet. Without the ability to warp, the battle would turn into a slug fest, ships trading blows until one or the other crumbled. It would cost a lot of lives, but Sara knew there was no other way to stop all the Teifen.

She hardly noticed the Teifen cruiser ahead of them, as Hon pounded the aft of the ship with round after round, until there were a number of white sprays, venting atmosphere. Cora followed up his pounding with an Aether bolt right up the rear of the ship. The bolt tore through the unprotected craft, and punched out the front in a burst of metal and fire.

The admiral sighed. "You're right, make your last jump. I'm activating the device in ten seconds."

"The warning has been sent fleetwide, ma'am," Mezner reported.

Sara searched frantically for the best place to be and decided they needed to be close to the dreadnought to retrieve their people. Then she saw a pack of cruisers headed the admiral's way, and knew she needed to protect the capital ship and the warp dampener onboard.

With a frustrated growl, she marked the location. "Jump."

CHAPTER 38

"THAT'S A LOT OF HORNS," Boon said, peeking around the corner of the corridor they were occupying inside the dreadnought. The five hundred Marines were spread along the wall of the vast, high-walled passage, awaiting orders.

"I was surprised we didn't find any troops along the way; I guess they were all here, waiting for us," Baxter said, consulting the map on his palm projector. "Gonders, take a look at this," he said, his second leaning in to study the map. "If this map is accurate, there are several ways around to come in from the sides. If we can flank them, the fight should go a little easier. I need you to make your way around here, and wait for my signal. We'll hit them from the front, then you can sweep in and overrun their position. We outnumber them two to one, but our numbers mean nothing if we all try to attack from one direction. The corridors are large, but we can still only fit so many in at a time."

Gonders studied the map for a second before nodding. "You should send Deej with a group of a hundred around this way. Keep the main force with you, and send another hundred with me. That way if the map turns out to be crap, we have a better chance of one of us being in position."

"Good point. Deej, you copy that?" he asked over the command channel.

"Got it, sir," came the immediate answer.

"What about Sir Reitus?" Gonders asked, flicking a glance in the Elif's direction.

Baxter considered. "Take him with you. He could be a help if the intel is bad."

"Yes, sir," Gonders said, motioning for the guard captain to join her.

"Right, get going, I don't want to take too long and miss our ride out of here," he said, checking his clock. They had been on the dreadnought for just under twenty minutes, and he knew the battle outside must be taking a toll on the fleet.

"I THINK WE'RE LOST," Boon said, cocking her head. According to the map, they were standing inside a wall.

Gonders motioned for the troops to hold their position. The hundred Marines took up the best defensive positions they could, kneeling beside the walls on either side of the corridor.

"Reitus, the map is no good," Gonders said, slightly accusingly.

Sir Reitus pulled up his own map, and studied it before saying, "The plans we stole for this ship were preliminary, it hadn't been built yet; they probably changed during construction. The overall layout should be close, however."

"I think he's right. The plans are almost correct, but it's like the measurements were off. I think we're actually in this passage," she said, pointing to the corridor that, according to the map, was fifty meters to their left.

Boon felt a flash of worry come from Gonders as she considered what to do next. Despite their current situation, Boon felt a swell of happiness. Gonders looked up at her, and Boon guessed there was a smile behind her faceplate.

"It'll be fine. Let's head this way, and if the corridor ends in a tee, then we'll know if your guess was right. We need to hurry; it's been five minutes, and we're only halfway there," Gonders said, making the decision.

She motioned for them to move out, and they moved to turn the corner. Gonders was in the lead, followed closely by Boon and Sir Reitus, with the rest of the troopers just behind them. When they were only a few meters into the new passage, a mechanical whirring noise came from behind them.

"Cover!" Gonders yelled, turning and throwing a shield to protect her, Boon, Sir Reitus, and the seven troops that had made it into the corridor with them.

A hail of slugs began ripping into the shield from above. A turret had dropped from the ceiling and was spitting rounds at them as fast as it could. Gonders was a good mage, but the unrelenting barrage was quickly tearing through her shield.

Boon reached out a hand, and powered the spellform Silva gave her from the hip pouch she was riding in. The new War Mage made a fist and jerked her hand downward. The turret and a large portion of the ceiling were ripped out, falling to the floor in a giant pile that blocked the passage behind them, and cut them off from the rest of the Marines.

The air was filled with dust and sparking wires. Boon stood with wide eyes at what she had done. This was the first time she had used her powers for real, and, if she were honest with herself, it scared the shit out of her.

"Durnt? Are you there?" Gonders asked over the open channel. "Anyone, what's your status?"

"We're fine, ma'am. Just a little shaken up. That was close. Is everyone okay over on your side?" Durnt responded.

Gonders let out a breath of relief. "Yeah, we're fine. Looks like you're going to have to find your own way. I'm sending you an alternate route now. Let the Sergeant Major know when you get there. We'll try and find another way."

"Yes, ma'am," he replied, dropping the line to give the new orders.

"Sorry," Boon said, chagrined.

Gonders patted her arm. "It's fine, ba—Boon."

Boon felt the rush of embarrassment from Gonders at almost calling her 'babe' in front of the others. It made her smile.

"Right," Gonders said, checking the map quickly before saying, "This way. Let's hope this is the right corridor."

The ten of them began to cautiously make their way, looking for hidden defenses. After traveling two hundred meters past where the map said there should have been a junction, they came to a turn in the corridor that ended in a four-way intersection.

Gonders gave in. "We're lost. This map is garbage."

"I apologize, Specialist. We had no way of checking the accuracy of the map once the ship was done." Sir Reitus offered a slight bow of apology.

"It's okay. We'll just have to find another way," she said, checking the corridors to each side. Then she looked down the one in front of them. "Well, which way do you think?" she asked Boon.

Boon put a hand to her chest. "Me? Why ask me?"

Gonders shrugged. "Because you're the War Mage?"

Alicia laughed. "That seems like flawed logic, but…" She stepped up to the intersection and inspected her choices. "I say we go this way," she said, indicating the left passage.

"Any particular reason?" Gonders asked, signaling the troops left and checking her rifle for the hundredth time.

"It seems nicer," she admitted in all seriousness.

She had noted that the walls were less dirty, and the doors were painted red, instead of the industrial gray they had seen so far.

Gonders looked down the other two passages, then said, "You're right…"

"I figure nicer means there are more important things to break. If we can't get to the prison, we may as well start some havoc to draw attention," Boon reasoned, then she cracked her knuckles. "Besides, I want to try out my powers."

"You know, for such a shy girl, you can be pretty scary."

CHAPTER 39

IT TURNED out that the ancient humans were not as fool-hardy as Sara had been led to believe. As soon as the jamming device was activated, Cora got a message from the core saying that warp was disabled, but that jumps could still be completed.

Sara took this news with glee, and they were able to begin systematically jumping to ships that needed the most help. First on the list was the admiral's flagship. They had taken considerable damage, and were barely staying in the fight. The fleet rallied to their position as fast as their gravitic drives would allow. The *Raven* disabled the destroyer that had been stalking the craft, and the admiral was able to finish it off. From that point, the battle turned in the humans' favor, but at a very high cost.

The Teifen were falling to the humans at a rate of two to one, with their superior firepower and shielding. However, two to one was still costly when it was considered that these were all the ships left in humanity's control, and that the Teifen had nearly unlimited ships in reserve. However, this battle was not to win the war, but to keep from being over-whelmed. The rate of loss was worth the outcome—for now.

Over the next twenty minutes, the balance tipped in humanity's favor.

As more of the Teifen were destroyed, more UHF ships were able to concentrate fire, and the toll on the Teifen fleet increased. The *Raven* played her part, covering her damaged sister ships by jumping in and hammering the enemy into submission, so that the defenders could finish them off while she jumped to the next ship in need. It soon became obvious that the battle was won, except for the hulk that was the dreadnought. Despite the constant hammering of the fleet, when they could get shots off, the dreadnought refused to go down.

Sara realized how lucky they had been, punching through the defenses so early on. She figured that the only reason for their success was that the shields on the side not facing the battle had not been powered fully when they attacked. It was a tactic the Teifen used often to conserve their Aether.

Now that it was obvious they could not win the battle, the dreadnought turned and began accelerating away to escape the warp disrupter.

"Captain, they're running," Mezner reported, her voice high-pitched with the stress of the situation.

A fleetwide communication interrupted Sara's reply.

"This is Admiral Johansen; all available ships, target the dreadnought."

"Shit," Sara said, slamming her fist on the command ring surrounding her, making the image in the viewing bubble waver for a second. "Get me Baxter on comms."

There was a crackling that she immediately recognized as rifle fire. "Baxter here," he said, his voice straining slightly.

"Baxter, the dreadnought is running. I need you to get

your men back to the rendezvous point. We're getting you out of there," Sara said, marking a jump point for Cora.

"Negative. We're pinned down and can't get away without unreasonable losses," he yelled over the gunfire.

"If that ship jumps, we'll lose you all," she argued.

"Maybe we can send you our location, like the prince did. You could come get us later."

"If that thing jumps into Teifen territory, our fleet won't come after you."

"Well… I guess we'll just figure something else out," he said with forced joviality.

Sara watched as every ship not engaged began firing directly on the retreating dreadnought. The shields were strong, but not invincible, and eventually, the aft section's shields failed. Hundreds of gauss rounds began tearing at the back of the ship, but the craft kept picking up speed.

"Whoa, what's happening out there? This beast is bucking like a stuck pig," Baxter said with concern.

Sara bit her lip with worry. "The fleet is targeting the dreadnought's aft section. Are you guys close to there?"

"No, we're kilometers away, still in the belly of the beast."

"Try and get to the emperor. I'll think of something. I'm not leaving you to die out there," Sara said, fighting back tears at the thought of losing him.

"I'm counting on it, ma'am."

A huge explosion jetted flames from the top right of the dreadnought's stern, the color and intensity matching the loss of a reactor. Then space bent around the huge ship, and it slipped into warp, leaving only the fading jet of plasma to mark where it had been.

CHAPTER 40

"CAPTAIN, we're not done. That concentrated fire left many ships vulnerable, and they need our help," Grimms said, snapping Sara out of her fugue state.

She shook her head to clear it and wiped the tears from her eyes. *When did I start crying? What is wrong with you, Sara?!* And then it snapped to clarity in her mind. *I...love him.* The thought of losing Baxter, now that she was finally accepting what could be, drove her rage.

"Right, sorry. Cora, new jump coordinates. Let's take these assholes down."

Pull it together, Sara. You'll see him soon. Somehow. Focus on the here and now; win this battle so you can chase him down and tell him how you feel.

Grimms relayed the battle's status as the *Raven* jumped into the heat of it once again, disabling a destroyer quickly before jumping to a cruiser that had just taken out the last UHF carrier, and sending a full set of twelve gauss slugs into its broadside.

"Twenty-seven... make that twenty-six Teifen ships remaining. UHF has forty-two ships still functional, and seventeen adrift. Six hundred escape pods are sending out requests for pickup, and we are seeing two hundred possible Teifen escape pods."

Sara gritted her teeth, marking the next position and ordering Cora to jump. They slammed a destroyer with Aether blasts and a volley of slugs, then a second volley, but the destroyer would not go down. Instead, it rolled to present fresh shields on their undamaged side.

How dare they come to my home and try to assert their dominance over my people? And for what? Pride? Greed?

She realized they had gotten caught up in a war so old, the reasons for it were as lost to time as those who'd started it.

My people are not pawns to be sacrificed on the altar of another's ambition. I am their protector, their War Mage.

She was greater than they could ever dream to be.

Sara powered a second spellform from Alister, shoving so much Aether into it, she felt a sucking in her soul. She let the torrent loose through the shield amplifiers. The rebellious ship in front of her, the one that had rolled to avoid more damage, bucked—its middle expanding like a balloon before bursting open with a blast of white-hot fire.

She put in new coordinates, and they jumped.

The gall of these pointy-headed little dictators.

They were bugs. A pestilence she would wipe from the galaxy.

She powered another spell, sending it through the amplifiers, and the small Teifen corvette they had jumped to was flayed open with a force blade.

They take and they take, never relenting. They took the Elif from us thousands of years ago, and lately their homeworld. They're trying to take Earth. And now they've taken Baxter from me.

She sent a force blast down like a hammer, blasting the shields of a damaged cruiser before Hon peppered it with slugs, ripping holes through the crippled ship. Its lights flickered out, and she sent another hammer blow down, crushing its reactors, causing them to envelop the ship in white-hot light.

"*You can't have him!*" she screamed at the micro-sun she had created.

She scanned the area, but couldn't find any more red icons. She checked again, her rage pushing her to find more enemies to kill.

The back of her head itched, but she ignored it, instead expanding the map and continuing her search.

She caught sight of something by her feet, and looked down, focusing on it. *Alister.*

He was standing with his legs spread in an aggressive stance, and was baring his teeth. Saliva was dripping from his pointy, white fangs. He looked like he should be growling, but she couldn't hear him; she couldn't hear anything but the pumping of her own blood.

Her eyes widened in shock.

In a quick motion, she reached down and plucked the frothing cat from the deck, squeezing him tight to her chest. She willed herself to calm down.

She had caught herself pushing against the edge of reason.

She used her breathing techniques from years of yoga and meditation. She breathed in through her nose and out through her mouth. She did it again and again, sending thoughts of calm to Alister as she reminded herself she was in control.

She stood, breathing with her eyes squeezed shut, for what seemed like forever, but she still couldn't hear anything. She knew that was a bad sign, but she could feel herself coming down.

Please don't let me lose it and start killing my friends. They're all I have right now. She loved these people; they were her family. They didn't deserve to die because she couldn't control herself.

Why the fuck can't I hear yet? How do I stop this?

She could feel tears running down her face, and she squeezed her eyes shut even tighter. She felt a cold paw touch her cheek.

"Merow," Alister said. He bunted his forehead to her chin and began to purr loudly.

"Are you okay? Sara?" Cora's voice was soft and cautious.

Sara blinked her eyes open and looked around the bridge.

Everyone was staring at her in complete silence. She wasn't in the rage anymore and could hear again just fine; she had just scared everyone to silence.

She cleared her throat. "Yeah. Yeah, I'm okay now. Sorry. I got a little carried away."

Grimms approached and slowly pulled her out of the command ring, its bubble dissolving the second she left it. He directed her to the captain's chair, and gently pushed her into it.

"Well, I have to say, that was something. I didn't know you could use the shield amplifiers like that," he said, sitting in the chair next to her.

Sara swallowed. "I didn't either, to tell the truth." She looked at all the shocked faces of her crew. "I'm sorry. I let my emotions get the better of me, there. Please forgive me."

Connors was the one to break the tension. He snorted a laugh. "Sorry? That was fucking amazing!"

The spell was broken, and the bridge all began talking at once.

Grimms leaned in close. "That was very close to catastrophic, wasn't it?"

Sara nodded, still slightly shaken. "I have to be more careful. I'm beginning to understand that I'm a tool like fire is a tool. I can provide warmth, and cook your food, and even allow you to forge iron, but I can also burn you to ash."

Grimms gave her a reassuring smile. "You just described every Marine I've ever met."

"Marines can tell the difference between friend and foe," Sara countered.

Grimms frowned. "You'd be surprised."

They fell silent, each brooding on their own demons for a time as the crew chatted excitedly about their captain's abilities.

Sara felt a ball of pain at the thought of Baxter being taken.

She wouldn't get to tell him how much she admired him. She wouldn't get to thank him for agreeing to bond with her and take on some of her burden.

He agreed to be by my side forever, to guard me, and for what? A small boost in power and a vague sense of my whereabouts?

She jumped up, spilling Alister to the floor. He gave her a disapproving look before noticing her expression and becoming excited.

"What? What happened?" Grimms asked, taken aback at her sudden movement.

She didn't answer right away. Instead, she focused her thoughts on Baxter and, more importantly, on feeling for where he was. *There.* Like a lighthouse in the dark of night, he shone in her mind.

She quickly stepped around the command ring and brought up the galaxy map on the holo projector. She zoomed in on a section, closer, until there were only a few stars on the screen. She highlighted one and zoomed in again.

It filled the table. A binary system with a red giant and a white dwarf, circling one another. She focused her feelings and reached out a finger, marking a spot in the empty system.

"The dreadnought is here. We need to go *now*. I don't know if it's going to warp again or if it's too damaged, but we can't lose it. Mezner, let command know where we're going. Cora, jump us away from this dampener, and then give me all you've got. Warp us there," Sara said, entering the command ring once more and powering it up.

Grimms stepped close. "Are you sure? You just nearly went over the edge."

She smiled at him. "I'm sure. I've got a handle on it; I can recognize the line now."

The colonel thought for a second before nodding. "I hope so. For your sake."

CHAPTER 41

AFTER TEN MINUTES and several flights of stairs, Boon and Gonders found themselves in a set of halls that were, for lack of a better word, gaudy. Thick, red carpets with gold fibers weaved in intricate patterns ran the length of the hall, and the walls were a pearl white, featuring overly ornate wainscoting and crown molding. The door handles were gold. The light sconces were gold. The pots holding exotic plants were gold. It was like looking into the bleeding mouth of a pirate with a good dental plan.

The ship had been rocked with explosions, making forward progress slow to a crawl. After the bombardment stopped, Baxter updated Gonders, saying that he had been talking with the captain as the dreadnought took major damage before it jumped out of the Sol System. The ship had been quiet ever since.

"I'm assuming most of the Teifen are busy with repairs, otherwise they would be all over the place. Either that, or this ship is way emptier than we thought," Boon said, noting the empty hall.

"Probably doing damage control. That last blast we felt

was a reactor going critical," Gonders said, motioning them to follow her.

She squat-ran to the intersection ahead. Boon followed, then Sir Reitus, with the seven Marines bringing up the rear. Gonders poked a finger around the corner, taking a look with her built-in camera.

"I've got two guards on a set of double doors. Reese and Trin, get up here—I need your sharpshooter skills," Gonders said over the group channel.

The two Marines came forward, peeking around the corner with their own cameras. One gave a nod and knelt against the wall, while the other stood ready and waiting.

"One, two, three," a gruff male voice—*Reese*, Boon guessed—counted.

On 'three', both Marines spun out into the open and took a shot each. Boon noticed their rifles had been silenced. It was not a feature that could be used in full auto, but it was perfect for sniping.

"Targets down," Reese reported. "Clear."

Gonders stepped out with Boon right behind her, and they quickly moved to the doors the enemy had been guarding.

Boon curled her lip at the gruesome splatters of blue blood that covered the white door. She looked down at the Teifen, the first she had ever seen up close. Their faces looked almost human—though the features were a little sharp—and they had roughly humanoid shapes, but that was where the similarities ended. The one on the right had legs that, for all the world, looked like a goat's; they even ended in hooves instead of feet. The one on the left had more human appendages, but it also sported a set of ram's horns, and a thick tail as long as its legs. Both were dressed in something like a battlesuit, but in white, and custom made for their peculiar anatomy.

"Be ready," Gonders warned, raising her rifle and reaching for the door handle. Two Marines lined up behind her, rifles ready. Boon grabbed the other handle as two more Marines lined up behind her. "One, two, three." They pulled their doors open at the same time and rushed the room, searching for enemies.

What they found was even more horrifying.

Packed into the room were at least fifty Elif, all of them bruised and bloody. They were standing in a tight pack in the center of the room, cowering at the sudden movement. Most of them wore what Boon knew was considered high fashion, but their clothes were ripped and ragged. These people had been abused thoroughly, and recently.

"Are there any Teifen? Are you alone?" Gonders barked from her suit's speaker.

The Elif raised their hands in surrender, and a small Elif woman said, "Only the ones on the door," as she saw the bloody corpses that had been their guards.

"Check the rooms," Gonders ordered the Marines, motioning to two sets of doors at the back of the room.

The four Marines moved quickly and efficiently, opening the doors and checking the rooms.

"Clear," one called, then "Clear," echoed the other.

Gonders opened her helmet's faceplate, allowing the Elif to see her face. Boon followed suit. Most had wide eyes of surprise at the sight of a human; some even recoiled, as if seeing a monster.

"Where is the emperor?" the specialist asked.

"He's not here. They keep him in another room down the hall," the same small Elif woman said.

"And you are?" Gonders asked, all business.

She took a bow. "I am Thia, handmaiden to the empress. They have taken me to attend my lady on occasion. She is not well."

Gonders opened the channel to the rest of her men. "Get those bodies in here and clean the blood from the doors. We're taking up a defensive position."

Four of the Marines that had entered the room with them walked over and dragged the Teifen bodies into the room, while a fifth began wiping at the blood with a scrap of clothing he'd found on the ground, previously worn by an unfortunate Elif.

"Sergeant Major, the prison is a feint. The emperor is up on the palace level. We have Elif prisoners here, and they have a location for his Highness," Gonders reported. She was quiet for a minute as she listened to his reply. "Copy. I'm sending our location and the updated map. You'll need to find a way around the cave-in, or blast it out of the way. We didn't run into any resistance on the way; I think the crew is busy with repairs." She was quiet another few beats, then said, "Got it, we'll hold our position."

"We wait?" Boon guessed.

Gonders nodded. "They're mopping up the last of the prison force then heading our way. As long as they don't run into any more trouble, they should be here in thirty minutes. Let's hope no one checks on the prisoners 'til then. Reese and Trin, I want you two posted at the end of this hall. Find something defensible with cover. It looked like the hall was a dead end; make sure it is. Everyone else, were digging in here until the cavalry arrives."

The Marines got to work without a word.

Boon couldn't help but feel like dead weight. She was not a soldier by a long shot, and these were the cream of the crop.

"What should I do?" she asked, a little embarrassed.

Gonders gave her a smile. "You, my dear, are the secret weapon. Just stay loose and be ready for anything. Thirty minutes is a long time in a war zone," she said, then leaned in and gave her a quick kiss on the lips before closing her faceplate.

Boon smiled, and closed her own faceplate.

I am a secret weapon, aren't I? Don't worry, babe. I'll make you proud.

CHAPTER 42

SIR REITUS and Gonders were moving through the prisoners, healing their various wounds. It looked to Boon like the knight was well-known. She had learned from Thia that everyone in the room had been someone of importance in the palace on Effrit. The Teifen had sent in a large force to take prisoners.

It had been hard to put together at first, due to Thia beating around the bush quite a bit, but eventually she'd told her that the Teifen liked to take high-class figures and turn them into their personal slaves. In the upper circles of Teifen society, owning slaves was a status symbol. The more important the slave was in their former life, the more value they had as objects. They were swapped amongst the Teifen lords like trading cards.

Boon realized that the Elif in the room were some of the most influential among Elif royalty. The value they held as trade goods would have made the governor extremely powerful. It also meant that the humans had a better chance of preserving the Elif government than they had first assumed.

Boon was curious about something. She leaned in close

to Thia and quietly asked, "If the prisoners are so valuable, why have they been so roughly treated? Most of these people have been beaten and not healed properly. I would think not damaging one's trophies would be a priority."

Thia grimaced and turned her back so that the others couldn't see what she said. "They were not *beaten*, not directly. The Teifen like to…" She paused, looking for the right word and wringing her hands. "*Break* their slaves… Make them subservient through degrading acts," she finished, and Boon saw a tear fall from her eye before she quickly wiped it away.

It took Boon a second to get Thia's full meaning, and when the truth finally dawned, she was gobsmacked. "The Teifen raped them? Oh my god. Were you…"

Thia shook her head quickly. "No. They left me alone, but only so I could attend the empress and her injuries. They would heal her, but only part of the way, saying the pain was to be a reminder."

The girl began to shake with tears, and Boon quickly engulfed her in a hug, careful not to hurt her with her armor. Boon wanted to comfort all the prisoners, but she only had one set of arms, and Thia was closest.

She felt a tear roll down her own cheek at the injustice delivered to these people. Silva cooed quietly at the pain and shock she felt from her Mage.

Boon was slammed into the present.

Up until now, she had just been along for the ride, following Sara or Baxter or even Gonders wherever they led her. But the revelation at the cruelty of the Teifen brought a clarity of purpose she had been missing. She could not sit by and let such evil exist in the galaxy. She was a War Mage, and with that came a responsibility to protect those who could not protect themselves.

She felt a burning rage twisting in her gut, wanting

nothing more than to be let free to ravage this entire ship. She wanted to crush it. To burn it. She wanted to make the Teifen pay for what they had done, and for what they would continue to do if she did nothing. She wanted *revenge*.

Boon looked at all of the Elif pressed closely together, and saw the signs of abuse that she had glossed over before. The torn clothing, the blood that stained inconspicuous places, the haunted look in so many eyes.

Then one of the Elif stepped to the side, and she caught sight of Gonders, laying a hand on a woman's shoulder as she sent Aether to heal her wounds. Her rage faded, changed into something less destructive.

She realized she didn't want revenge; she just wanted the Teifen to stop.

Boon was not bloodthirsty; in fact, she could hardly stomach the sight of blood. But she would gladly wade through a river of it, if it meant that less people would suffer in the long run. The one thing that living in a religious commune for the first eighteen years of her life had taught her was that, sometimes, violence is the answer. It was an odd thought to take away from a group of pacifists, but that revelation had created a seed of truth, deep within Boon's soul.

Seeing the world and *wishing* it would change, instead of *acting* to make it change, allowed for the same amount of violence.

This was made clear on the day Boon decided she was leaving the commune. A local farmer had come with a complaint that the commune's sheep herd had wandered into one of his berry fields and was killing the bushes by stripping the leaves from the plants. The leader of the commune said that it was the right of the sheep to eat from the land, that he would not stop the natural order of things, and finally said that if the farmer wanted to keep the sheep out, he should put up a fence.

The farmer argued that the project would cost a fortune, considering the field's size, and he became angry, which Boon thought was a completely natural reaction, and he punched the leader in the face.

The leader called in the authorities, and they came and took the farmer away. Everyone else thought this was a fine solution, and praised the leader for not striking back at the farmer, but Boon knew the truth.

He *had* struck back; he had just used someone else's hands.

She had decided then and there that she would not let others fight for her rights, if she could do the fighting herself.

Boon patted Thia gently on the back, and cooed softly to her as she watched her guard heal the broken.

"Ma'am, we have guards coming your way. A lot of them. Looks like twenty-one in total," Reese said over the open channel. "We can take out a few, but not before they are able to get away. You have thirty seconds before they get to the door."

"Shit. Okay, people, we have a fight on our hands. Hemmet, get these people to that side of the room and out of the way as best you can. Sir Reitus, I need you to provide a shield barrier for the men to fire from, here," she said, indicating an angle facing the door. "I'll take this side. Reese, you two open up after we attack; go for targets in the back of the pack first; maybe they won't notice their compatriots falling behind them if they are focused on us. Boon…"

"Don't worry, I can handle myself. In fact, I'll throw the first punch; I can take a lot of them out in one blow if they don't see it coming. Reese, let me know when most of them are directly in front of the door," Boon ordered, stepping up to face the doors, as Silva slipped into her hip pouch and prepared for battle.

"You heard the woman, Reese," Gonders said, producing a shimmering golden shield that her men could kneel behind while still having a clear line of sight on the door.

"Yes, ma'am. Ten seconds. They've noticed the missing guards. The leader is approaching the doors, followed by a few... *now!*"

Boon sent a shot of Aether into the spellform she had requested from Silva. The shape blazed in her mind, and a blast of invisible force blew both doors outward, ripping them from their frames. With lethal force, she sent them flying into the five Teifen standing on the other side.

The doors slammed into the lightly armored guards, throwing them back against the corridor wall. Boon didn't let up on the spell, instead shoving the doors harder. There was a *crack* and *boom* as the doors were shattered under its weight. Splashes of blue blood sprayed out in all directions from behind the splintered doors.

There was a brief second of stunned silence, then more Teifen began to drop, as Reese and Trin picked off targets from their hiding places at the end of the long hall. The room suddenly filled with chattering rifle fire, and most of the Teifen were cut down before they could even raise a rifle.

Boon stepped out into the hall, checking to make sure they were all down. "Clear," she and Reese announced at the same time.

"It's a good bet they know we're here," Gonders said, checking her arm tablet and noting it had only been twenty minutes since she had talked with Baxter. "Right, start throwing any furniture you can get from the surrounding rooms out into the hall. We're making a barrier. Sir Reitus, I'll need you to be on shielding duty, since you Elif are exceptional at shields. Reese, Trin, stay on overwatch, and let me know the second you see anything."

"Aye, ma'am," Reese agreed.

"You're forgetting about your biggest asset, Gonders," Sir Reitus said, stepping up to her. He pointed at Boon. "She can hold off an army."

"Not for forever, and the more we push her, the less time she has. This will work just fine. You don't need a cannon when a twenty-two will do," she said, grabbing a chair from against the wall and carrying it into the corridor.

Sir Reitus considered that, then picked up a chair of his own and followed.

CHAPTER 43

THE THUDDING of many heavy boots filled the corridor. Boon began to stick her head around the corner, then remembered the camera in her glove, and slipped a finger around the edge.

Instead of fear at what she saw, she felt exhilaration. Fifty or more Teifen were running down the corridor, headed their way.

"Here they come," she shouted over the open channel.

They had only been able to erect a quarter of the barrier, when the Marines were forced to take what little cover they could behind potted plants, or in doorways. Sir Reitus put up a low barrier across the corridor and readied his own rifle.

Seeing an opportunity, Boon decided she should do as much damage as possible, as *quickly* as possible, and stepped around the corner to face the oncoming horde.

"What the hell are you doing?" Gonders shouted to her, but she was barely listening.

She powered a shield in front of her, and then quickly powered a second spell, sending a force blast down the hall. The front seven or eight rows of Teifen had nowhere to go, and were smashed backward with the blast, tumbling into those behind them and bringing the whole group to a stop. A large portion of the downed Teifen groaned in pain and rolled around on the floor, but just as many quickly got to their feet, and, in a heartbeat, the corridor was filled with rifle slugs.

Boon's shield deflected the incoming fire, but the constant barrage blocked her view, and made targeting a second spell difficult. She sent another force blast blindly down the hall, and was satisfied with the sound of tumbling Teifen, but the fire on her shield continued.

Unfortunately, she had not gone through magical combat training. She could cast pretty much anything at a thought, but she had never learned the art of actual killing. Using force the way she was, was akin to beating an armored man with a bat; you could knock them down, but it didn't hurt them very much.

However, there was something to be said for just using a bigger bat.

Boon sent a third blast down the hall, but this time, she dumped a huge amount of power into it. She felt her well sucking dry from the spell before she unleashed it blindly.

This time, there was not the sound of tumbling bodies, but the roar of ripping metal and composites. Mixed in were the sound of screams and the splashing of blood. The rifle fire stopped all at once, and she was able to finally get a clear view again.

The corridor was no longer corridor shaped; instead, the floor bowed, and was scraped clean of its gaudy rugs and golden planters. The walls were misshapen as well, some even ripped open to show the room behind. The lights in their area had all been smashed, or their wiring had been sliced, because the once brightly lit corridor was now dark where they stood. But silhouetted against the backdrop of the end of the hall, further down, Boon could see the mangled corpses of fifty Teifen.

"Oh, god. That was one hell of a blast," Gonders said, peeking around the corner. She looked at the panting Boon. "Are you okay?"

She was; in fact, she was *wonderful*. She felt like she could do this all day, except for the ever-so-slight headache that was forming. She reached up to scratch at the back of her neck before remembering she was wearing armor.

"I'm good. You guys okay?" Boon asked Gonders' blank helmet, and got a nod in reply.

"I know we have a fairly defensible position here, but I think we should press on, toward the emperor. The Teifen know we're here and that we have the prisoners, so they know we have someone that knows his whereabouts; if it were me, I would assume the emperor was next on the rescue list. If we wait for Baxter and the rest of the troops, the guards might get so entrenched, we'll never be able to get them out," Boon reasoned, reaching into her hip pouch to pet Silva.

Gonders nodded. "I was actually thinking the same thing. Get back here, in cover, and I'll contact the Sergeant Major," she said, pulling Boon back around the corner.

She opened a channel to Baxter and awaited his reply, which was nearly immediate.

"This is Baxter. How are you holding up, Specialist?" he asked, puffing with exertion.

"Good. Boon just tore the fuck out of a hallway and killed fifty guards, but she seems fine. We think the emperor is going to be hard to get to if we wait it out here for too long. With Boon backing us up, I think we can at least secure the room. The handmaiden pointed it out on our map, and it looks like the area will be defensible, if we can take it before too many guards show up."

"What about the Elif prisoners?"

"I'll leave the men and Sir Reitus behind to look after them. If me and Boon cause enough trouble, it should keep the heat off them."

It took a second before Baxter replied. "I agree. You trust she can handle it? We're twenty minutes behind you."

Gonders looked Boon up and down before replying. "She can handle it. If it's too much, we can pull out. I think we need to move on this now, though."

"Do it. We'll see you soon."

THE ROOM the emperor was being held in was not far, but it marked a whole new level of gaudiness in the palace. The carpets had transitioned from red with gold trim to gold with red trim, along with the walls, doors, and ceilings. You name it, it was gold.

It was starting to give Boon a headache.

"You okay, babe?" Gonders asked, making Boon snap her head up from where she was pressing it into her palm.

"Yeah, just a headache. This color scheme is making me queasy. I'm fine, really," she said, knowing it was a lie. A small lie, but still.

Gonders had surprised Boon with how quickly she had begun calling her 'babe'. They had spent an hour or two talking in the captain's cabin. To Boon's surprise, Isabella had been thinking about approaching Boon for a date since their first day aboard the *Raven*. Beneath the hard, muscled exterior of the compact woman was a beautifully tender person, who cared deeply for the well-being of others. Without even trying, Boon had found the perfect person to become her guard.

Gonders pressed herself against the wall at yet another

intersection and pointed her finger camera around the corner. She pulled it back and let out a breath. "Well, I knew the easy part had to end sometime. Take a look," she said, sliding down the wall to let Boon see.

She copied the camera trick and took in the scene.

The room Thia had shown them had double doors that faced a large, circular atrium that soared up three stories. This was the place; however, instead of the empty space the map showed, the atrium was full of Teifen, piled up behind portable bulwarks.

Boon did a quick count, and stopped when she got to thirty and wasn't even halfway through. She also spotted several auto turrets—some portable, and some coming from hidden compartments in the walls and ceilings.

"Well, shit. How do we do this?" she asked, still looking over the atrium.

"The only way that keeps the emperor alive; hard and fast. The longer we wait, the more enemies there will be. Can you handle this? That's a lot of weapons fire we'll need to deflect," Gonders warned.

Boon gritted her teeth. "I can do it," she said, trying to work out a plan.

The previous fight had taught her that she needed to expand her mind, as far as what was possible. After smashing that hall with a giant force blast, once she'd had some time to think, she thought up ten other ways she could have killed them that didn't involve using so much Aether.

"Could you shield us both for a short time? I have an idea, but I'll need to use two spells to pull it off," Boon asked, looking at the other woman.

Gonders took another quick look at the situation. "I can, but not for long. Ten seconds, fifteen at the most. How long will you need?"

Boon bit her lip, thinking. "That should be plenty," she decided.

She quietly jogged back down the corridor they were in until she came to one of the large plants. She reached into the pot under the giant, fern-like foliage and found what she was looking for. She had Silva create a shield bubble with the top cut off, making a floating bowl, and began scooping handfuls of the small, decorative stones from the planter into it.

Gonders kept watch as she worked, making sure that the Teifen were staying put. It took Boon three of the planters to fill her fifty-centimeter globe, but eventually, she had the small stones packed tightly to the top. She had Silva close the globe, then she returned to Gonders, the globe of stones floating along beside her like a pet.

"Okay, I'm ready," she said, taking a breath and finalizing the plan in her mind.

Gonders looked at the globe that was seemingly moving under its own power, and asked, "If you can move that around without it being attached to you, why do we need to go in there at all? And what exactly is your plan, anyway?"

"Well, I got the idea from Sara. I'm going to fill the shield will these small pebbles, hover it above the Teifen, and then I'm going to fill it with air, like, a *ton* of air—like, five hundred atmospheres' worth—and then I'm going to drop the shield so that the decompression flings the rocks out in all directions," Boon said, proud of her clever contraption.

Gonders just nodded a few times, thinking. Then she reached into one of her many pouches and pulled out a cylinder slightly larger than her fist, showing it to Boon.

"Why not just use this?" she asked, presenting the grenade to her charge. "Don't get me wrong, your idea is good, but it puts us in a lot of danger, for an effect that we can recreate with a few of these."

Boon's face flushed crimson, and she was glad there was an opaque faceplate hiding it. "Right. I kind of forgot about those. I'm no good at battle tactics."

"That's what I'm here for, my dear. This is what I propose…"

CHAPTER 44

Tornak Reem, The Under Captain of his Excellency, the Grand Governor, was on edge. The ship was under attack by an unknown force. There were reports that the newly acquired Elif slaves had been taken, and no one had heard from the five squads sent to recover them. There wasn't even a battle reported, they'd just gone silent.

He had been ordered to keep his Excellency's new toys safe at all costs, but was then promptly ordered to send three quarters of his men to assist in fighting the fires that were raging through the aft of the ship. The lucky shot those humans got off had hit a reactor, causing it to lose containment. The resulting chain reaction of reactor failures had cut their power output so much that the ship was barely able to keep life support running. And now he was expected to defend these pathetic slaves with only six squads.

He stomped back and forth in front of the double doors, checking to see that his troops were staying alert, while his tail whipped back and forth in irritation. He hadn't even been allowed to stop and properly armor his men. He was only able to get the four auto turrets because the armory had been on the way, and the officer in charge owed him a favor.

Humans had come aboard his ship, and even now were stalking the halls; the ancient enemy of legend, in the flesh, here and now, and he had to send all but sixty of his men away to fight fires.

He ground his teeth in frustration. *I wish the devils would just show themselves already.*

One of his troopers was approaching, a female named Dren. He admired the way her white battlesuit fit her form, especially the way it accented her hooves and muscled arms. When this was all over, he would call her to his rooms.

Dren stepped in front of him, a sly smile on her face as she saluted, arms crossed over her chest, and gave a respectful bow. "My Lord, the fires have been put out in the main reactor room, but—"

She stood up straight and looked him in the eye, just as her head exploded.

Tornak sputtered and stumbled back, spitting pieces of bloody skull and brain matter from his mouth. He stared wide-eyed at Dren's headless corpse. He watched it fall to its knees, and then topple over sideways.

All his troops were staring in horror.

That's when a black cylinder, two fingers round, hit him in the chest and fell on Dren's slightly twitching body. He saw two other soldiers rubbing their heads where similar cylinders had hit them.

"Incoming!," he yelled, right before all three grenades went off in rapid succession.

Only Tornak's quick spellwork saved him; dozens of his troops were not lucky enough to have the ability of Aether focus.

He threw up a hastily put together shield that absorbed

most of the blast and shrapnel, but it was quickly over-whelmed, burning a deep red before winking out and letting the tail end of the fiery blast envelop him.

He screamed in pain as the white-hot phosphorous burned his hide-like skin. He landed in a heap against the doors, cracking several ribs in the process, sucking in air at the pain.

The auto turrets began to fire in quick bursts, but only got off a few rounds before they were either cut in half with an unseen blade, or crushed to semi-spherical balls of scrap. His men were firing in long, frantic bursts, yelling and screaming at one another for help or cover. Two troopers were behind the portable barricade to his right, taking aim and firing in unison, running through their ammo cartridge quickly. He opened his mouth to yell at them to check their firing discipline, when the entire barricade was pushed back-ward with incredible speed, smashing the two soldiers to pulp on the wall beside him.

That's when he realized there must be mages in the attacking force. His men needed his skills, needed him to combat magic with magic.

He sucked in another breath and pushed himself to his knees. He was able to get a good view of the battlefield from behind the barricade in front of him, but his mind would not allow what he saw to make sense.

There were only two of them, and they were small. Very small, like children. *No, not children; females.*

They were covered head to toe in midnight black armor, similar to what the Elif wore, but these two were somehow more sinister with their small stature. Only one had a weapon, but she wasn't using it—she was instead creating a shield wall that moved in front of them as they stalked into the atrium.

He had heard of such things in the histories, but had always assumed they were fables. The Teifen could make shields, but once they were made, they could not be moved. Even the Elif, who were blessed with the ability to create powerful shields, could only make them stationary.

The moving shield and its creator were a horror to behold, but were nothing compared to the demon it protected.

This demon had no weapon. Instead, she wielded spells from both hands. She sliced with one, and cut three of his troops in half with a force blade, then she made a fist with the other, forming a shield around two more of his troops, and shrank it rapidly, crushing them to death in an instant. Not only was she casting two spells at once, but she was using her shield as a weapon.

His troops were being mowed down in the confusion of the surprise attack. Already, half of them were dead, and another ten were dying. He was so far outmatched that he decided it was better not to even try.

I will do the one thing I can to beat them... I will take their prize.

With a burst of speed that made his ribs scream with pain, he quickly pushed his way into the slaves' rooms and slammed the door, locking it behind him—knowing in the back of his mind that a lock would do nothing to stop those spawns from hell.

He saw the female first; she was standing beside a chair that she had occupied the last time he'd seen her. She clutched at her torn dress, her eyes wide with horror, remembering his past abuses to her. She began backing away from him, but she was not the prize the two intruders were looking for.

Perhaps he is hiding, like the sniveling coward he is.

It was no matter, the humans would be denied them both. He would just have to start with her, and find the male after.

He pulled his sidearm and pointed it at the screaming woman. Then he pulled the trigger.

The shot went wide when he was tackled from the side and pushed to the ground by the cowardly male. If Tornak were not in such a damaged state, the slave could never have taken him down so easily. With a backhanded swing, he smacked the slave as hard as he could, and the weak man was sent crashing into a table.

The woman screamed again, and Tornak raised the pistol to her face. Before he could pull the trigger, however, a pain erupted in his back. He twisted, roaring again at his broken ribs grinding together, and caught sight of a broken piece of table leg, sticking from his back. The male had rammed it home and was still trying to push it deeper.

Tornak raged. Grabbing the man by the throat, he slammed him to the ground. Then he reached back and, with another howl, pulled the wooden spear from his back. He looked at the dripping blue blood, then down at his attacker, who lay dazed at his feet.

Snarling, he rammed the bloody end of the table leg into the chest of the Elif emperor.

Boon blasted the doors open with a small force spell, just in time to see a large, horned Teifen, covered in blue blood, ram a pointed stake into the emperor's chest.

"No!" she screamed, slashing at the Teifen's chest with a blade of force that split him in two. She rushed forward, falling to her knees beside the wide-eyed emperor.

Without thinking, she ripped the stake from him and opened her gloved hand, pressing it to the bare flesh of his neck. She began dumping power into the spellform that Silva provided, squeezing her eyes shut with the effort, but the Aether would not flow.

She tried again, but nothing.

Opening her eyes, she met the emperor's glazed, dead ones. She was too late. Only a living body could be healed.

She began preforming CPR, but with every compression, blood gushed from his chest, and she was forced to accept the truth. He had been stabbed through the heart with a fist-sized stake; he was dead before she'd even gotten to him.

A tall, thin Elif woman fell to her knees on the other side of the emperor. Her face was pale white with shock as she stared into her dead husband's eyes. With a wail of anguish, she buried her face into his neck, and began to heave with sobs.

"Shit. Boon, we have a problem over here," Gonders yelled through their comm link.

Boon tore her eyes away from the weeping empress and looked over to the door just in time to see Gonders throw a shield over the open doorway. It immediately started sparking and distorting with golden waves as concentrated gunfire beat at it. The number of slugs slamming into the shield increased exponentially over the next half a second, rapidly turning the shield orange, and then red in the blink of an eye.

Boon threw up a second shield behind Gonders' just as it was overwhelmed, and caught the incoming fire. She rushed to the panting mage's side and, through the distorted barrier, she could see Teifen pouring through one of the passages leading deeper into the ship.

"Oh, crap. Let me see what I can do. You take a breather," Boon said, noting that her shield was starting to turn a little orange. She pumped more Aether into it, then sent a force blade out through the atrium. It was hard to see, but she did catch the flash of golden orange light as a shield absorbed most of the blast.

Shit!

"They have mages."

CHAPTER 45

MULTIPLE FIREBALLS BLASTED the shield right in front of Boon's face, making her take a step back in surprise. Her shield had blocked the blasts, but it was costing her a considerable amount of Aether to keep it up.

She sent out a stream of smaller fireballs—almost at random, her visibility was so bad. She could see flaming figures running before falling to the ground, but she also saw just as many attacks splash off shields.

She was half-blind and firing at random. Not to mention that she had been using attack spells nonstop; her headache was getting worse by the second. She knew that was a bad sign, but there really wasn't much she could do about it.

She sent out some more fireballs, and was rewarded by a volley from the enemy.

"Isabella, I need you to find us a way out of here. Do any of those doors lead to an exit?" She figured the room wouldn't be used as a prison if there were multiple ways out, but it never hurt to check.

She kept up the 'fight', blasting anyone she could pick out from behind the constantly distorted shield. There came a point where she was blasting with such regularity that she entered a sort of Zen state, and the world around her fell away.

It was just her and the fire.

The enemy shoved her, and she shoved back, but harder. She wouldn't let them win—they didn't have the *right*. They were murderers and rapists. They would burn for their sins, and she would personally usher them through the gates of hell.

She sliced, and coated the atrium in ice, then melted it with fire, then started the whole process again. She could hear the beating of her heart in her ears. The ragged sucking of air into her lungs. The swelling of power in her mind's eye.

She hadn't even noticed that the shield had stopped taking fire, and was now clear. She just aimed and blasted. Aimed and blasted.

Her face hurt from the smile that was plastered on it, but she couldn't seem to stop.

Aim, blast.

A Teifen was enveloped in flame, burning to ash before it hit the ground.

Another was frozen solid.

Another was cut to ribbons.

Then there were no more; just a sea of blue blood and burning bodies. She searched, but found nothing. So she searched again.

There, coming from the passage, a whole group of them.

She raised her arms and focused on the new group, ready to blast them to a bloody pulp, when she was dragged down from behind. She threw up her arm, but her effort was blocked. She tried to focus on the new enemy, but they were wrestling her down to her back, and she was not strong enough to stop them.

They're going to make me pay for what I did to their friends.

They're going to make me their slave, like the Elif. They're going to—

"Boon! Alicia, snap out of it. You got them," the person above her said.

She recognized that voice...

Wait...I don't know any of the Teifen.

She was on her back, her arms pinned above her head, and a woman was straddling her chest, holding her wrists.

Why does she seem so familiar?

With a quick movement, the woman's faceplate popped open, and slid back. "Alicia. It's me. It's Isabella."

I know that name. It's the name of someone important. I need to break free, need to find my love.

The woman leaned in and kissed her hard on the mouth. When she leaned back, a tear rolled off her nose and landed on Boon's face.

She stopped struggling, and blinked. She was still confused, but starting to come around. Then she was kissed on the mouth again, and desire flooded in, pushing the rage back a bit.

"Come on, Alicia. I know you're in there. I can't have lost you on our first mission, I'm a better soldier than that," Gonders wept, leaning in once again to kiss Boon.

This time, something cracked free, and Boon kissed her back.

Gonders laughed and sobbed at the same time, as she pulled away with a smile on her face. "I thought I lost you there for a second," she said, still dripping tears.

Boon cleared her throat. It was beyond dry.

From screaming, she realized. Then she said, "To be honest, I think you did. But it's good to know I can count on you to bring me back."

"Anytime, babe," she said, kissing her again.

"You all right, Boon?" Baxter asked, coming through the broken and charred door.

Gonders was pulling Alicia to her feet, but she spun quickly at the voice, going into a defensive stance.

"Baxter? When did you get here? I didn't realize the cavalry had arrived," Boon said, noticing for the first time that the atrium was now held by the Marines.

Both Gonders and Baxter gave her a slightly concerned look, before Baxter asked Gonders, "She was that far gone? That's what you're supposed to keep her from doing."

Gonders held up her hands. "What was I supposed to do? We were being pounded, and I had no way to attack. It was either let her go, or be killed. I was keeping an eye on her; I kept her from attacking *you*."

"I almost attacked you?" Boon asked in horror.

Baxter gave her a hard look of assessment. "You're not used to your powers yet, but from what Sara has said, it'll get easier. Just try to keep your head about you, okay?"

"Got it. What about her," Boon asked, pointing back to the empress, only to find her gone. Instead, she saw the body of the emperor, covered with a sheet from the bed. "Where did she go?" She looked around the room in a panic.

Gonders put a hand on her shoulder. "It's all right. We already sent her back to the others. They've set up a stronghold, and have half the men guarding the prisoners. We're just waiting on word from the *Raven*."

"I can feel Sara getting closer," Baxter told them. "We just need to hold out a little longer."

Gunfire broke out in the atrium, drawing everyone's attention. The team rushed to the door and saw a large group of Teifen coming down one of the halls, then fire came from another. The Marines had set up quick defenses, using the barriers the Teifen had brought, and were well defended. Not to mention there were half a dozen mages with the Marines, covering and healing as best they could, while still getting the occasional blast down one of the hallways.

"Shit. Looks like our break is over. Get over there and defend the second hall," Baxter ordered, slamming his faceplate closed and taking cover before aiming and firing his rifle.

Boon and Gonders closed their faceplates as well, and took up position with a squad of Marines that was happy to have them. Then they settled in for what was going to be a drawn-out fight.

CHAPTER 46

THE MARINES WERE HOLDING their own, now that they had the defensible position inside the atrium. Baxter was assessing the battle, while also healing the occasional Marine and then moving on. He looked over at Boon and saw that she was doing the same. With each healing, she seemed to become more like her old self.

That was a good thing; Baxter had seen on Colony 788 just how far a runaway War Mage could go. And according to Gonders, he'd nearly been on the receiving end of the small woman's considerable fury only a few minutes ago. That sent a chill down his spine.

War Mages are truly a double-edged sword. Sara and I are going to have to come up with some kind of training to keep them from losing control. If that's even possible.

Their position, while defensible, was not perfect, and he was losing Marines at a slow but steady rate. Already, two dozen men had died before a mage could get to them; the constant use of Aether was running the mages dry. There were fewer and fewer shields, which was driving up the number of his injured troops. He had brought two hundred men with him, but they were slowly being picked off.

Eventually, the mages would not have any Aether left, and the real toll of this battle would start creeping up.

Baxter pulled his hand away from a Marine who'd had a round pierce through a ruined plate of armor on his arm. The healing was not complete, but the soldier would be able to continue the fight. Baxter reached for a second man, this one hit in the lower torso, and was beginning the healing process when the entire ship rumbled and shook.

"What the hell was that?" someone asked.

Baxter finished the healing with a smile on his face. "That was an explosion, deeper in the ship," he said. He closed his eyes, and there she was. He could feel his captain, not far away; he was pretty sure she was on the ship.

"They're falling back. Something has them spooked, I can see them heading in the opposite direction," one of the Marines said, peeking around the barricade.

Baxter's comm chimed, and he answered immediately. "This is Baxter."

"Sergeant Major, this is Grimms. Damn, it's good to hear your voice. How are you holding up?" Baxter was greatly relieved to hear the gruff voice of his commander.

"Better now that you're here, sir. We have fifty or so high-born Elif, along with the empress, that need extraction. Unfortunately, the emperor didn't make it."

He watched as the Teifen left a small force behind, while the majority of them ran off to fight a new battle.

There was another rumbling explosion, and the lights flickered for a second before stabilizing again.

"Sir, are you attacking the ship?" Baxter asked, trying to figure out how the *Raven* could be doing that much damage.

"We are taking out defenses and turrets, but what you're probably feeling is the captain. She's tearing a hole in the top of the ship as we speak. The dreadnought is dead in the water; right before it jumped away, a reactor was punctured, and we're pretty sure it set off a chain reaction that disabled the whole thing. The shields and weapons systems are down, so we're picking off what we can before they can get power to them.

"The captain has a plan to take out the whole ship, but she's going to need Boon's help. I'm sending you Captain Sonders' location; you need to get Boon to her ASAP. Send the prisoners with as many Marines as you can spare to drop them off for extraction," Grimms said.

"Yes, sir. They'll be on their way shortly. It should take the whole group thirty minutes to get there."

"Good. That gives us some time to trim this tin can of some of its thorns. Grimms out."

Baxter opened the battalion-wide comm channel. "The *Raven* has arrived. Deej, I need you to get the prisoners and your people down to the drop-off point for extraction. I'm sending the rest of the troops down to meet you. Your pick-up ETA is thirty minutes, so don't dilly-dally." A cheer went up before he cut the comm, and addressed the two hundred Marines in the atrium.

"I want a hard push to overrun the remaining defenders. Mages with enough juice for shields go out front. We're going for a legionnaire push," he ordered.

The legionnaire push was a formation used to rush opponents. It consisted of two mages providing a low shield and a high shield, with a slit large enough for the barrel of a rifle to fit in between them at chest-height. It was a quick attack formation because it depended on a mage being able to shield against the enemy's combined firepower for the entire rush, while also not going too fast, or the riflemen would not be able to keep their rifles in the slot.

Baxter took point on his side, along with Specialist Oriel.

He saw Gonders explaining the maneuver to Boon, and decided she was a good choice, seeing as Boon had more Aether at her disposal than the rest of them combined. Only fifteen riflemen would be able to attack during the rush, due to the constraints of the corridor, but the rest of the troops would follow behind to overwhelm the target in close combat.

"I'll take low shield," Baxter told Oriel, and she nodded agreement. Low shield took the most damage, and she was a force bolt specialist, not particularly strong with shields. "On my mark," he said, checking that Boon's side was ready. He was impressed to see that she was doing both shields, and also a bit envious.

"Go!" he shouted, bringing up his shield along with Oriel. Fifteen Marines piled in behind them and slid the barrels of their rifles into the slot and began firing. The entire group began to advance at a steady, quick walk. The return fire was intense, and Baxter had to pump quite a bit of Aether into his shield, but with his newly deepened well, he was able to keep it up.

The Teifen began to panic when the Marines were halfway to them, and continued firing wildly from behind portable barricades. The Marines stayed calm, picking their targets as they presented themselves, and cutting the Teifen's numbers in half by the time they had made it three quarters of the way down the corridor.

The last of the Teifen broke, running for safety, but this just presented easier targets, and they were cut down with slugs to their backs.

Baxter would have to thank Sara when he saw her. This formation would not have worked if she hadn't drawn so many of the enemy away with her attacks.

He could feel the occasional burst of gleeful determination coming from her, as she presumably tore through the enemy. But Baxter knew she wasn't invincible; even a lucky shot could be the end. He needed to get to her, and soon. She had a habit of trying to bite off more than she could chew.

It had taken a few minutes, but the battle was finally over. Fifty Teifen lay dead or dying in the corridor, and no more were on their way.

"Gonders, Boon, you're with me. The rest of you, get your asses down to the pick-up, double-time. You've got twenty minutes before the *Raven* gets there. Move it, people," Baxter ordered, and the Marines began moving out.

Gonders and Boon fought against the flow and made it to his side.

"We need to meet up with Sara," he urged them. "She's close, and causing all sorts of trouble, but I don't know how long she can last. You're going to be our main source of offense for this trip, Boon. Are you up for it?"

"Do I have a choice?" Boon asked sarcastically, scratching at Silva's head where it poked out of her hip pouch.

Baxter shook his head. "Nope. Let's go."

He started picking his way over dead Teifen, and led the women deeper into the ship.

THEY ENCOUNTERED ONLY small groups of Teifen along the way, and dealt with them quickly, either by having Boon rip them in half, or the much simpler move of putting a few slugs through their thick skulls.

The deeper they went, the more lavish the decorations that filled the halls. They were obviously headed toward the Teifen governor's seat of power.

They entered another huge atrium, easily five hundred meters across, and a thousand long. They entered at the midway point of the massive, open area, where there were trees growing from a center strip of grass-covered park that was lined by walkways along each side. The ceiling was a clear material that showed the twinkling of stars outside. The entire structure was breathtaking.

Except for all the bodies.

There were hundreds of dead Teifen strewn about the floor. There were even a few broken bodies stuck in the branches of the trees. It didn't matter if the Teifen were wearing armor or just battlesuits; they were flayed open or charred all the same.

Baxter could feel Sara to their right, and pointed that way. "She's down here. I think she's in rough shape... Her thoughts have gotten darker."

They began to jog cautiously, not wanting to be taken by surprise, but everywhere they looked, only the dead stared back. It seemed the fighting had really happened at the end of the atrium, because the body count became obscene the further they traveled.

"I think I see her," Boon said, pointing through the trees.

Baxter squinted as he jogged; the girl was right. There was a huge, three-story set of double doors standing open. Inside the room was a figure in black armor. She was in a fighting stance, but her left arm hung limply, and there was a small pool of blood on the ground where it was dripping from her fingertips.

Baxter picked up his speed, the others keeping pace.

As soon as they broke through the trees, they saw Sara getting hammered by multiple spells, thrown by unseen enemies. Fire and ice and force blasts slammed into her shield from all angles.

Baxter watched her go down on one knee, and could see her shield burning red from the abuse, then it winked out. Before he could even shout, a force blade slashed through the air, raking across her chest and throwing her onto her back. Her armor was split open, and blood ran from the gash in her torso.

Alister was standing next to her body, his stance low, but he was ultimately undefended, with Sara so out of it.

Baxter roared in his helmet, but before he could do anything, Boon flung herself forward with her own force spell, flying through the doors as another bolt of force sliced through the air toward Sara and Alister.

CHAPTER 47

BOON LET the force spell die and powered a shield around Sara, Alister, and herself as she slid in close on her knees, her armor sending up sparks from the stone floor.

The force blast shattered against her shield, but she paid it no mind, instead opening her glove and pressing her bare hand into the open gash of Sara's armor, coating her digits in sticky, red blood. Boon poured Aether into the healing spell Silva provided, hoping she wasn't too late, like she had been for the emperor.

The Aether flowed, filling the spellform and rushing into Sara. Boon choked a laugh of victory as her captain's eyes opened, though they were still dazed from the impact. It would take her a few minutes to come out of her stupor.

Alister 'merow'ed, and jumped onto Sara's chest, nuzzling her face. Somewhere along the way, Sara's faceplate had been damaged and removed. *Probably in that massive fight out in the atrium*, Boon thought.

She turned just in time to see several spells slam into her shield. She had to feed it more Aether, but it held firm. She surveyed the room.

A throne was on a raised dais at the back of the one hundred and fifty-meter square space, perched in front of giant windows that looked down the spine of the dreadnought.

Standing in front of the throne was a figure Boon assumed must be the governor.

He wore white and gold armor that covered him completely, which was then covered by long, white robes that hung to the floor. He was more or less human-shaped, but he had a long, thick tail that whipped angrily back and forth as he stared down at Boon and the prone figure of Sara. His face and horns were encased in a helmet that featured a blank, white faceplate.

Though she couldn't see his face, Alicia guessed his expression would be one of surprise. That thought made her smile cruelly.

Surrounding them in a semi-circle were ten Teifen, all of whom were obviously mages. They wore similar armor, though no robes, and their stance implied attack rather than pride, unlike their ruler.

Boon didn't hesitate. She lashed out with a force blade, catching the right arm and leg of the nearest mage, cutting them free with sprays of blue blood. The nine others all began to return the attack at once.

Two of the mages dropped from slugs to their necks as Baxter came over her comms. "We can snipe from the door, but try to keep them busy."

In answer, Boon lashed out again, while her shield was battered to a burnt orange. She shot off a fireball at another mage, but it splashed against a hastily erected shield spell. Another round of spells slammed into her own shield, and she struggled to keep it up, almost losing it before she could focus enough Aether.

Another mage dropped to a rifle slug, but his demise

caught a compatriot's attention, and a few turned to deal with the snipers. Boon took the opportunity to send out another force blade, and caught one of the distracted mages in the shoulder, slicing his arm off.

The barrage on her shield continued, and she became overwhelmed.

Another fireball pushed the limit of the shield too far, and before she could reinforce it, her protection fell. She was immediately struck with a bolt of force to the chest, and staggered to her knees. She fired a bolt in return and caught the Mage in the face, crushing her white faceplate into her skull, dropping her to the floor, dead.

Another force bolt hit Boon just before her shield came back up, dazing her and making it too hard to concentrate and power the spellform. Silva gave a squeak of fear and anger from her spot in the hip pouch in reaction.

Boon could see the governor walking across the floor toward her and Sara, his gait slow and steady.

He stopped right in front of her, and raised a hand. "Die, human," he growled, and shot a bolt of force right at her face.

But the bolt hit a shield—a shield that Boon didn't remember making.

Then she felt a hand on her shoulder, and looked up to see Sara standing behind her. She had a hand on her own armor, closing the ripped steel and composites with a mending spell. Then, reaching down, she opened Boon's faceplate, and touched her finger to her cheek.

A warmth rushed through Alicia as Sara healed the broken bones and bruised muscles she didn't even realize she'd sustained.

"I forgot to keep it balanced," Sara said with a smile just for Boon.

The governor slammed her shield again, but it would not

budge. Sara checked the room and saw there were only two mages left.

Baxter and Gonders have done well.

She quickly and viciously lashed at the last two Teifen mages with force and fire spells, until their shields were overwhelmed and they were burned down with the relentless attacks.

The governor, sensing that the mage in front of him was not the same battle-worn person that had broken through his doors only minutes before, decided that perhaps diplomacy was the better option.

"Stop. This has gone quite far enough. You dare come here and attack me?" he boomed, standing as tall as he could.

"Oh, shut up, you worthless piece of shit," Sara growled, and snatched him up in a shield bubble.

The governor immediately lashed the bubble with force, trying to break free. Sara began shrinking the bubble, causing the governor to become almost hysterical with panic.

"How are you doing this? Stop! This doesn't need to happen. We can make a deal," he pleaded, as the space in the bubble became cramped.

"Have you told your emperor about us? About humanity, and our return?" Sara asked, stopping the shrinking as if she were considering his words.

"He knows there are humans again, but not where you are," he blurted, his voice full of relief that the shield had stopped shrinking.

"Why wouldn't you tell him where we are?"

He didn't say anything at first, so Sara resumed the shrinking. Then he nearly choked, he was trying to tell her so fast. "I was in a position to take the throne from him; with the victory over the Elif, I was already in favor with the other governors. If I could have just added you to my victories, my ascension would have been assured."

"So the Teifen emperor has no clue where we are?" she pressed, needing to be clear.

"No. You were to be *my* victory. But we don't have to do this! I can keep you hidden from his fleets," he pleaded.

"No," Sara said coldly.

"No?" he asked. "I can make you rich."

"No. You need to be put down; your cruelty has no limits." She turned away, and the governor began banging on the shield and yelling curses at her back, but Sara was looking down at Boon, paying him no mind. "We are War Mages. That means we need to do what is best, not always what is right. Do you understand? We have a duty to protect our people, and if killing is the way we have to do that, then so be it."

The governor pounded harder on the shield, his voice becoming frantic, "You can't do this. You shouldn't even be here," he screamed.

Sara turned around slowly at that last statement, and shot daggers of hate at the uncomfortably compressed ruler. "Why is that? Is it because your people tried to hunt us to extinction thirty thousand years ago? Is it because you turned our allies against us, and forced them to make a bio weapon that sloughed the meat from our bones?" She stepped forward until her face was right in front of his, trapped behind her shield. "Or should we not be here because you mistakenly thought us weak?"

The governor stared into her eyes and recoiled in fear at what he saw swimming in their depths. "You have no idea, do you? We didn't *force* anyone to turn against you. We didn't have to," he said quietly.

Sara frowned. "Lies. That's all you have left, isn't it? Just the lies you tell yourself so you don't have to be the monster in your own story."

He actually laughed at that. "No lies, War Mage." He

took an uncomfortable breath, and stared her down. "The true monster stares at you from the mirror."

The shield collapsed to the size of a basketball, with a crunching finality. After a moment of quiet reflection, she let the shield bubble fade. The sound of splattering as the liquefied governor fell to the floor filled the now silent room.

Then Sara fell to her knees in exhaustion.

CHAPTER 48

BAXTER WAS by Sara's side as soon as she hit the ground. "We need to get her out of here. She's spent. Gonders, call the *Raven* and have them wait for us. I can carry her…"

Sara put a hand to his faceplate. "I'm okay. It'll just take me a few minutes to get my strength back. It's good that healing Boon and mending my armor brought me a little back toward center, because we can't leave 'til we make sure this ship is destroyed and Earth is safe," she said with a tired smile.

"Okay, then we need to get to the reactor room, or maybe the armory. We need something large enough to destroy this thing," Baxter said, trying to come up with a workable solution.

"That won't work. There are far too many enemies between here and any one of those places," Gonders reminded him, punching holes in his half-baked plans.

"I have an idea. It's going to be a little rough for me and Boon, so I'm going to be counting on you two to get us out of here," Sara said, looking to Baxter and Gonders. She took a deep breath and pushed herself to her feet.

"Okay, but how are we leaving, if we're not going to meet the *Raven*?" Baxter asked.

Sara smiled and cracked her neck. "The same way I got in." She pointed at the ceiling.

"Oh, god. Nothing is easy with you, is it?" Baxter asked, hanging his head.

Sara slapped him on the back. "Better get used to it, life-bonded guard of mine."

She led them out the double doors, and down the long atrium, until they came to the far end, to a hall that was closed off with blast doors. "This is where I came in. They closed it off to keep the ship from decompressing, but there is a hole that leads right outside on the other side of these doors. We'll set the trap, then blow the door, and it will blast us clear before our nasty little surprise can take us with it."

"We'd better hurry. I'm sure there are more guards somewhere on this ship," Boon said.

"Right. Here's the plan. Gonders, I need you to put us in a shield bubble, so we can survive out there; I lost my faceplate in the fight, so no airtight suit for me, and Alister and Silva don't even have suits." Alister jumped onto her shoulder and gave a 'Merow' to the assembled mages. "Silva, where are you?"

The ferret stuck her head out of Boon's hip pouch, and chittered before crawling around Boon's torso and up onto her shoulder.

"Hello, darling. Do you remember those four spells Alant taught us?" Sara asked her. Silva chittered and rolled her eyes. "Okay, you don't have to be such a jerk about it. The fourth one, the one me and Alister did—not the binding one, the other one… you know which one I mean?"

Silva chittered again, and Sara took that for a 'yes'.

"Okay, I need you to give that to Boon and cast it right

here," she said, pointing to a spot in the air between them. "I'm going to make a shield to contain it, then start powering the spell. I need you to keep the spell right here as we move away."

"Got it," Boon said, and cleared her mind, preparing to cast.

"Baxter, I need you to blow the doors once we get the spell going," she said, then leaned in and kissed his faceplate where his mouth would be. "It's so good to see you again. I thought I might have lost you."

"Not a chance. I knew you would come," he said, gently squeezing her arm.

With a smile she looked back at Boon. "Ready?"

Boon nodded, and Sara formed a shield bubble slightly larger than a human head. She nodded back to Alicia, and the girl began powering the odd spellform that Silva gave her. She gasped at the result.

A tear opened up in the space between them, instantly spewing forth a dark blue substance that filled the shield bubble, attacking the sides with incredible ferocity, and turning the shield orange, then red.

Sara grunted and powered her second spell. It was a modified force spell, designed to press in on the shield bubble. The air warped around the shield just as it failed; instead of the blue substance spilling out, it was trapped in the sphere of force. The two powers fought one another, the blue substance pressing out and the force pressing in.

Sweat had sprung to Sara's forehead, and she was squinting with concentration.

"What is that?" Gonders asked, leaning in to take a closer look.

"Aether," Sara said simply.

"As in *pure* Aether?" Gonders asked in wonder.

Pure Aether would not stay stable for long. It wanted to be absorbed by space-time. Usually if a mage were to concentrate their own Aether on a spot, it would evaporate almost as quickly as they could channel it.

"How are you making so much?" she asked Boon.

"I'm not. I'm just holding open a hole in reality and letting it come through. This isn't taking much power—for me," she qualified, jabbing her chin at Sara, who was obviously struggling. "We need to go now. How about that shield, babe?"

Gonders nodded and, a second later, a large bubble formed around them. Baxter had everyone lay against the back of the shield, facing the door.

"When I blast the door, we are going to be sucked out. This will keep us from being slammed into the shield. Are you ready?" he asked Gonders, who gave him a nod. "Okay. Here we go."

At first, nothing happened… then a red line appeared, in a circle slightly larger than the shield bubble, at the center of the blast door. The glow grew in intensity until it was nearly white. In a sudden rush, the door failed where Baxter had super-heated the metal, and the center circle was sucked out. The rushing air pulled them toward the door at an incredible rate, then out into the giant hole Sara had ripped into the ship on her way in. Baxter used a force spell to push them up and out of the hole as momentum carried them away from the ship.

Sara was sweating and shaking with the effort, pouring more and more Aether into the force spell that was holding back the building pressure of Aether pouring into their reality. By the buzzing in her head, and the muted sounds of the others' voices, Sara knew she was pushing herself over the line to madness, but she could see that they were not far enough away from the dreadnought, and the longer she waited and maintained the spell, the larger the blast would be.

"Push," she mumbled.

Baxter leaned in. "What?"

"Push," she said again, unable to say more as she fought against the tide of power she was holding at bay.

Boon got it. "We need to move away faster. The blast will get us, too, if we don't put more distance between us and the ship," she told him, while forming a second spell and powering it. She began pushing the shield, and they gently accelerated.

"More," Sara grunted.

Boon pushed harder, accelerating them up to a full *g*, but it wasn't enough. After more prompting from Sara, she really let loose. She didn't want to hurt anybody, but she figured around three *g*s of acceleration should do it.

They were smashed to the edge of the bubble as it rocketed away from the dreadnought.

Sara was at her limit. She had fed more Aether into that spell than she'd known she had. She could feel the last dregs of her well drying up, but she wanted to wait as long as she could.

After a few more seconds, she couldn't take anymore. She screamed before blacking out completely.

THE FORCE SPELL ENDED, letting loose a torrent of Aether in an explosion of a blue substance that passed through anything it touched, expanding outward in an ever-growing sphere. It passed through the metal and composite of the ship. Through the bodies of tens of thousands of Teifen, both living and dead.

It spread out into space, reaching as far as it could for

kilometers in all directions. Everything it touched was saturated with pure Aether, and as Aether likes to do, it fell through the fabric of reality, back to its own plane. As it did, it took with it everything in that cloud, leaving only pristinely empty space behind.

CHAPTER 49

Sara awoke warm and comfortable, a thick blanket pulled up to her chin, and Alister curled up beside her. It took her nearly a full minute to realize she was in her bed on the *Raven*. The lights were dimmed, making the transition from sleep to wakefulness a pleasant one. She felt more rested than she could remember since first stepping on the ship.

The sound of a book page turning made her aware that she was not alone in the room, and she turned her head to the side to see Baxter, dressed in a tee-shirt and athletic pants, sitting on her couch and reading a book by the light of a small lamp on the side table.

He was so engrossed in the book that he didn't seem to have noticed she was awake.

She watched as he turned another page and took a sip of something hot from a mug.

The entire image was so contrary to everything he presented about himself; except that it was exactly who he was.

Alister lifted his head and saw that she was awake, then stood and stretched all four legs and his back as he walked to the edge of the bed and hopped down to the floor. Sara watched him trot over to Baxter and hop up onto the couch to curl up next to the big man. Baxter gave him a distracted pet, then turned the next page.

Sara was overwhelmed with a feeling of rightness.

She carefully slipped her feet from under the covers and sat up on the edge of the small bed. She was in a tee-shirt and a pair of shorts that she didn't remember changing into; if she were honest, she didn't care who had done it, just grateful that they had. She stood and quietly walked to the couch, dragging the blanket behind her.

Baxter looked up from the book. "You're up," he said, starting to put the book down.

"Don't. Stay right there, I'm coming in." She knelt down on the couch beside him, relocating Alister onto his lap. Then she pulled the blanket over herself and snuggled into his side.

"Do you want to know what happened?" Baxter asked, looking over at her as she rested her head on his shoulder.

"The fact that you're sitting here reading a book while I sleep is all the information I need," she said, closing her eyes and breathing in his soapy smell.

He didn't say anything, only patted her cheek affectionately before settling back in.

She was almost asleep again when she heard him turn the next page. Then she truly was asleep.

ISABELLA GONDERS WAS STANDING in Alicia's new cabin, waiting for her to finish getting ready in the small bathroom.

The cabin had been assigned when Alicia's status as a War Mage became known to the rest of the ship. Captain Cora had said it was 'proper' for a 'resource like Boon' to have some privacy, plus there was a ferret to consider.

Isabella didn't mind at all; it gave them a place to be together without bunkmates getting in their business.

Alicia had told her they were going out for drinks—even if the drinks were non-alcoholic until they got back to Earth—so she had found something nice to wear. To the shock and awe of everyone she had passed on the way there, it turned out that Gonders owned a few dresses. She even had shoes that weren't boots. The dress and shoes were both black, though; she wasn't crazy.

"I hope you like it," Alicia said, nervously opening the bathroom door and stepping out. She was wearing the blue dress Sara had gotten for her.

Gonders' eyes widened. "You look beautiful."

Alicia's face flushed. "Thanks. Oh, you look amazing," she said, looking up and seeing Gonders for the first time.

It was the specialist's turn to flush. "Thanks. You ready?" she asked, holding out her hand.

Alicia took her hand and squeezed it. "You bet." She leaned in and gave her a quick kiss on the cheek.

They headed out into the hall, toward the cafeteria and dinner, both of them smiling so brightly, they could blind an unprepared onlooker.

———

GRIMMS TOOK A SIP OF COFFEE, and looked over the report, his brows furrowed.

"It's not that bad," Cora said.

"It's not good," he retorted.

"No. No, it's not good, but at least we were able to rescue the empress. And fifty-three high nobles. They can rebuild with that."

Grimms took another sip, laying the tablet down on the ready room's desk. "There are only twenty-seven battleworthy ships left in the fleet. The rest either need to be overhauled completely, or scrapped. It's going to take a year to get back to what we had, and even *that* was barely enough to defend from an already damaged armada. Next time, they could send a thousand, or ten thousand ships. We need help. The Elif are broken, the Galvox know humans exist again, and the Teifen are actively hunting for us. Unless we get a miracle, I don't see how Earth will survive."

"We're not the only humans out here. What about the second dreadnought that humanity sent out at the end of the last war? We could always go and find them. Maybe they've gotten by better than we have on Earth?" Cora suggested.

Grimms thought about that. "They may not be anything like us, or want to help us, but it's worth a shot. I'll include the idea in my report when we arrive." He paused, considering what he needed to say next. "Captain, the real question is… what are we going to do about Sara?"

"What do you mean?"

"I mean she attacked the Elif embassy; there are going to be repercussions. No one is above the law," he admonished.

Cora was silent for a while.

"The more I look at the histories on this core, and see how the galaxy worked in the old days before the war," she began, "the more I think she just might be."

"You think she's above the law?" he asked, flabbergasted.

"According to the core," Cora said, her voice full of concern, "she *is* the law."

AUTHOR'S NOTE

Dear Reader,

Thank you for following Sara and Cora as they expanded their repertoire and made a statement the Teifen will never forget.

Boon is coming into her own. What will her new future with Gonders hold?

The War is changing…

And all is not right in the universe.

The Elif are gathering their remnants, preparing to take back their home. But will there be as much resistance as they first thought?

Come join Sara and Cora in Harbinger, book three of the War Mage Chronicles.

Is the galaxy as isolated as they once assumed?

Find out today!

Thanks,
Charley Case

P.S. My cats are judging me for not paying attention to them and writing all day… but if you were to leave a review, I could rub that in their faces.

P.P.S. You can find me on Facebook to stay up to date on what's happening… and see pictures of my judgy cats.

facebook.com/CharlesRCase

Printed in Great Britain
by Amazon